Annette Higgs is a writer living in Sydney, Australia. She was born and grew up in Tasmania, leaving on her eighteenth birthday to study literature and law at the Australian National University in Canberra. She has lived, worked and studied in Sydney, London and Italy, and holds a Doctor of Arts from the University of Sydney. A Pushcart nominee, her short work has appeared in literary journals and anthologies in Australia, the USA, the UK and India. Her novel *On a Bright Hillside in Paradise* won the 2022 Penguin Literary Prize.

on a bright hillside in paradise

ANNETTE HIGGS

VINTAGE BOOKS

In the nineteenth century Tasmanians referred to Aboriginal people with three main terms: Aborigines, Blacks and natives. These terms can be offensive today. They are retained in the speech of the characters in this book in order to authentically reflect the way in which people spoke in the 1870s.

VINTAGE

UK | USA | Canada| Ireland | Australia
India | New Zealand | South Africa | China

Vintage is part of the Penguin Random House group of companies whose addresses can be found at global.penguinrandomhouse.com.

First published by Vintage, 2023

Copyright © Annette Higgs, 2023

The moral right of the author has been asserted.

All rights reserved. No part of this publication may be reproduced, published, performed in public or communicated to the public in any form or by any means without prior written permission from Penguin Random House Australia Pty Ltd or its authorised licensees.

Cover photography courtesy Getty Images
Cover design by Christa Moffitt © Penguin Random House Australia Pty Ltd
Typeset in 12.5/18 pt Adobe Garamond Pro by Post Pre-press Group, Brisbane

Printed and bound in Australia by Griffin Press an accredited ISO AS/NZS 14001 Environmental Management Systems printer

 A catalogue record for this book is available from the National Library of Australia

ISBN 978 1 76104 973 6

penguin.com.au

We at Penguin Random House Australia acknowledge that Aboriginal and Torres Strait Islander peoples are the Traditional Custodians and the first storytellers of the lands on which we live and work. We honour Aboriginal and Torres Strait Islander peoples' continuous connection to Country, waters, skies and communities. We celebrate Aboriginal and Torres Strait Islander stories, traditions and living cultures; and we pay our respects to Elders past and present.

To my mother Dorothy
(1935 – 2022)
who first told me the stories

'There remains in the back-blocks of Tasmania and in collective memory an experience of homemaking that [it is] important to honour.'
— James Boyce, *Van Diemen's Land*

'And what we do not know the air will tell us, the air will tell us.'
— David Malouf, from the libretto for the opera *Voss*

Contents

In the barn	1
Eliza	11
Jack	65
Susannah	133
Eddie	193
Echo	241
Author's Note	*307*
Acknowledgements	*309*

In the barn

Kentish Plains, north-west Tasmania, 1874

Starlight spilled down the flanks of the mountain. Gradually, lopsidedly, the sphere of a gibbous moon rose above the rocky ridge, casting silver light below. A stage seemed set.

In the moonlight a creaking wagon pulled by lumbering bullocks weighed down by their yokes rolled along a track. Following bush trails, other carts and wagons headed in the same direction. People tramped the tracks too: husbands, wives, some with babies; girls, boys, little running children. Lines of light marked out the course of the crowd. Hurricane lanterns swayed from the wagons while young men held aloft flaming torches of pitch-dipped manfern stumps blazing like captured stars.

The bush soon opened out into Duggan's paddocks and a brightly lit barn appeared on the hillside. All the trails of light converged upon it. The farm boys brought their flambeaux and stuck them in the ground around the perimeter of the barn, forming an irregular ring of light.

Inside the barn, lanterns flickered in the lofty rectangular structure, the largest in the district. A murmur rose as the crowd pushed their way in. People jostled, found positions. The air glimmered yellow, fading to an indoor twilight in shadowy corners. With the autumn harvest not far off, a store of hay would soon fill the space, but tonight it was empty, ready.

Underfoot, a layer of chaff carried the faint scent of vegetative decay. A row of blue-painted wooden chairs from Mrs Duggan's kitchen stood ranged along the front of a low, makeshift platform. Duggan himself, short and fat, supervised these chairs, making sure no-one sat on them. He spread his arms wide and asked the women to keep back, keep back, please. The chairs seemed to promise something special, something mysterious.

Wives and mothers wedged themselves onto hay bales set out around the barn walls. They roosted, chattering in low voices, their children sitting cross-legged on the floor at their feet. Nearer to the front, bearded men clustered in groups by the platform. It had no decoration, no props, no sense of a stage or an altar. It was a clear, open space of possibility waiting to be filled.

Younger boys, adolescents, lounged against the barn walls, nonchalant. They formed a tight knot close to the doorway and the starlight outside, ready to escape if the show turned out to be a lot of rubbish after all. A skinny boy with a prominent Adam's apple picked up a straw and chewed the end of it, one ankle crossed over the other. As a rustling in the air suggested proceedings were about to begin, another boy leaned close and urged him towards the front. But the boy with the straw shook his head. The other shrugged and pushed forwards alone, elbowing others out of the way.

A commotion arose. Two figures in black coats and flowered waistcoats entered through a side door near the front of the barn. Anticipation rippled through the hundred-strong crowd; heads craned, pleasurable shivers quivered up the backs of necks. The murmuring increased – then died away at some inaudible cue, as if they had all paused at the edge of a precipice.

The two men, strangers who had arrived in the district unannounced a week ago, stepped up onto the platform. The older man, clutching a Bible against his waistcoat, stooped as he climbed awkwardly, even though the platform stood only about a foot off the ground. His shaggy white beard gave him the look of an elder, a Moses figure, about to impart mysteries. He stood to one side, lifted his shoulders and stared over the crowd with glittering eyes. The other man, spry, trim, with a hint of red in his whiskers, leaped to the front of the platform and like a young commander of troops, raised one arm. The crowd hushed expectantly.

'Brothers and Sisters,' he began, 'may the Lord bless us as we meet together.'

He spoke with a musical Scottish brogue, an attractive deep baritone. The sound of his voice, muffled at first by the smoky air full of chaff dust, the odour of cattle and the gentle anticipatory murmurs of the crowd, gradually grew in volume with a power that cut through the warmth and close fuggy smells.

He raised his chin. 'Bless the singing of your praise, the reading of your Word!' The words resolved, became clearer, and took on a sing-song rhythm. 'Bless our prayers and let them be heard! Bless us as we meet together, dear Lord!'

Shuffling noises filled the barn, the soft sounds of a hundred people breathing. The sharp odours of perspiration and anticipation joined the animal smells of the barn. The mesmerising voice spoke on, words of peace and rest and blessing and promise. The preacher strode up and down, turning now and then with a wide gesture of his arms to encompass everyone.

Echo Hatton, fourteen years old and thin as a stick, sat on a disintegrating hay bale wedged between her grannie Eliza and her mother Susannah. She huddled against her mother's generous breast as she had done as a little girl and fingered the small treasures she kept in her pinafore pocket: a stone from the creek, a few dried mushroom caps. It was as if the preacher made her uneasy. Looking up, she saw her mother's eyes wide and staring, her mouth open, her pink lips damp with a slick of saliva. The baby on her mother's lap slept, forgotten. Echo stared at the other women, the other mothers and daughters and grandmothers. They all bent like sunflowers towards the front of the barn, attracted by the speaker with the waving arms.

The rhythms changed. The preacher's sing-song prayers metamorphosed into a hymn. Round, deep notes reverberated through the golden air. Within a few minutes some in the crowd, women with shining faces, joined in. Low murmuring spread among the grandmothers and children, the bearded men and the young girls. Soon the pull of the hymn had reeled everyone in. '*What a friend we have in Jesus, all our sins and griefs to bear!*' Those who didn't know the words hummed. The old hymn lulled with the rhythm of a mother rocking a baby in her arms. '*O what peace we often forfeit, O what needless pain we bear, all because we do not carry, everything to God in prayer!*'

As the last chorus died away, the yellow light of the kerosene lamps flickered in the dusty air.

The young preacher intoned into the quiet, 'Come unto me, all ye that labour and are heavy laden, and I will give you rest. Take my yoke upon you, and learn of me; for I am meek and lowly in heart: and ye shall find rest unto your souls. For *my* yoke is easy, and *my* burden is light.'

These were the words of Christ from the Book of Matthew, he reminded them, waving his Bible aloft; words addressed to everyone here tonight as much as they were back in the Biblical days. 'For my yoke is *easy*, and my burden is *light*,' he repeated. He strode up and down the platform, his patterned waistcoat flashing under his coat. His mesmerising voice, starting low, rose in volume. His tone, gentle and persuasive at first, grew in force and urgency. Throwing both arms wide, he stepped forwards as if he would plunge into the crowd.

'Come unto me says the Lord!'

Spittle flew from his lips.

'And I will give you rest!'

An uneasy stir rippled through the crowd at this. Women turned to each other, wiping away tears. Cheeks were flushed, eyes glistened. Some of the young men leaning against the barn walls chewing on straws threw the straws to the ground, lifted their shoulders, and pushed their hats back on their foreheads. One or two widened their stances and crooked their arms akimbo, fists on hips. The women sitting on the hay bales began to rock back and forth to the rhythms of the singing, the preaching, the praying. The air in the barn thickened, warm and stuffy; the dim lights trembled. Female voices began to cry *ahs!* and *ohs!* and other noises, strange and guttural.

The girl Echo could no longer make out what the preacher was saying. The pure sound of his voice reverberated around the barn like a rebounding answer, though the question remained mysterious. His words seemed full of promise and rightness and peace and rest, though how these blessings would come upon them wasn't clear. Perhaps a miracle was about to happen. The girl's mother, Susannah, began to sway like the other women, moaning a little.

'You all right, Mother?' Echo whispered, grabbing her arm above the elbow.

Susannah didn't answer. She stared at the two preachers, both pacing rhythmically holding their arms out to the crowd, waving their Bibles high. The smaller children hunched their knees to their chins, wide-eyed. In the middle of the crowd a woman stood, stretched out her arms, and swayed as if she might fall. An inarticulate note rose from her, hovered in the air – an entreaty of some kind? – joyful and fearful at the same time. As the younger preacher stepped down from the platform and moved to greet the woman, the crowd parted. She pressed forwards and fell into his arms with a gulping sob. Leading her to the row of blue chairs, he bent over her, spoke low, patted her shoulder. She went on sobbing. As the preachers' vivid chant – *'Come unto me, all ye that labour'* – spread ripple-like through the barn, other women followed. They stumbled to the front, huddled on the chairs and dabbed their eyes. Singing started up again, *'Blest be the tie that binds, our hearts in Christian love . . .'*

Another woman leaped to her feet, an eruption from the sea of people. She sobbed and cried, shook and screamed, struggled against her family who tried to hold her. The crowd around her shrank back, but the younger preacher called reassurance, 'The Holy Spirit is upon her!' Faces turned with fascination to watch the weeping woman. Helping hands lowered her to the ground, held her shoulders. She drooled and groaned. 'Our sister is blessed!' cried the preacher, and the people turned to him in wonderment at the strange spirit he had brought among them.

Beside Echo on the hay bale, Susannah bent forwards and groaned low. Echo scooped the baby from her mother's lap so it wouldn't roll unregarded to the barn floor. Susannah's eyes, bright with tears, stared at the platform; the flesh of her cheeks quivered. Panicked, Echo looked around for help, for her father or her brothers, but she couldn't see them anywhere. Susannah continued to groan, as if she were in pain.

The old grannie, who had been intently observing the show, seemed to notice her daughter's affliction. 'Ay, what is up with you, Susannah?' she asked, grabbing her wrist.

People began to stand and move; the barn became a confused crush. When Echo looked towards the young men near the barn walls hoping to spot her brothers, what she saw made her flinch. Shouting and waving their balled fists, the youths seemed drunk, or angry. The hubbub became frightening. An unseen wind had infiltrated the barn, blowing out several lanterns. Susannah's face wavered in and out of Echo's sight as if lit by flashes of fire. The girl closed her eyes and screwed up her face.

How long all this went on, no-one afterwards could really remember. At times it seemed brief and events flashed past; at other times it seemed the night stretched on and on. When the people of the district looked back, this evening always seemed like an island in an ocean of days. It seemed to mark a before and an after.

Finally, when supplicants filled all Mrs Duggan's kitchen chairs, when the hubbub in the barn had resolved into a dazed aftermath, the preachers raised their arms and pronounced a blessing. Boldly upright, open palms outstretched, eyes raised heavenwards, they covered the people in benediction. 'The Lord bless you and keep you; the Lord make His face to shine upon you and be gracious to you; the Lord turn His face towards you and give you peace!'

Sighs of *peace!* rippled through the barn. There was more shuffling. Neighbours turned to neighbours and embraced. What a fine thing is a revival! And to think their own district had been touched!

Descending the platform, the two preachers approached the row of women on the blue chairs, sank to their knees, took work-roughened hands in theirs, and spoke in low, intent voices. The women wiped their eyes with dirty handkerchiefs and the edges of their skirts. Husbands moved towards them hesitantly.

Near the barn door, a tall young fellow with an angular face and a battered hat pulled low on his forehead stepped out into the cold starlight and spat. Eddie Hatton followed him, pausing to take a deep breath. Pulling his tobacco pouch from his pocket, he unwrapped his pipe and pressed a pinch of shag into the bowl. 'Got a light?' he asked the tall fellow, who obliged by reaching into his britches pocket for a box of matches. Eddie offered his tobacco pouch in return, and the fellow filled his own pipe. Eddie watched closely, but the bloke took only a modest pinch.

'What d'you reckon about all that?' Eddie asked.

The tall fellow sucked in a lungful of smoke, then puffed out slowly. 'Wouldn't surprise me if they was all drunk. Acted like it, didn't they?'

Eddie snorted in agreement. He wasn't sure if the fellow was referring to the preachers or their audience, but he agreed either way.

Eddie's older brother, Jack, had stayed inside the barn. Moving against the tide of the departing crowd, he pushed towards the platform, as if he wanted to speak to the preachers. But they had their backs to him, bent over the women. Hesitating, Jack turned away to join his father who was making his way towards Susannah and the children. As Noah Hatton came up to his family, his face inscrutable behind his thick beard, Susannah held out her arms.

'Oh, Noah!' she whimpered.

She said no more and he stared at her, looking unsure.

Echo held onto the baby, her face screwed up in puzzlement. Eventually, Noah patted his wife's shoulder and said, 'We'll go home now.'

Jack leaned close to his father, his face rosy. 'Did you see, Father? Did you see?'

Noah looked from his shaken wife to the bright visionary eyes of his son. He shook his head, and said again, 'We'll go home now.'

On the way home, walking beside the rolling bullocks with his whip on his shoulder, Jack began singing the last hymn. His voice, not long broken, skidded across the notes, sometimes falsetto like a child and sometimes growling like a man. *Blest be the tie that binds, our hearts in Christian love . . .*'

It sounded tuneless and ugly, but his grannie, surrounded by little children in the back of the wagon, seemed to like it. 'Bless me heart alive, it's a lovely one, Jack,' she called over the creaking of the wheels. 'A person can really hum along with that one.' She gave a little cackling laugh.

Echo gazed out into the darkness though she couldn't see much. One hanging hurricane lamp cast a faint glow on the track ahead. The moon came and went behind greyish clouds. Eddie, walking alongside the wagon, smoking, said nothing until Echo leaned over and asked him, 'What do you think, Eddie?'

He turned towards her. 'I reckon they put on a good show, young Eck.' He nodded once, his lips twisting into a half-smile she couldn't interpret.

The family drove on, home to their farm in Paradise.

Eliza

1

A clang of cast iron resounded as the door of the stove swung open. Red coals hissed, as did a barely audible curse (perhaps because of a splinter) as an old woman pulled a piece of kindling out of a pile. There was a crackle and sparking of the replenished fire as it began to roar a little, the thunk of the stove door pushed to and re-latched, and finally a sigh. This last, contented. The ancient old thing, small and bent, backed her rump into a wooden chair beside the stove. She had completed her task and, despite the splinter, regarded it as a job well done.

A grey old woman. Her grubby apron, dusty and faded, covered a worsted dress that had seen her through at least a decade and long lost its colour. Her eyes, however, were small, bright, black beads peering from wrinkled cheeks. Her grandchildren – and there were many, coming in and out of the kitchen where she sat – sometimes noticed their grannie's eyes glittering, and then they would ask her to tell them a story of the old days. They knew when Grannie's eyes began glittering she'd readied herself to remember, or perhaps to invent. She liked to do both.

Eliza Walters was tolerated in the farmhouse of her grown daughter Susannah and her daughter's husband Noah and their brood of eleven children and adolescents. Eliza herself had borne fifteen children, twelve who survived; she'd always lived among a large family. In fact, she knew no other mode of life. Well into her eighties – or thereabouts, the details of her birth being hazy – Eliza had taken refuge with her daughter Susannah, the only one who would take her in. Her own husband had thankfully died and all her other children had grown and, as children do, left her.

Though Eliza's eyes glittered beside the replenished stove, the moment was not one for storytelling. A growing commotion in the yard disturbed the kitchen and caused Susannah, who'd been chopping root vegetables for the pot, to rush outside. Eliza found rushing impossible, her legs stiff with age, her fastest pace a slow shuffle. She was obliged to wait for news to reach her. The sound of crying came through the kitchen door, flung wide when Susannah rushed out. Eliza's granddaughter Echo ran into the scullery, emerging moments later with rags in her hands. She dashed back out to the yard. Susannah's voice cried, 'Oh, what has happened?' Then Eliza's tall grandson Eddie stood in the doorway, a wet rag held to his nose and his shirt all bloody.

Eliza straightened in her chair. She pulled in her chin and peered at this awful sight. 'Ay, Eddie, what you been doing?'

He didn't seem to hear her.

The kitchen filled with people. Another tall grandson carried in the little girl Lottie, holding her limp body in his arms. Lottie's skin was as white as a sheet on washing day. Eliza watched, a pain squeezing her heart, as he lowered the child onto the sugar-bag mattress at the far end of the room. Susannah, following close behind, let out a tiny wire of sound like an injured bush creature, perhaps a wallaby dying of a shot wound. Anticipating mourning, Eliza thought, familiar with the pain of such things.

'Ay, Echo,' she said to her granddaughter, 'what be now?'

Echo didn't answer.

Eliza watched the boys stand aside, push their hats back on their foreheads, let the women step in. Echo scurried outside to the water barrel, then rushed back. Susannah bent over her injured daughter. Was that limp little body dead or alive? Eliza, gripping the arms of her chair, waited to see. Then Lottie began to whimper and a thread of hope pattered through everyone, through mother and sister and grandmother.

'Oh, Jack,' Susannah said to her eldest son, 'whatever happened?' Jack, who had carried in the child, waved a hand towards her right foot. Susannah gasped and bent over the little one, muttering, 'What has happened? What has happened?'

Between the bent figures of the family, and because she sat low in her chair, Eliza could see the child's ankle. She narrowed her eyes, trying to focus. Things were cloudy these days but she could see the bone poking up, forming a pointed mound where there should be no such thing. Lottie stopped whimpering and seemed to subside into a faint. Eliza watched Susannah gingerly examine the ankle. Her old heart still felt gripped, but it was not the time for painful hearts, nor for explanations.

'You will need a compress, Susannah,' she called, and levered herself out of her chair. With a clatter of cast iron, she set a black pan on the stove top and ladled water into it. 'Eck,' she said in a tone of command, 'bring some fresh gum leaves, girl.'

Echo hurried out to grab a handful of leaves from a young eucalypt. Many sprouted along the fence line of the yard. Eliza prepared a compress of rags soaked in warm water steeped with eucalyptus, the catty perfume quickly filling the kitchen. Susannah wrapped the child's broken ankle to loosen the muscles. She then pulled and set the bone as swiftly as she could while the child seemed insensible. Lottie woke with a scream when her ankle was straightened. Susannah wiped her white face with a damp rag. Echo hovered at her mother's elbow, fetching bowls and cloths, offering to warm a broth, make tea.

The boys and their father had retreated to the yard, Eddie with the wet rag held to his bleeding nose.

'Poor little blighter,' Eddie had muttered as he passed Eliza by the stove.

'Yes,' Jack had replied, 'but Mother'll fix her up.'

In the big kitchen, where Eliza's own sugar-bag mattress was rolled out each night, the women continued to tend the injured child. The grandmother opened the stove and used a fire shovel to extract a portion of hot coals that she placed on an iron pan, keeping them hot on the stove top. Broken bones were no small thing in the bush, without a surgeon or doctor to set them properly and nothing but bush remedies to ease the pain.

Echo bent beside her sister, smoothing the damp hair back from her white forehead. Lottie seemed feverish. The old woman took a handful of sheep's wool from a basket, where she kept such things in reserve, and placed it on the pan full of hot coals. Then she sprinkled the wool with a little sugar. Smoke filled the kitchen with the odour of sweet lanolin. Susannah, bustling, took the pan and held her child's broken ankle in the fumes, watching Lottie's face. Would it soothe? After a time, the child's breathing settled, so perhaps it had worked.

2

Eliza had been born in Maidstone, in Kent – so she had always been told by her own mother, who had herself been born in County Clare in Ireland. Telling her tales as an old woman, Eliza liked to dramatise her stories with *constant drizzle* and *caramel mud* and *skies like dirty linen*, but she didn't really have true memories of Maidstone.

When she was but a little child, well under ten years certainly, her father Richard Wise had *unwisely* (she would say, telling the story) assisted a certain Benjamin Walters to hold up an inn and make off with the day's takings. The story was told over and over in the family, as the central and defining event of their lives – the event that saw both men transported as convicts to New South Wales and thence to Van Diemen's Land. The details varied with each telling. Sometimes the perpetrators dashed away on a stolen horse but were captured at the crossroads, like romantic bandits. Sometimes it was all the fault of Ben Walters, who bungled things, waking the landlord while trying to grab one last bag of coppers. Sometimes they stole a fortune, heroically; sometimes they stole a pittance and were poor victims of a harsh penal system.

'Ay, kiddies, let me tell you about the time them old fellas frisked a crib and got nabbed.'

Eliza's grandchildren listened, alert, when she spun these yarns, sitting in tense silence as if hearing a ghost tale, wondering how it would end this time. But Susannah, having heard the terrible story told over so often in her own childhood, always interrupted, said she didn't need to hear it again. 'Forget that old story, Ma,' she would say.

Often enough Richard Wise himself had retold the tale – whether to frighten or impress, Eliza never could tell. The public house he and Ben Walters had held up was near Maidstone. Breaking in through the scullery window, the linen bags full of pennies and ha'pennies, the shouts of the awakened landlord and the way they had to break out of the house as roughly as they'd broken in – old Richard liked to tell that story, the only story that cast him as hero. They'd done the deed at three o'clock in the morning, and armed too, which made their sentences worse. Ben Walters' sentence was *transportation to the outer colonies for life*; Richard Wise received *mandatory death*. When she reached this part of the story, Eliza would lean forwards and whisper the dreaded sentence in a low rasp. *Mandatory death.*

'Think on it,' she'd say. 'Them two buggers with the heavy bags of coppers, diving into the night forest to escape, chased down by the landlord and his ostler too, them bags busting open and spilling onto the forest floor, all them coins hard to see in the *caramel mud*.'

She knew the haul too, having heard the numbers recited so often. 'There was seven hundred pennies and one thousand four hundred ha'pennies,' she told the children, as her story climaxed. It seemed a fortune to her.

Those were the numbers read out in the charges against the men at the Maidstone assizes. They never spent as much as one of those ha'pennies themselves. 'Father was lucky though,' Eliza would say. An appeal for mitigation was granted – perhaps someone argued the aching poverty of his wife and children, the little child Eliza among them, but no-one in the family knew for sure. Mercifully, they thought, *mandatory death* was commuted to *transportation to the outer colonies for fourteen years*.

'Oh, he had stories to tell, he did,' Eliza confided. 'He liked to make our skin crawl with tales of floggings and chain gangs. But it weren't true, that part. When he arrived in Van Diemen's Land he were assigned to a farmer on the Norfolk Plains, who sent him out to the remote regions. He became a shepherd, watching over a motley collection of sheep what ran wild out there, living in a rough hut and shooting at the Blacks if they come around with their spears and firesticks.'

Eliza had hair-raising stories of this time, heard often as her father, growing old, sat by the fire with his pipe between his teeth.

'Them natives was *warlike*,' Eliza said, 'and *collisions* occurred.' She chewed at the inside of her cheek to ease her gums. 'It were the taking of their women, I reckon. They wanted *revenge*.' She lowered her voice on the last word. She'd honed the story to a razor-sharp edge, and it resonated with the fear and the horrors of those old days.

'That's enough now, Ma,' Susannah would cut in whenever Eliza got to this point. For her part, if anyone asked about her family, Susannah always replied they were immigrants and free men. 'It's my story, ain't it?' Susannah would say. 'I can tell it as I want.'

After the sentence pronounced at the assizes, Eliza's Irish-born mother gathered her five little children and followed her husband to the colonies, sailing on the convict transport as families were sometimes permitted, if they chose such a fate. What choice did she have? Eliza would ask, rhetorically. 'To stay in Maidstone, destitute?'

Like the *dirty linen skies* of England, Eliza nurtured faint memories of the sailing ship, *Earl Spencer* transporting two hundred convicts, her father among them. They were two months on the open sea, sometimes seeing port but not allowed to disembark, the rough salted food and hard biscuits, until the ship sailed through the heads of Sydney Harbour and unloaded its cargo of felons and their families.

Then the brig to Van Diemen's Land, the hut in the bush near Launceston where her mother sheltered with her children while Richard Wise, convict shepherd, worked out his sentence and earned a conditional pardon. As for food, there were scraps from the farm where her mother worked every hour of daylight, and root vegetables the children cultivated in a rocky patch of soil outside the hut. Sometimes there might be a bit of bacon, or flyblown mutton unwanted at the farm – but not often, Eliza would tell her grandchildren, gesturing to the luxurious bounty of the side of bacon hanging over their own stove. There were trails through the Van Diemonian bush filled with strange plants unknown in Maidstone, strange animals, the seasons turned about, an unfamiliar night sky. How strange it had been to have even the stars look different!

Eliza's mother always said she preferred the bush hut to living in the town, where she might have worked as a domestic servant. In the town, she said, people didn't like to hear an Irish accent. They didn't want their servants to come saddled with children. And she couldn't have grown potatoes.

'Oh, she could make the praties go far, my mother could,' said Eliza.

Eventually, with his conditional pardon, Richard Wise returned to his family. In the three years following, three more babies were born. He expanded the vegetable patch and took up hunting for wallaby, and for badgers, which made good stewing. From time to time a weather-beaten man wearing a kangaroo-skin jerkin would stop by the hut. Maybe two or three such men would arrive together, slap Richard Wise on the shoulder, exchange low words. These were mates who had *come over* with Wise, fellows who had ganged with him, who'd been assigned with him in the bush. Together again, they'd guzzle home brew, and something stiffer too if it were to be had. The men would eat the thin larder bare and cuff the children if they came too near.

They spun their yarns. Stories of men in a lonely shepherd's hut deep in the mountains, alert to the cunning Black warriors who could sneak up on a hut dragging their spears with their toes so they couldn't be spotted, who might throw a firestick onto the bark roof and burn down the hut, and its occupants too, and maybe all the bush for miles around. The child Eliza had absorbed the fear behind the stories, the horrible fright of fire, used like a weapon – all to steal the flour store, or a few ragged sheep, carcasses found butchered.

'They oughta stick to hunting their own game,' the rough men would grunt. 'What did they eat before the white man came? Kangaroo! They oughta stick to hunting kangaroo and leave the white man's sheep alone.'

The natives lived together in big families, and slept by their fires at night.

'That were the best time to get 'em,' one of the old lags would reminisce. 'There were safety by attacking first, before they could throw their spears, or a firestick. It were needful to go in with guns firing, to shoot any that did not run away quick enough, women and children too. Then we'd push them Black bodies into the fire.'

The drinkers toasted their own bravery and guile. With bad rum, they erased memories of fear and culpability. Huddling together, they devised stories to explain the unexplainable they had encountered in the Van Diemonian bush. Then they called for the woman of the house to find more food, to submit to their hands. The child Eliza, listening, stored away these stories of two worlds colliding.

'It were a desperate frenzy all round,' she told her grandchildren, years later, whispering the stories, passing on the fear, passing on the mysteries of it.

3

Eliza's son-in-law Noah Hatton was, in her opinion, a hard disciplinarian. She'd known him to take a stick to the bare calves of disobedient children, or banish an older boy to the bullock shed all night. The transgression might be some mistake that cost the family dearly: losing a few pigs on the way into town, or storing the spuds poorly so they went black over winter. Once he even squared up to his son Eddie, that time Eddie came back from town with a rolling gait and smelling of hard liquor – and the boy only fourteen. Drunkenness was a terrible black mark in Noah's eyes. Eliza suspected he'd suffered at its hand as a boy, as had her own brood. Oh yes, Eliza knew enough about the effects of the drink, that she did. But Noah never approached the temper of her own husband – that was a blessing to all.

She'd heard it said – the story had been abroad in the district around the time Susannah married – that Noah's own parent was transported for smuggling kegs of brandy. This may have been true, though Eliza didn't know for certain. Stories were not always told straight in the bush, especially when the convict stain was involved. Though he never spoke of his father's history, Noah always insisted on truth-telling. That was another thing about him. Eliza rarely told her stories in his hearing.

'He's harder on fibs than anything,' she said to Susannah one day, when Noah was in a dark mood and they weren't sure why. 'Though what he counts as fibbing is hard to know.'

She puzzled over this silly prejudice. For her own part, she loved a good yarn and was unconcerned about the ins and outs of it – stories worth telling usually had a kind of truth to them, one way or another. But Noah was always grumbling to his children about lying. 'Don't you fib to me!' he would growl.

To give her son-in-law credit, he did make a point of teaching his boys to box, and in a proper manner too. Eliza had watched them sparring in the yard, on those days when they moved her chair out to the corner by the cow byre. She approved of this proper boxing. Boys should be handy with their fists; they would likely need the skill.

On the day the boys brought Lottie in with her injured foot, Noah Hatton's temper had come to her mind. Eliza watched him as he gazed down at the child. He didn't say a word. She'd stared hard at him, trying to detect any twist or grimace, any desire for revenge on those who had injured Lottie, but she couldn't tell with that thick beard of his. He'd just stomped out to the yard, calling for Eddie and Jack. She wondered if the sight of the poor white-faced child had brought back uncomfortable memories, but she knew better than to ask Susannah about that.

When Lottie's ankle had been straightened and she'd subsided into a faint, or a stupor, or perhaps (if the child were lucky) a sleep, Eliza sat back in her chair by the stove. Through the still-open kitchen door she had a view of the blue mountain that loomed over the farmyard, growing grey-silver now as evening descended. Voices were raised out there, and she sensed an air of agitation. In a sudden eruption, Eddie strode into the kitchen and grabbed a hurricane lamp hanging from a nail on the wall. His appearance startled Eliza and she jumped a little in her chair.

'Ay, Eddie, what has happened?' she asked.

He glanced over at his grannie but didn't reply. He seemed in an awful hurry.

Things fell quiet in the yard for some time. In the kitchen the crackle of the fire and Lottie's soft sleeping breaths were the only sounds. Susannah had by this time managed to get all the little kiddies into their big shared bed and asleep, and she'd fed the baby until she too slept. Then voices rose again outside, Noah's deep tones among them. Susannah left Lottie's side and went out into the yard. Through the open door, Eliza could see her standing in the dusk, talking with her husband and sons under the frowning brow of the mountain. Then with slow steps she returned to the kitchen and her interrupted task of watching over her injured child. The apron bib across her wide chest was damp, and Eliza could see the tears still running silently down her cheeks. Echo had been out in the yard too. Now she slipped back in and joined her mother beside Lottie. Eliza hadn't seen the girl go – she was a sly one, that Echo.

'Ay, what has happened, Susannah? Tears don't help nothing.'

Susannah turned her wet face to her mother. 'The boys lost the sale money, Ma,' she said, 'and it seems we'll all starve if Eddie don't find it on the track. He says he'll go back to look in the daylight.'

Echo hefted the iron kettle onto the stove top with a thump. 'We won't starve, Mother,' she said gruffly. 'We got the mutton birds.'

At this remark, Eliza sniffed. Yes, a cask of mutton birds stood in the larder, still half-full. You couldn't mistake the tide-pool stink of them. Noah had managed to buy them from a boat that came into Emu Bay and the family had been living on them for weeks. Mutton birds were good eating. Eliza ran her tongue over her few black teeth. She liked the fatty birds. The smell of them sitting salted in the cask, or boiling on the stove top, didn't bother her. Those birds did indeed taste like mutton, she reckoned, and there hadn't been real mutton around here for quite a while.

'Plenty of them birds left, ain't there, Susannah?'

Susannah lifted her apron and wiped it across her wet face. 'We have to conserve them, Ma, now the sale money's lost.'

The three women in the kitchen fell quiet, until they heard the child on the mattress groan. Blinking, Eliza watched Susannah sponge Lottie's damp forehead, then try to settle the broken ankle comfortably. The little one would be all right, she reckoned. She'd seen worse.

4

When Eliza was thirteen years old, or thereabouts, Benjamin Walters turned up at the Wise family hut. Transported with Richard Wise for the same crime, Walters had been sent out shepherding in the Central Highlands. With a few dogs to hunt the kangaroo, a man could live independently out there. Ben expected to have his conditional pardon soon, that's what he told Richard Wise. Taking Eliza by the elbow, lifting her from the tree-stump seat next to the fire, her father stood her before Ben, then in his thirty-second year. Ben looked her over. Being so young and underfed, she presented small and skinny in those days. After a long moment, Ben nodded.

'Your husband,' said Richard Wise to his daughter.

Ben was assigned to a place in the Midlands, the farm of Mr William Barrett, and Eliza would live with him there. Before leaving Launceston they were married in a brief ritual in an Anglican church, as arranged by Ben's master, who was known to be particular about his household and didn't tolerate the irregular. Eliza remained proud of her wedding all her life. She always insisted on the *Anglican church* when she told the story. It was respectable. It made up for a lot. 'Though,' she usually added, 'I wouldn't wish a husband like mine on any girl.'

The years that followed, bearing child after child, living from the land – badger stew, stolen mutton, potatoes and turnips and parsnips, no sugar to be had – Eliza had plenty of stories to tell of those times. A husband often brutal with his words and hands, and he drank too. Her grandchildren seemed to believe all she told them. That life she described resembled their own, though they had a cast-iron stove instead of an open fire, and planks underfoot in the farmhouse instead of packed dirt; and their father did manage to get hold of a bag of sugar or flour from time to time.

'And you got the rabbits!' she'd remind them. Rabbits were much more numerous now. They were everywhere. Eliza regarded the spread of rabbits as a great thing.

Of her husband – Benjamin Walters, ex-convict – she spoke only a little, and repeated the same epithets. 'That old Ben,' she would say. 'That old brute. That bastard. I wouldn't wish a husband like mine on any girl.'

Benjamin and Eliza Walters lived all their married life on the edge of the bush. At first, Ben, still working out his sentence, remained assigned to Mr Barrett as a farm labourer, digging and planting, clearing and harvesting. The master allowed them a hut. 'Only two rooms for all of us,' Eliza said, 'but a sound roof. And we had the garden. It weren't bad at all.' She made that hut, her cherished home, sound nearly as fine as Paradise.

'Trouble were,' she said, 'Ben would go on the grog, and then Mr Barrett weren't beyond giving him a good thrashing.' One time he even hauled Ben before the magistrate, a charge of drunkenness and insolence. Ben argued with that magistrate. 'He were a great one for arguing,' Eliza said, cackling. 'He were a feisty one.'

Ben failed to win the argument and ended up on a road party for three months. That meant leg irons.

Left to her own devices, with all those children to feed, Eliza resorted to *borrowing*, as she called it. The grandchildren always snickered at this part of the story. 'It were only a shilling or two, when they come my way,' she'd say. 'I were in distress, weren't I? I helps meself to a few shillings what ain't needed. Them Barretts had plenty, didn't they? As to the finding out, why, of course, that were uncomfortable if it happened. I always promised to pay it back. Me husband, he were so angry when he come home and found people complaining to him of me borrowings. I got a good thumping them times. He even put a notice in the paper once!'

'What did it say, Grannie?' one of the children would always ask, though they all knew it well.

Eliza couldn't read or write, but Mrs Barrett, the master's wife, had read the notice to her, in a voice that was supposed to sound a warning. But the thought of her name in the newspaper had greatly impressed Eliza. It still did. She'd memorised the words. '*I do hereby caution the Public not to give credit to my wife Eliza Anne Walters, as I will pay no debts she may contract after this date. Benjamin Walters,*' she recited, then laughed with glee. 'The master put it in for him,' she usually added, in a tone indicating that the children should be impressed.

When Ben got his ticket of leave they stayed in the bush. He tried looking for work, whatever he could get on the farms, but there wasn't much about. Emancipists were thrown on their own resources, no longer fed by the government or their masters. There were plenty of them too, competing for work, hard put to survive. Of course the masters preferred convicts, who were cheaper. The Walters stayed away from towns. As more prosperous white settlers surveyed, ring-barked and cleared, they would up sticks and move deeper into the forest. 'You'd think there might be work in town,' Eliza said, 'but not for old lags there weren't.' There was only name-calling, and worse if you didn't watch out. 'It were better in the bush.'

They grew praties and turnips. It would've been all right, living out there, but for the drinking and the fists that came out with the grog. Drunkenness always landed Ben Walters in trouble, his whole life. He couldn't help himself, couldn't keep away from the town. After months grubbing a living from potatoes and cabbages, and giving Eliza yet another baby, he'd hitch a ride on a cart into Launceston. She knew he mooched around the docks, talking to the sailors, asking about Home, putting up with the jibes. Those insults were the lot of an old lag like him. Eliza, wife and daughter of convicts, had heard them often enough herself.

And he'd drink — oh, how the man could drink, thought Eliza, half-dozing. Shaking her old head, she remembered the drunkenness of ex-convict Ben Walters, so often arrested and thrown in the Launceston lock-up to sober up. Three days of solitary confinement he might get, or a five-shilling fine he couldn't afford. It was true that Eliza fancied a nip of the grog herself if it were on offer, though Ben didn't leave much; *she* had little chance of finding oblivion in the drink. Nowadays things were no different. Noah Hatton forbade it in his house, except for the home-brewed ale he made himself. It'd been years since Eliza had tasted liquor.

Sitting beside the stove, thinking back on those days, she wondered if she missed her husband. Sometimes she thought she did. It hadn't been all fists and curses.

5

With autumn closing in and frost covering the farmyard in the early mornings, the steep face of the mountain in Paradise turned pewter in clear light. Sitting on her chair in a patch of sun in the yard, Eliza watched the mountain change. She often sat there podding a bowl of peas or top and tailing some beans. Out in the yard she could see what everyone was doing, and listen out for news: an injury when the boys had been splitting timber, tidings of a new baby at a neighbour's house, or of bad prices at the sale yards.

This particular autumn some news arrived – and with it a vibration of possibility, a sense of portent. Two strangers had turned up in the district. Nobody knew they were coming but they'd arrived unannounced at the Clarke place, riding up the bridle track from Kimberley's Ford – so Eddie told them at tea time. He'd heard all about it. It was not uncommon for travellers to seek a bed and a bite of food at a farmhouse or hut, especially at night or in bad weather, but these two had decided to stay on in the district. Eddie reckoned they'd come far, maybe even from Launceston.

'We would've taken them in, wouldn't we, Susannah?' Eliza said. 'Two strangers, ay?' No-one responded to this remark, but Eliza was used to that.

Susannah poured tea from a big enamel pot. Echo cleared away the debris of the meal, scraping rabbit bones from the plates. Eliza's little black eyes noticed the girl lingering near the adults. Flies buzzed in the air of the kitchen; they were such a curse.

'Cover the milk, Eck,' Eliza said. 'If it's left uncovered a minute them varmints drop thick into it.'

'They come to the Clarkes' place,' said Eddie of the two strangers. 'You reach their place first when you come up the bridle track. Ernie Clarke got a surprise when he saw them, riding good horses and in waistcoats and hats. He tells me they are preachers, but I don't know what kind.'

The Clarkes' farmhouse had more rooms than the Hattons', as well as a shingle roof and a proper verandah. They grew pumpkins and beans down the slope in front.

'Them two must have thought they were onto a good thing when they walked up through them vegetables,' Eddie said.

'They arrived at teatime,' Susannah said. 'Mrs C. is telling everyone about it. She's right pleased to have them. So I heard.'

Eliza was always impressed by how Susannah knew the latest news, how it seemed to come to her on the air.

'What are they doing now?' Jack asked, leaning forwards on his elbows. He seemed mighty interested.

'You can ask Mrs C. yourself,' Susannah said. 'Them Clarkes are coming over here tonight. The preachers are going out somewhere, doing visits, I believe, so the Clarkes are coming here. For a game of cards.'

'For a good gossip, you mean,' said Eddie, and he laughed.

'I would certainly like to see them fellas,' Eliza remarked to no-one in particular.

When the neighbours arrived at the Hatton place that evening, their bullock wagon creaking into the yard and their smaller children tracking mud into the kitchen, Bert and Emmeline Clarke were happy to tell the whole story of the preachers over again. Their names, announced Emmeline, were Fenny and Braithwaite, a Scotsman and an Englishman.

'Of course we took them in,' she said. 'Wet through, they were! Had a rough time crossing at the ford – it ain't ever easy, as you know – and at first they thought they'd have to camp out along the track. But they prayed, so they told us, and God delivered them to a warm house by sundown.' She sat back, looking pleased with the idea of her house being the answer to prayer.

'Whatever are they like, Mrs C.?' Susannah asked. 'Are they – gentlemen?'

She sounded doubtful. Eliza, in her chair by the stove, cackled to herself. The only gentleman Susannah had ever known was Mr Stanton at Chudleigh, where Noah used to work mucking out pigs and ploughing rough ground and keeping the Stanton family in vegetables and bacon. What's more, Susannah only knew that Mr Stanton was a gentleman because his house had two storeys and was made of stone, and had four tall columns in the front. It presided over acres and acres of the best farmland outside of the Midlands, built by convict labour and farmed for Mr Stanton by convict descendants.

'They certainly are gentlemen, to judge by their way of speaking,' Mrs Clarke said, 'and they really knew their Bible verses. That Mr Braithwaite told us how he was converted – in London!'

At this mention of London, of Home, the adults fell quiet for a moment, their faces lively with imaginings. Eliza pricked up her ears.

'Yes, he was *down and out* in the gutters of London, then he *heard the Word* and was saved,' Emmeline Clarke went on, breathlessly.

Eliza would certainly like to meet this fellow, newly arrived from London, someone who had recently seen *skies like dirty linen*.

The thwack of playing cards on the tabletop broke this momentary spell. Bert Clarke shuffled expertly. The four adults sat, ready to play a hand of pinochle. Eddie leaned against the mantle, Jack cleaned his boots by the fire, and Echo, who should have been in bed since she had to be up early for the milking, pottered by the stove.

Listening again, thought Eliza, watching the girl.

A fire crackled in the open hearth at the other end of the kitchen, spreading the scent of woodsmoke through the room.

'Did they read the Bible to you?' Susannah asked.

'Well, before we had our tea they said the nicest grace, I ain't never heard such a one before,' Emmeline Clarke said. 'Then after tea we sat around the fire and they commenced reading from them psalms. I ain't never heard such lovely Bible reading since we come to the colony.'

'Is they Anglican?' Eliza piped up. 'That would be a fine thing.'

Emmeline Clarke turned and blinked at her, but seemed not to understand the question.

'That Wesleyan fella what was here three months back, he weren't bad,' remarked Noah. 'I was quite partial to his way of preaching.'

Bert Clarke didn't seem too impressed by the Wesleyan. 'That old fella ain't nothing on these two,' he said. 'These two is the real thing. As good as that Moody, I reckon, the one as gets the big crowds in England.'

Noah nodded; his beard settled into his chest. 'The papers say that Moody is a regular fine showman.'

'I heard the singing of these two were very fine,' Susannah said. 'Is that so? I like a good singalong.'

'Oh, yes,' said Emmeline Clarke. 'And they say we don't need no minister like the Anglicans – we can look after ourselves, they say!'

Noah scratched his beard and considered this idea. 'You mean no ordained fella telling us how to do things?'

'That's right,' Bert Clarke said, 'nor what to think.' He laughed happily.

Eliza listened with interest to this discussion of the competing merits of the different religionists. It brought to mind her own marriage, which was the last time she'd had anything to do with an organised church. Although her wedding ceremony had been conducted rather quickly in a side chapel of St John's in Launceston by a poor-looking chaplain, still a proper church counted for something she felt.

'What're these preacher fellas doing now?' Jack asked, looking up from his boots.

'Well,' said Mrs Clarke, leaning forwards over the cards, 'they held a meeting at our place the night after they arrived. Word spread like a grass fire, it did. Several families come over, the Vineys and the Powletts, and we had such a nice meeting, with readings and hymns. During the day those fellas go out riding, circulating round the district, you know, socialising and holding prayers if requested. They are out again tonight, over to the Miller place.'

'I reckon they'll turn up here pretty soon,' Bert Clarke said.

Eliza saw Jack lower his eyes to his boots and rub the leather with concentration. The boy – sixteen now, so really a man – had a thin torso, his chest almost concave. Eliza watched him, the muscles of his forearms visible under his pale skin. So little fat on his bones, and fuzzy facial hair sprouting on his upper lip. She wondered what he was thinking. His face rippled between soft and hard, wavering, at that curious turning point Eliza had seen many times in her own sons, the moment when boyhood begins to recede behind the approaching man. Sitting there, not looking up, Jack gave the impression of deep thought.

His brother Eddie, on the other hand, merely grunted, pushed himself off the mantle and turned to leave. Echo watched the boys, eyes darting from one to the other. The old woman quivered a little with happy anticipation. Strangers in the district! Something, she felt, was bound to happen now.

6

The strangers reached the Hatton place within a few days. Eliza heard their horses' hooves as they trotted into the yard. It'd been years since she'd heard proper horses; not many kept them in this district where the mud tracks were treacherous. She recognised the jangle of stirrups and harness and sat up alert, keen to observe these strangers up close.

Susannah had been looking out for the visitors and had tidied her kitchen in readiness, yet their arrival seemed to fluster her. She called for Echo, shouting more brusquely than usual. When the girl scurried in from the yard she had bits of fern in her unbrushed hair – been rolling around in the bush again. The baby coughed, a rasp like an unoiled hinge.

The visitors seemed to fill the doorway, to block out the daylight for a moment. Then they moved and became mobile shadows against the bright day. Susannah bade welcome and invited them to sit at her kitchen table, and they doffed their hats like gentlemen and sat. The baby snuffled. The men introduced themselves.

'The bairn isn't well?' inquired Mr Fenny politely. He was the red-bearded one, Eliza gathered, though she might have mis-heard.

'She's a little rheumy,' replied Susannah. 'I confess I'm a mite concerned, it's not lifting as I'd hoped. Three days now she's been like this.'

The baby gave another faint cough and Susannah gathered her from the cradle.

'I can suggest a new remedy, Missus, if you'd be interested,' Mr Fenny said. 'I have the recipe for a very good plaster. Over at Scottsdale, where we were at work last month, it has been used to great effect.'

Susannah perked up. 'Oh, sir! A new remedy? I'd be right pleased. Her little chest is as scratchy as bark.'

Eliza pricked up her ears too. Like all bush women, she always welcomed news of fresh remedies. For a few minutes the men conversed politely about the remedy, about the district and the neighbours, and told how they'd been up at Table Cape last summer. In response to Susannah's questions, they spoke of the weather, and the prices, and how they planned to travel back to Scottsdale by boat. It was better than what Noah read in the newspaper, Eliza thought.

The white-bearded fellow, Braithwaite, then asked if Susannah would like to hear a Bible reading. So far they'd taken no notice of Eliza on her chair in the corner. She spoke up now, startling them, and they turned surprised faces to her. 'May we hear that one about the loaves and fishes?' she asked in her faint voice. 'I like them stories about miracles,' she added with what she hoped was a friendly smile.

Mr Fenny raised his ginger eyebrows and nodded pleasantly in her direction. 'We would be most happy to oblige,' he said, and pulled out his Bible with its black leather cover, rubbed soft. 'A miracle is a fine thing to think on, I agree with you.' He turned the beam of his wide smile full upon Eliza, and she smiled back at him, gratified.

The two men lay their Bibles on the Hatton kitchen table and turned the filmy pages to the Gospels. They took turns at the reading. Both had fine, sonorous voices, the younger one's Scottish accent musical and entrancing. The older one's English voice woke vague memories of Eliza's childhood.

'*And they that did eat of the loaves were about five thousand men,*' concluded Mr Braithwaite. He nodded towards the old woman. 'A fine miracle, Missus, and shows what the Lord can do for us if we have need of Him.'

Eliza sighed with satisfaction and decided she liked the white-bearded one best of the two.

Mr Fenny looked across to the stove where Echo lingered, listening and watching. 'Young lassie,' he said, 'come over here to the table and show me what you've learned at school. Do they not teach you to say the *Lord's Prayer*?'

Certainly Echo knew that one. Hadn't the child gone to the school in Sheffield for years? Eliza had always felt in awe of Echo's schooling.

'Of course,' Echo said in a rush. 'I know plenty of verses besides. I can do the whole of Psalm 121.'

'Oh, well done!' said the preacher. A grin split his red whiskers. He had muttonchops and a moustache.

'Come on then, Eck,' the girl's mother said, waving her hand at Echo. 'Come and say it then.'

Stepping away from the stove, looking suddenly shy, Echo clasped her hands behind her back.

'We would very much enjoy to hear the grand old psalm, wouldn't we, Mr Braithwaite?' said the Scotsman.

'Oh, yes, Mr Fenny. I came all the way to Tasmania, I crossed at the ford, and rode my horse up to this door here, just on purpose to hear this young lady repeat Psalm 121.' He smiled at Echo encouragingly.

Biting her lip, Echo lifted her shoulders and repeated the psalm with no mistakes. *'I will lift up mine eyes unto the hills, from whence cometh my help. My help cometh from the Lord, which made heaven and earth.'*

From her corner, Eliza looked on with delight. That Echo was a smart girl.

7

The family almost forgot to load Eliza into the wagon on the night they went to hear the preachers in Duggan's barn. Susannah was wrapping the baby and herding the small ones out the door when Eliza heaved herself from her chair and began to shuffle towards the door too, pulling her shawl around her shoulders.

'Ay, Ma! You don't want to come out in the wagon at night,' Susannah said. 'I'm feared it will be too rough for you.'

'You ain't leaving me behind, my girl.'

And so Eddie lifted her into the wagon where she sat in the tray propped up by small giggling grandchildren and the wagon lurched down the rugged tracks towards Duggan's place. As they neared the barn Eliza could see other families converging on the same place, boys carrying flaming torches, carts swinging hurricane lanterns. She hadn't been away from the Hatton farm for many months; she hadn't been among such a crowd for as long as she could remember. It seemed to her the whole district had turned out. Her papery old skin tingled with anticipation.

When the boys had staked the bullocks, Eddie lifted her again and carried her up the short rise to the barn. She could feel the muscles in his young arms as he held her against his chest.

'Heave ho then, Grannie,' he said.

Eliza never mentioned it to anyone, but she liked Eddie best. Such a strong boy and the kindest of them all. Inside the barn he set her down on a disintegrating bale of hay pushed against the wall. Many of the women found seats like this, while their children sat on the floor. A pleasant sensation clenched Eliza's insides as she took in the scene: neighbours filling the barn, the warm air, the yellow light, the odour of rotting chaff and sweaty men, the anticipation.

'So many!' she whispered to Susannah, and pointed out one or two she recognised – Tom Bailey the blacksmith, that Mrs Mason from the next farm. Susannah nodded, absorbed in the scene too, looking around for friends. The Coleman girls were there, Eliza saw, and their father with them, that old lag. Respectable now and owning land too – people said he was rich, certainly more prosperous than Noah Hatton, who only leased. It was true though, Eliza mused, that the Coleman girls and their brothers did cop a good deal of haranguing. She'd heard it herself, especially after their grannie came to live with them from Wybalenna on Flinders

Island. It wasn't easy to have a convict *and* an Aborigine in the family. You got it coming both ways. The Coleman boy Percy, Jack's mate, stood tall and skinny among the crowd near the door. That boy always held his head high.

When the preachers stepped onto the platform, Eliza found herself so pressed between the bodies of her family that she couldn't see the men at the front. The barn filled with a sea of sound. The rising of the preacher's voice, the lilt of the hymns, the rhythm under the music, the subterranean rumble of people murmuring, the warmth of the golden barn – all worked on the old woman's senses. Drifting on a tide of sensations, she sensed vague promises in the preachers' tone. The gist seemed to be that everyone could depend on the Lord's forgiveness if they went converted. Even the old lags, or so Eliza understood – those who'd made a few mistakes in their time, which included just about everyone. She'd always assumed she'd earned a rest in the next life, after all her work and trials in this one. This rest would surely be forthcoming in heaven, that's what she'd always expected. But now she wasn't so sure. Was there something else she needed to do? The sounds filling the barn turned into a humming, a soft murmur of indistinguishable words.

Blinking watery eyes and trying to see what was happening, Eliza's attention was caught by Susannah wriggling beside her, trying to stand up. She saw Echo grab the baby from her mother's lap, and none too soon. Eliza gazed up into Susannah's face, startled at the strange expression on it, and reached for her daughter's wrist. 'Ay, what is up with you?' she asked.

Susannah's eyes were glittering and streaming tears, but of course Susannah was always crying. Her mouth hung open. Echo managed to pull her mother back onto the hay bale.

'Ay, Susannah, what has got hold of you?' Eliza asked again.

Before she received an answer, ructions broke out at the front of the barn. Women began moaning and crying and one or two seemed to collapse. Many began to push to the front, to the row of chairs set out there. Men shuffled around the perimeter of the scene like sheepdogs who'd lost control of the flock. A bubble of glee rose up in Eliza's throat as the women took over the show. One woman then another and another stood and pushed forwards, the men standing back with expressions of awe and astonishment. Susannah struggled to her feet again and Eliza managed to get upright too, hanging onto her daughter's wrist.

'Ay, Susannah! Let's go!' she hissed, and the two of them began to stagger through the crowd towards the front. A wind seemed to be blowing from somewhere, whipping the skirts of their dresses against their thighs. It was hard to see anything much, the way the light flickered. The singing began again, '*The Lord will come: the earth shall quake, The hills their fix-ed seat forsake.*'

'Ay, we're going to be saved, Susannah!' Eliza cried in delight, pushing onwards. Her heart began to pound. She slipped on some loose chaff underfoot, but someone reached for her elbow and righted her. The people were singing about the Second Coming of the Lord: everyone would rise and the saved would be in heaven together. The moment had come! Perhaps she was going to head for heaven right now. It could be so – the way she felt so light and everything was flashing brilliantly, and maybe she would be raised up by that breeze she could feel, even stronger now. '*The Lord will come: a dreadful form, with wreath of flame, and robe of storm.*'

But the next thing she felt was Echo pulling her back onto the hay bale, insisting she sit down – Susannah too. They hadn't stumbled more than two steps, although it had felt like the *stairway to heaven*. It had certainly felt like that.

Afterwards, in the wagon on the way home, with the trembling excitement of the barn behind her, she felt as if she'd lived through a tremendous moment. Lucky she'd lived to see it, that was what Eliza thought.

Soon the preachers began offering 'immersions', and the first of them took place in the Dasher, the creek below the Hatton farm. Eddie again carried his grandmother down to see the show.

'Thank ye, Eddie,' she said. 'Me limbs is a bit stiff these days.'

He found a stump to sit her on, said, 'You'll be all right there, Grannie,' and went off to climb a tree to get a better view of things. Perched on the stump, Eliza had a fine vantage point from which to watch that Mrs Mason wade into the Dasher in her best house dress. What a sight! Several women lined up for the same treatment, and Eliza squinted, trying to recognise them. She thought she saw Mrs Miller, Janie's mother, and one or two of the Coleman women, though what were their married names? A black hat bobbed in the creek – one of the preachers, the younger one she thought, standing plumb in the middle of the waterhole and dunking all the neighbours who lined up. It was quite a sight, such an entertainment they never had before in the district.

Eliza had heard of immersionism – Wesleyan Methodists talked of it. Some had lived near her hut, back when she was raising her family. Them Wesleyans were the first preachers to come into the bush. Eliza sighed. She wasn't sure the Wesleyans were proper, nor that fellow standing wet to the waist in the Dasher. But you had to go to town for a proper church, and she hadn't been to town for years now, and what's more she had no wish to ever go to town again. Towns were not ever welcoming, in her experience. Eliza preferred bush people.

'There was never any Anglicans come,' she mused to herself, 'just them Wesleyans, and now these fellas with the immersions. And that show in the barn.'

The memory of the night in Duggan's barn produced a fluttering in her little round stomach, an unruly combination of thrill and doubt. Having admired the Anglicans for so long, she now felt guilty, like a backslider, for having been so taken in at the revival. The Anglicans, after all – they came from England, as she did, the land where she'd been born, that her own mother always called Home, and most people too for that matter.

But that white-haired preacher Mr Braithwaite, the one she liked, he came from England also. You could tell from his voice, and that story he told about being saved in the gutters of London. Where the *skies are like dirty linen.*

Eliza sat on the stump on the hillside in Paradise and listened to the women on the creek bank below singing, '*Shall we gather at the river . . .*'

8

The days drew in and the hours of daylight grew shorter. Eliza overheard her family discussing the preachers who had now left the district and retired to the big towns. It was a great pity, but she supposed they preferred the towns in winter, where they didn't have to do any rough riding and the beds were warmer.

The days at Paradise were duller without them; there was

little news, and Susannah seemed less cheerful. Eliza wondered if her daughter would have liked to repeat that night in the barn. Certainly Eliza herself would like another go at that *stairway to heaven*. When she thought back on that time, she felt she might've missed an opportunity. If only she could have got to the front, to that row of blue chairs, and had the preachers bend over and tell her how to be sure of being on the right side of the Lord when He came again. With all the goings-on in the district lately, His Second Coming might not be too far off.

At Paradise, under the mountain, Noah Hatton worried about his reserves of hay. Eliza listened to him grumbling, listened to him wondering if there'd be enough to keep the animals going through the winter. She knew he had hessian bags of spuds and turnips in the shed, stored since the last harvest. The vegetables were becoming withered in the cold, but at least the family had something. Eliza had known worse times. Sitting in her chair by the stove, by far the cosiest spot in the kitchen, she noticed Noah watching her, a thing he never used to do. Whenever he came into the kitchen these days, the air seemed to tauten. Susannah said he was worried about them starving, but she often said that, as she tried to make the root vegetables stretch.

'That Noah is waiting for me to go,' Eliza muttered to herself. 'It would be one less mouth to feed.'

The next time the boys gathered in the kitchen, cleaning their guns or boots, Eliza called to them. 'Ay, Jack! Ay, Eddie! You boys had better set some snares. Get some rabbits.'

Eddie looked up and grinned at her. 'We set plenty of traps, Grannie.'

'You got to go round them every day,' she said, giving a decisive nod, trying to impress upon them the need to take her advice.

Jack and Eddie set their rabbit snares and spent endless frosty mornings going round the traps to see if there would be meat to go with the turnips. Sometimes they managed to shoot a wallaby, or catch a badger near its burrow, and that meant a tasty stew. Snow fell on the mountain as if to remind the family how close they were to the highlands. The mountain's silver flanks grew mottled with icy patches. Occasionally a white blanket settled across the yard itself and Echo complained when she went out to milk Bessie in the early morning. But snow didn't last long on the ground at Paradise, not like up in the highlands. It would be deep on Middlesex Plains and out towards Cradle Mountain. Percy Coleman had brought his sheep down from there, Jack said, and Percy reckoned it would be a freezing winter this year.

Eliza huddled into her corner and waited to see if there'd soon be rabbit stew.

It had been raining cats and dogs but it finally let up, the day that Susannah's favourite, young Amos, got into trouble. Eliza understood why Susannah preferred the little fellow. He was the only one among the children with blond hair, and he had a chirpy way of asking questions, of laughing at any little thing. Also, he was still young enough to let Susannah embrace him. Soon he'd be too old for that, but for now he was half-baby, half-boy.

At first, when the catastrophe happened, Eliza had trouble working out what had occurred. All she saw was the big boys going out with their guns and their little brother running behind, headed to the traps. Then not long afterwards one of the big boys carried in the small body, just as had happened when Lottie's ankle got broke.

Eliza saw blood seeping through the boy's shirt. Susannah let out a scream at this awful sight and raised her hands to her cheeks. Eddie said not to worry, it was only a bit of shot, she could pick it out soon enough. And Susannah did set quickly to work, cleaning the boy's pale skin, preparing to extract the shot from his shoulder and back. She'd done such jobs before, though on a grown man, not the body of a skinny little child.

'Too small to go rabbiting,' Eliza muttered. She didn't like the look of this. Her stomach lurched but she knew enough to ignore it. Though shaky in the legs, she levered herself from her chair and went about preparing her remedies. 'Crying won't help nothing,' she advised Susannah, but the shocked mother took no notice. Eliza didn't repeat her advice. She'd often enough seen Susannah find release in tears. She shed them so regular and seemed strangely better for it.

Together they worked on the boy, stripping off his shirt to expose his skin and wash his back and shoulder. Eliza held two long clean nails in the flame of the fire to sterilise them. Then, bending over the child, they began picking out the shot that had peppered his little body. Each small wound they splashed with kerosene then covered with rag bandages.

'Will he be all right?' Susannah whispered. 'Will it be enough?'

Eliza examined the boy's white face and listened to his shallow breathing. She mixed a salve of her own recipe: melted beef suet, castor oil, eucalyptus and a sprinkle of boracic powder. It was the best remedy for skin irritations; perhaps it would help take away the redness flowering across the child's back.

Emmeline Clarke arrived – who had summoned her? – and the women conferred in low voices. Mrs C. recommended sassafras tea, but Eliza said that would only thin the blood.

'I reckon he'll be all right if you picked out all the shot,' Emmeline Clarke said, looking doubtfully at the unconscious child.

Eliza gazed down at Amos too. She thought they'd got all the shot – unless some had gone deeper, and you couldn't tell about that. The main worry, in her opinion, though she didn't say so, was the quantity of blood that had soaked his shirt. She wondered if the big boys had hung about before bringing him in. And she wondered which one of them had shot him – though no doubt it had been accidental.

Eliza's instincts turned out to be right, though she'd rather have been wrong. Amos lay quiet, becoming paler, his breath faltering, the hours passing, Susannah up all night beside him. But it did no good. Had they missed some of the shot? Would it have helped if they'd had some strong brandy to dose him? It was no use repining on it. By morning Amos was dead, and there was naught to be done but mourn him and bury him. Susannah lay on her bed, unspeaking, and Echo had to prepare the breakfast and feed the little ones.

That night, sitting in the kitchen, Eliza listened as Noah questioned Jack. Susannah had roused herself at last and sat by the fire, white-faced, feeding the baby. Jack insisted he and Eddie had warned Amos to keep out of the way, that neither of them had seen the little fellow go down to the warren.

'He was too small to go rabbiting,' Jack said, his arms lying along his knees and his head hanging down.

'But who fired the shot, Jack?' Eliza asked, because his parents had not. They raised their faces for his answer.

Jack ducked his head, stood up and sighed. He shoved his hands in his pockets and paced back and forth across the kitchen. 'I don't know,' he replied at last. 'We both of us fired, there was rabbits running about. I don't know which of us hit him.'

Eliza's eyes darted across to Noah. He was harder on fibs than on anything. She wondered what had happened out there in the wet paddock. She wondered how Susannah would keep going – but of course she would. There was the baby, and the little ones.

When the neighbours heard Amos had gone, they came over to say how bad they felt and offered to help dig the pit. Susannah cried at night, cried rivers of tears until Eliza wondered how they weren't flooded out of the house. Susannah insisted that Amos be buried under the celery-top pine in the home paddock next to Caroline. She wanted prayers too, and Echo, the best of them at reading, found one, '*We which are alive and remain shall be caught up together with them in the clouds, to meet the Lord in the air: and so shall we ever be with the Lord. Wherefore comfort one another with these words.*'

It sounded like the Second Coming to Eliza. If that event were close, as the preachers had promised, they might all see Amos again sooner than they reckoned. There was comfort in that. Eliza thought she would remind Susannah of this, if she ever stopped her weeping long enough to listen.

The service was a lovely one, with Echo's reading and Jack saying a prayer over the grave. It was just as good as the service that the old master, Mr Barrett, had spoken over the grave of Ben Walters when he finally died of the drink. 'Rest in peace,' Mr Barrett had said, and Eliza sometimes wondered if Ben had been granted so much.

The old woman sighed. Amos was only a little mite and angelic too; he would surely go to heaven. With the winter come, and now this death upon them, it was hard to recall what had made everyone feel so hopeful, that time in Duggan's barn. Certainly it seemed as if Susannah had forgotten that night. Lately she'd stopped talking about the immersions, and about everyone going converted. Even Jack no longer spoke so much of the Second Coming, but that might have been because Eddie objected and called it 'God-bothering'.

When Amos's burial was done, Eddie helped Eliza back to the house, up past the outhouse by the back fence line. She heard the bush beyond, rustling. A chilly breeze had sidled up, appropriate for a funeral day, a reminder of the cold winds that blow through family life from time to time.

9

That winter seemed so long, with Susannah slow to recover from the loss of the little boy. Noah didn't take it too well either; Eliza supposed it brought back memories of the other one they'd lost, and that being his fault. He wouldn't care to be reminded of that. Daylight hours were short and evening hours dark. Eliza often dozed in her chair, but she would brighten up after tea and spend the hour till bedtime telling stories to the small children, to keep them out of their mother's way and give Susannah some respite to work through her grief. Screwing up her wrinkled forehead, Eliza tried to recall some of the old tales of faeries that her Irish mother had told, but often as not the details became mixed up with her own memories of the Van Diemonian bush.

'Once, deep in the bush, there lived an old man,' she said, beginning a story without really knowing where it would end, 'who wore kangaroo skins as his clothes. His house was in a big old King Billy pine, two hundred years old, which had a hollow trunk. It opened up like a tent flap, and it was big enough for him to live in there. Each evening after dark the animals of the forest came to his tree to see him, and in the end he even learned some of their language.'

'What talk do animals have, Grannie?' one small boy asked.

'Oh, you've heard them. The grunt of the badger, the snick-snick of the wallaby, the shriek of the devil – and the yip-yip of the tiger!'

The boy jumped with pleasurable fright. Eliza had seen plenty of tigers in her time, and she recalled their strange wide jaws and the way they snuck through the undergrowth. She considered them fearsome beasts. They could devastate a chicken coop if they got in. One small girl, leaning against Eliza's knee, sucked her thumb in concentration. The children bent forwards to hear their grannie's low, wavery voice.

'If you go into the bush after dark and you follow the animal tracks by moonlight, you might come right up to his front door in the tree,' Eliza said. 'But don't go in! This old man has lived in the bush for so long, he can no longer tell the difference between a bush animal and a little child. He might eat you for his dinner. All the mothers tell their children this story, but some children don't believe it.'

The little ones laughed.

'Once, there was a girl living near the bush,' Eliza continued, 'who didn't believe the story, or perhaps she just forgot. This girl had ten brothers and sisters, and when she went to school she got into all kinds of trouble and was called names because of her dirty fingernails and her ragged old pinafore. She preferred to play alone and to make her own games in the bush. One afternoon, she stayed so late among the ferns – looking for mushrooms, I reckon – it was too dark to find her way home. She tried one path, but it stopped at a big fallen log, all covered in moss. She tried another, but it petered out at a creek, too deep to cross. She wandered around and around, becoming more and more mixed up and hopelessly lost. Clouds came up and covered the moon and the bush fell as dark as midnight. She sat down where she was and burst into tears.'

The children sat quiet and thoughtful.

'When the girl had cried out all her tears and was exhausted, she finally fell asleep. She slept all night, and all the next day, and into the next night. When she woke up, she felt a hungry pain in her stomach as if she hadn't eaten for a week. Maybe she'd slept for a year! At last, the girl remembered the story of the old kangaroo-skin man and his home in the tree trunk. But instead of being frightened by this thought – as her mother had meant – she longed to find the cosy tree trunk!'

'I want to find it too!' cried a small voice. The others shushed him.

'So when the clouds cleared,' Eliza said, 'and the moonlight and stars came out enough for her to see a little, the girl peered around for the animal paths. Soon she found a narrow track through the ferns that looked like a wallaby had passed that way, or maybe even a person long ago, and she followed it. Sometimes she lost the trail. But she always found it again, and after some considerable time had passed she came to the great King Billy pine with the hollow trunk.'

Her audience gave several small gasps.

'Around the opening in the trunk she could see all the bush animals gathered. She saw possums and wallabies, currawongs and badgers, potoroos and them spotted quolls. She didn't see any devils or tigers – she might have hung back if she did. But instead she walked straight up to the tree and sang out, "Hello! I'm lost! Can I come in?" She was a brave little child. From inside the tree she heard a deep voice, which answered her, "Yes! Come in, little lost one! Welcome home!" Well, in she went and what do you reckon she found inside that big tree?'

Eliza waited, but no-one answered. They waited for her to tell them of the mystery inside the tree. She lowered her voice for this part.

'Inside that tree was just like the inside of a big house, with a staircase and a huge fireplace with logs in it, and a long table loaded up with good things to eat. There was even windows! And when the brave little girl looked out through those windows, do you think she saw the bush in the night? No! She saw daytime, and *skies like dirty linen* and that's how she knew she had reached home at last.'

Eliza paused. She wondered if she'd lost control of the story, which was supposed to be about the dangers of the bush. She sucked in a breath and looked deliberately around at the faces of the children. 'And her family never saw her again.'

The children shuddered and giggled. The story trembled in their minds, both fearful and thrilling. Eliza leaned back in her chair by the stove, feeling a little tired now. It had been a long story, as it turned out.

10

Amos had been buried for several weeks by the time winter began to lift. Spring arrived, mild and warm, and Susannah could leave the house doors open at last. Lime-green shoots appeared in the paddocks and fuzzy-furred joeys were seen poking from the pouches of the wallabies. Susannah seemed to wake from her grief, to respond to mornings without frosts, to regain her cheerfulness. Her apron dried out in the sunshine. Eliza asked Eddie to place her chair out by the byre in the yard. Watching as Susannah pegged out the laundry, she basked in the fresh air of Paradise, felt the faint sap of spring even in her ancient veins, and wondered aloud if they'd go for a picnic soon.

'Them picnics down at Dunn's Swamp we had fine times,' she remarked to the yard. 'Everyone down there on a Sunday afternoon, all the food to share, and spreading blankets on the grass. It were mighty fine down at Dunn's, like an English park it were.'

Susannah had never seen an English park. Eliza wasn't sure she had herself, yet she felt there was no higher praise.

'Yes, we had good times at Dunn's,' Susannah agreed.

'We'd take a feed and have a real good tuck-in,' Eliza went on, and heaved an elaborate sigh. 'Them picnics! Our only pleasure.'

Susannah thumped a pair of her husband's britches on the washboard and scrubbed vigorously. She gave a grunt of disagreement. 'Well, that's not true, Ma. What about the dances we had sometimes, in someone's barn? We might do that again now spring is coming. All them smoky kerosene lamps, and Bob Williams playing his mouth organ.'

'Oh, yes! And Tom the Smithy with his accordion. Lot of work, to clear out a barn for a dance, but Duggan does it sometimes, like for that revival.'

Susannah thumped the britches on the washboard again and let the mention of the revival go by without comment. Eliza had never been able to get her to discuss that night, though she'd tried often enough. Susannah seemed to regard it as some kind of secret.

'And what about the woodchopping?' Susannah said, changing the subject. 'You always liked the woodchopping, Ma.'

'You are right! Our Jack's a fine chopper, a fine one. He's often been the winner.'

'Yes. So don't tell me them picnics were the only things we had for pleasure.'

'But they were good, ay, Susannah? Down at Dunn's Swamp. Going there in the wagon, all the kiddies, boiling the billy with the neighbours.'

Many other things went on at those picnics, they both knew.

Susannah chuckled. 'And some playing kiss-in-the-ring too.'

'And rounders.'

'And singing.'

'Ah, we sang the good old songs,' Eliza said. She leaned back in her chair, gazed vacantly across the yard, and began to hum. She began singing, her voice, a low wobbly contralto, thin with age but still velvety. The words seemed to drift from her. '*Come all you gallant poachers that ramble void of care.*'

'What's that you're singing, Grannie?' Echo asked, slamming the gate of the chook pen.

'*That walk out on a moonlit night with your dog and your gun and your snare. The hare and lofty pheasant you have at your command. Not thinking on your last career upon Van Diemen's Land.*'

'Where'd you learn that song?'

'Me husband used to sing it,' Eliza said. She stopped then, and went back to gazing across the yard and into the bush beyond the fence.

The two preachers returned to the district with the spring. When she heard this news, Eliza brightened, hoping there might be another revival, or some more immersions, and Eddie might take her to see the show again. It had been a long and dreary winter, what with losing young Amos and the frosts thick in the mornings and the tall trunks of the ringbarked trees around the house casting long shadows. Those ghostly trees would never sprout again, but it was with pleasure that Eliza watched green shoots begin to emerge in the vegetable patch.

She wondered if this might be her last spring. This thought didn't concern her too much – it was hardly any surprise – but she did think she would prefer the Lord to carry her into the clouds in His Second Coming rather than join Amos in the muddy soil of Paradise. What had been happening with preparations for His coming? What had the converted of the district been doing about that, ay? Maybe now the preachers had returned some proper action would be taken. Eliza felt ready.

Although the farmhouse began to bustle and hum with activity, no-one offered to take Eliza anywhere. In fact, it was all she could do to keep track of where everyone else went. The big boys constantly had something brewing. As the weather warmed, Jack was always going off somewhere, often as not with the family Bible wrapped in an oilskin cloth.

'It is a bit of a blessing, in one way,' Eliza remarked to Susannah. 'When he's at home, he's always fighting with Eddie.'

The change that had come over the boys puzzled the old woman. They never used to squabble so much. But she'd raised sons herself, sons long gone now, she hardly knew where, and she understood they grew up different no matter what you did. And now, another thing – here was that young fellow Henry coming around, courting Echo, or so it seemed.

The first time he visited, Eliza had been surprised out of her skin: a strange young fellow she'd never seen before, ushered into their kitchen by Echo. It had taken her only a moment to see which way the land lay, of course. The boy was awful good-looking, though he needed a new hat. When Echo brought him in, Susannah was at an old black pot on the stove, stirring something. The skinny young fellow, with a face carved like the sides of the mountain, stood among all the small brothers and sisters, clutching his battered hat. Eliza watched him shift his weight from one leg to the other and twist his hat brim in scarred brown hands. He had an air to him she hadn't seen for years, but she recognised it straightaway: that mixture of grim poverty and independence found in bushmen from the back country. Tall, with a high forehead and thick rough-cut hair, he was certainly a handsome boy. It didn't surprise her that her granddaughter was taken with this young fellow, poor though he looked. Echo, making tea, rushed and dropped the teaspoon, spilling smoky tea leaves on the floor.

'Watch out, Eck,' her mother said. 'What's the matter with you?'

Over in her corner Eliza watched on with amusement, one hand resting on her little pot-bellied stomach.

'Sit down, won't you?' Echo said to Henry, waving him towards the chairs at the family table.

Henry perched on the edge of a chair, still hanging onto his hat. Susannah turned at last from the stove, picked up a toddler and secured him on her hip, stood solid in her kitchen, and eyed this fellow who had come to court her daughter. Eliza watched her give him a long, frank inspection, head to toe, casting her gaze over his ragged waistcoat and his britches tied up at the knee with string. Henry took this inspection calmly, returning Susannah's gaze with a mild expression, his face tucked in on itself, keeping its counsel.

After he'd drunk his tea and gone, Eliza's black eyes darted from Susannah to Echo. 'He's a good-looking one, Eck, that's for sure,' she said.

Echo blushed. 'I don't want to talk about him, Grannie.'

'You needn't peck up like that. It's natural enough.' One of her low chuckles escaped her.

Echo grabbed the teapot and hurried outside to empty the dregs.

When these visits of Henry's had gone on for a few weeks – he came most Saturdays, and sometimes on weekdays too – Noah expressed doubts about the boy. It was obvious, from his threadbare clothes and the way he had no steady work, that Henry was even poorer than the Hattons.

'He's only a rabbitoh,' Noah told Echo.

She stamped her foot and said he was a prospector, he could strike it rich one day.

'I don't want you marrying a rabbitoh,' Noah said, stubborn. He thought for a moment. 'Nor a prospector.'

'I got to marry sometime,' Echo replied sharply. But she seemed unsure.

'Is he converted?' Susannah asked. Those who had converted and those who hadn't was a great topic of conversation in the district.

'I ain't asked,' Echo said, flushing, 'and I've got to finish this mending, those girls are so careless with their things. I don't wish to talk about it anymore.'

'Is his father a convict?' Eliza asked, but Echo had left the kitchen.

Most people had a convict or two in their family, like her own. It didn't mean much, but there was no doubt it could attract taunts from some. Eliza wondered why Noah should object to a rabbitoh. 'Rabbits is good eating,' she said to herself.

11

Spring had come in warm and wet and Noah was fussing about his wheat crop. He was feared of the smut taking it, as well he might be, thought Eliza, with the weather like it was. Vegetables were doing well, the peas in the vegetable patch winding up the tea-tree stick trellises. Luckily the frost hadn't got them, and Eliza hoped for peas to pod again soon. When the rain stopped she liked to sit outside, basking in the warmth of the spring sun. Her bones seemed often to ache these days. She used to be able to take a shuffling walk around the yard on her own, leaning on a stick Jack had made for her, but this spring she needed someone to help her. If he were around, Eddie would often walk with her, though it made slow progress for a young fellow.

The preacher with the red beard, that James Fenny, had been back to the house. Eliza had sat amazed when he started in with his praying in the kitchen; she'd hoped for another Bible reading, another one of them miracles. They could use a good miracle around here, after Amos. But they all seemed more worried about the wheat. If Noah had asked her, she could have told him this winter would be too wet to sow, but he never asked her advice about anything. In any case, it appeared that the Lord had answered that preacher's prayers, and the wheat looked like it would dry out and not get the smut after all, so that was something.

One morning, watching from her chair in the yard, Eliza saw the family bundle themselves into the bullock wagon. Jack had hitched only two animals, Blue Boy and Lion, so that meant it was probably a trip to town. Noah and Susannah climbed in, and Echo too, with Jack at the head of the leader with his stock whip. Eddie, staying behind, stood in the kitchen doorway.

'Where you all going?' asked Eliza, into the hubbub of departure.

Jack called to the bullocks, '*Haw! Haw!*' The wagon wheeled about and heaved out of the yard and onto the track.

'Where they going, Eddie?' Eliza asked again.

He looked over at her, frowning, then strolled to the byre and peered in to check on the milk cow. Taking a straw from the manger, he squatted beside Eliza's chair and picked at his teeth. 'They are going to dunk their selves in the creek,' he said, not without a note of disgust.

'They going to get *immersed*?' Eliza asked, surprised. 'All of 'em?' She wouldn't have thought it of her own family. And why hadn't Susannah told her about it?

'Mother and Echo,' Eddie said, shortly. 'Jack already did.'

'Already did!' Eliza exclaimed. 'Crikey me!' People were not telling her the news as they should.

The two sat silently in the yard for a few moments, with the mountain overhead and the ringbarked trees rustling. The foothills had the air of a ghost forest.

'What do you reckon, Grannie?' Eddie asked at last. It seemed to dawn on him that the old woman might have an opinion about these developments.

'Well, Eddie,' Eliza said slowly, 'I got to say, I'm a bit startled. True, it were a right good time, that revival in Duggan's barn. Best show I ever seen. And I was certainly pleased to hear news of the Second Coming.'

Eddie grunted but didn't say anything. He chewed on his straw and waited for more.

Eliza squirmed a little, sat up straighter. 'But all this Bible reading every night, Eddie – and this getting immersed! I don't think they do that in the Anglican church.'

Eddie laughed. 'I don't reckon they do.'

She considered this. All along, the preachers and their goings-on had seemed a little taboo. That explained why it all felt so exciting. Though it was obvious Eddie didn't think much of it.

'You won't get immersed, will you, Eddie?'

He snorted. 'Not likely! I got work to do. I ain't mucking around with that God-bothering.'

Eliza settled back in her chair. Always plenty of work to be done on a farm, that was for sure, and Jack had been away a lot lately what with his scripture meetings and whatever else was going on. If anyone had asked her, Eliza would have told them to look to the farm, or how could they be sure to survive the next season? She thought about explaining this to Eddie. He sometimes asked her advice; that might be why he was her favourite.

'And some of them new Christians ain't all that *Christian*, it seems to me,' Eddie remarked, breaking the silence between them.

Something about the way he said this made Eliza think he was about to confess a secret.

'They get all caught up in theirselves,' Eddie went on, 'and regard theirselves as better than the next man.'

'That is surely no good, Eddie. And it ain't what the Bible teaches, I don't reckon.'

He glanced at her. 'Did you used to go to church, Grannie?'

She sighed happily. 'That time when I were married.'

He chuckled. 'But any other time?'

'Oh, no. There weren't no church where we lived, except a Wesleyan chapel over at Latrobe, but me husband weren't one to go to chapel.' Eliza looked into the middle distance, peering into the past, remembering her husband who took her to church to marry her.

'But you learned them Bible stories, didn't you?'

''Course I did. My mother told us them, as I told me own children. We were Anglican in the old country, or so my mother said, though she were Irish.' Eliza felt her thoughts muddle for a moment. Sometimes it was difficult to sort out her memories.

'There's Irish over to Railton,' Eddie said, 'and at Vinegar Hill.'

'We lived at Maidstone. The skies were *like dirty linen.*'

Eddie chuckled again, then stood and stretched. 'I don't like this God-bothering that's infected everyone. It's like they all drank a potion and become bewitched – or poisoned, more like. I just want to get on with things, and no-one saying I'm lesser than them because I choose to mind my own business.'

His tone had become bitter. Eliza wondered what had occurred.

'Well,' she said, intending to comfort, 'whatever happens in this life, you will surely be rewarded in heaven, Eddie.'

He surprised her with a snort. 'I don't place no reliance on that. I reckon we got only one life, and it's a good idea to get on with things.'

She considered her favourite grandson, his skinny neck and bobbing Adam's apple, and saw a faint look of Ben Walters, something she hadn't noticed before.

'You should go out on your own, Eddie,' she suggested. 'You got a girl?'

Eddie looked down at her, his face bright with surprise. 'I think you're right, Grannie.'

She wasn't sure if he meant the part about going out on his own, or the part about getting a girl.

12

Summer warmth embraced Eliza, dozing in her chair in the yard. Echo was elbow-deep in the wash-day tub, flushed red in the face. When Eliza roused from her nap she watched the girl for a while, slapping the children's pinafores and overalls on the washboard. Henry had not been to the farmhouse for some time. She mentioned this to Echo, and asked where that Henry was, and the girl screwed up her face, ugly.

'He's gone to the mountain country for the summer,' Echo replied, shortly. 'He's trapping possums.'

The slap of wet clothes on the washboard seemed intended to fend off more questions about Henry. Eliza regarded her eldest granddaughter for a few long minutes. Of late she'd noticed Echo's temper was sharper than usual, though she'd always been a grumpy sort of girl. Now, however, Eliza detected more than grumpiness. It seemed more like worry.

'You poorly, Eck?' she asked. 'You could try some of my tonic if you'd like.'

Percy Coleman had brought some pepper berry leaves and twigs down from Cradle Mountain and given them to Jack for his grannie's aches and pains. Percy said to make a tea of them; his own grannie was an Aborigine, that's how he knew the best remedies.

'Pepper berry is good for colic,' Eliza said. 'You suffering?'

Echo slapped the shirt she held onto the washboard and told her grannie, rudely, that she didn't have no colic. She paused in her work and straightened up. Eliza watched her push one fist into the small of her back and stretch.

'You could try it, Eck.'

Echo gave out a deep, irritated sigh. Then she seemed to decide that her grannie knew plenty about such things, and said she would try some pepper berry tea.

'Good idea,' Eliza said. She added softly, 'And I hope that Henry comes back soon.'

Eliza felt the reality of her thin, life-hardened body. Her aches and pains were not getting any less, despite the pepper berry tonic. Sometimes, dozing, wandering in her memories, she missed much of what went on around her. Yet there were other times when she saw more than they did themselves. Eddie had moved out to farm potatoes at Staverton, a development that hit Eliza hard, and Susannah too, but at least put an end to all the fighting between him and Jack. Before he went, he'd brought that girl Janie Miller to see them, the one who had been Echo's schoolfriend. Eliza gave the girl a good looking-over and formed her own views on why the boy had decided to move out to Staverton. Remembering Eddie, her favourite, she heaved a sigh and wished she could see him again. He'd only come back to Paradise that once, to return the borrowed bullocks, and Eliza certainly wasn't going to get over to Staverton; it was too far out, on the edge of the world.

So it came as quite a surprise the day Eddie arrived back at the farm driving the new cart with their cart horse Creamy pelting into the yard like a wild thing, Echo next to him on the driver's bench. Eliza watched as Echo took a bundle from the cart and thrust a baby into Susannah's arms.

'Whose mite is that?' Eliza asked.

No-one answered. But she was gratified when Eddie turned to her, sitting by the stove. He smiled, though it seemed that the smile was an effort, that the boy's face hadn't creased for a smile in quite some time. He came over and took her wrinkled hands in his, and asked, 'How are you, Grannie?' and she had heartswell and hoped he was going to stay for a while.

Eddie was still stopping at Paradise when the men had to dig the burial pit in the new town cemetery. The whole family went in the wagon for the service, which Jack led because the preachers had moved on. Standing beside the grave, Eliza leaned on her stick and looked down into the muddy hole. Burying was always a sombre thing. She heard the thin whimper of a baby wrapped under a coat – poor scrap of a thing, brought out on a wet morning like this. The people gathered around the grave sang, '*When all my labours and trials are o'er, And I am safe on that beautiful shore.*'

Eliza expected to be buried herself soon. It couldn't be far off. If that *stairway to heaven* she'd glimpsed at the revival was never to be hers, if she missed the Second Coming, she supposed she would simply wear out one day and expire with a sigh. She would have preferred something more colourful, more celebratory, like that golden night in Duggan's barn. And there was still a niggling worry: that the Lord might not welcome her into heaven. He'd have to be willing to forgive a few things.

As for getting immersed like so many others, she reckoned she was too old for that trial. Surely He couldn't demand that of her? Hadn't she put up with enough in her life? These thoughts made her uneasy but she took comfort in the idea that at least she'd been proper married, in an Anglican church. Her one good thing. She felt that would count for something when her turn came.

Jack

1

A bird's eye view of the town of Sheffield on the Kentish Plains would have shown one long, muddy road passing for a main street, the crossbars of the fenced sale yards (filled with animals on sale day), half-a-dozen men in hats standing about in small clusters as if sprinkled onto the scene, a farmer leading a white cart horse and a couple of loose dogs running alongside. On one side of the main street stood a substantial-looking timber building with two storeys and a verandah. Opposite it was a smaller wooden building with a steep pitched roof. In the middle distance a backdrop of strange white tree trunks clustered and rattled like skeletons in the breeze. Behind the town the mountain, blue and hazy in the autumn sunlight, overlooked the district, the rough tracks converging on the muddy main street, and the farms embedded here and there on the low hillsides. Much of the area appeared good farming land, broad grassy plains and plenty of open country, but here and there a plot had been cut out of thicker, scrubby forest and stood isolated in a patch of cleared ground, the startling white trunks of the ring-barked trees surrounding a wooden hut.

In Sheffield's main street a crowd had gathered. Tuesdays were sale days. The autumn morning had dawned cold and the first frost of the season lingered in the shadows. Jack Hatton, a tall sixteen-year-old, was there with his brother Eddie. They'd driven a small herd of pigs into town, about a dozen fat piglet boars, now enclosed behind the fences of the sale yards. The grunts of the boarlets and the bleats of Percy Coleman's sheep, which he wanted to sell for mutton, combined in a loud racket. Sweaty animal odours hung in the air along with the scent of tobacco from the pipes. Beards and hats clustered along the fences. Sitting on a top rail, Jack pulled a tobacco pouch from his pocket and began filling his pipe. When he had it fixed to his liking he said to his mate, 'You got a light, Perce?'

Percy Coleman leaned against the fence, staring out under his hat brim, his face hard to read. The reading of Percy's thoughts often preoccupied Jack, who had a desire to be like his mate, to know the things he knew. For example Percy, who was several years older than Jack, had far more experience with animals and the ways of the sale yards on Tuesdays, the deals done on the sidelines, how to ensure a decent price for what you had to offer.

Eventually, after a slow turn of his head, Percy pushed himself off the fence and reached into his pocket. The sharp sound of a match being struck flared into the cold morning air and yellow flame singed the shag in Jack's pipe, sending a tendril of leaf-scented smoke up past his hat brim.

'Ta, mate,' Jack nodded thanks.

Now and then he glanced towards the schoolroom door. The Union chapel building with the steep pitched roof doubled as a schoolroom and class was due out soon. There was nothing much of interest in the main street of Sheffield beyond the sale yards, the inn, the chapel, and the blacksmith's shed and forge. Jack noticed his brother Eddie sauntering across to the sale yards and staring over at the schoolroom door. Jack wondered why.

'We going to get these pigs sold, Jack?' Eddie asked, as he reached his brother. 'I'd rather be gone before them Dunstans get here.'

The brothers were a year apart but people often told Jack they looked similar from afar. That was probably because they were both lanky and thin. Jack, being the eldest, tried to hold his chin higher so people wouldn't confuse him with Eddie, who often stared down at his boots. Jack watched the prominent Adam's apple in his brother's throat rise and fall as Eddie chewed the side of his tongue. He was still watching the schoolroom door.

The auctioneer climbed onto his wooden pedestal. His breath issued in cloudy bursts. Pointing to the animals as they were offered, calling the names of those offering them and those whose bids he heard, he made short work of the sale. The Hatton pigs sold soon enough, though at a disappointing price. Jack often found the price disappointing, but it was never worth driving the pigs home again. You had to take what you could get. Pigs were unruly brutes.

The sale ended. No sign of the Dunstan boys. Jack and Eddie were supposed to wait for their younger brothers and sisters to come out of school. Meanwhile Jack suggested they spend a few pence from the sale proceeds on a couple of pots of ale. The brothers strolled over to the inn with their big mongrel dog, Rags, trotting behind them. As long as they stuck to the innkeeper's home-brewed ale and steered clear of the grog, their father didn't mind them having a drink.

'You coming, Percy?' Jack asked.

Percy's sheep had sold well, better than the pigs, and Jack saw him counting a palm full of coins.

'I reckon,' he said, and turned to walk beside the brothers.

At the inn Eddie paid for two pint pots, making sure of the

change. He carried the pots back to his brother and handed him one.

'How'd you go today, Perce?' Jack asked.

Percy Coleman took a long slow slurp from his pot and let out an *Ahhhh* sound. He looked pleased with himself. 'Pretty good. You know I'm going in with me brother out at Mount Claude? He's got a tin lease. This profit from the sheep will finally give me enough to buy into his lease. The Great Spur Tin Mining Company. You want to come in with us, Jack?'

Jack felt a thrill travel up his insides. The Coleman brothers were always taking up mining leases and it sounded like tin was the new bonanza. It had been gold in the Minnow for a while. The idea of finding gold had mesmerised Jack. He had a divining rod, he could find water pretty well, and an old bloke had told him the stick was good for gold too – if you had the touch. He reckoned he did; he wanted to try anyway. You had to try. But he could only dream for now.

'Nah, Perce, you know I ain't got no money,' he said.

The thrill inside him subsided as quickly as it had come. He had wanted to go in with Percy on the Minnow lease but his father had put his foot down. 'Half-baked idea,' Noah had said. But Jack believed in Percy; he was a smart one. He knew more than anyone else in the district, even more than the first farmers who'd been here for fifteen years. Percy got a lot of secrets from his grannie. Sometimes he'd let Jack in on something, something really useful, like the gold. But Noah had called it a 'dreamers' enterprise'.

Jack took a swig of his brew, wiped the back of his hand across his mouth, looked up, and saw the Dunstans coming up the street. He nudged Eddie. They both steadied themselves for the inevitable taunts. Nothing could be done.

The three Dunstan boys eyed the Hattons as they came into the inn. The Dunstans all wore hats, dirty britches held up by suspenders, worn woollen waistcoats and rough jackets. None was old enough to have grown more than faint stubble. The other farmers, fresh from the business of the sale, grinned among themselves. Jack knew they were waiting for the show to start. And soon it did.

Arthur Dunstan, veering to pass behind Eddie, jogged his elbow. Eddie's beer splashed onto the dusty verandah and he looked down at the patch of beery mud spreading around his boots.

'Bloody convicts,' Arthur muttered as he ducked past.

Eddie's quick temper flared, as Jack knew it would. Arthur Dunstan hadn't gone two steps before Eddie had put down his pot and grabbed him by the armholes of his waistcoat. He brought his face to within an inch of Arthur's long, pointed nose. A rising tide of mottled red tinged Arthur's cheeks.

'Let go of me, you bloody convict,' Arthur hissed into Eddie's furious face.

'Take it back, you mongrel.'

Over at the bar, Percy Coleman also put down his pint pot. He walked across the dirt floor of the inn and leaned in close to the two boys, his hands on his hips. 'Cut it out, lads,' he said softly. 'You are disturbing our drinking.'

Eddie gave Arthur a shake, then let him go. Arthur shrugged his shoulders, sneered, and pulled at his waistcoat. Before he moved off to join his brothers, he edged close to Eddie again. 'Convicts and Blacks stick together, ay?' he hissed.

The older men, standing with their elbows resting on windowsills or along the bar, pushed their hats back on their foreheads and continued to watch the show. Jack glanced towards Percy, but he might not have heard Arthur's jeer for all the notice he took of it. The beer in Jack's stomach churned in gassy turmoil and he grabbed hold of his brother's arm. 'Come on, Eddie, leave him.' Jack had a better idea than brawling here in front of an audience. 'We'll get 'em later.'

'Good advice, young 'un,' Percy said, shoving his hat back on his head. He drained his pot and left.

Jack's last remark had been loud enough for the Dunstan boys to hear. They understood, Jack could tell, from the way they stood there grinning.

Later. At the ambush rock. A showdown.

Jack's sister Echo had emerged from the schoolroom and crossed the street in time to see the whole exchange – and to hear Jack's parting shot. Rags, waiting outside the inn, gave her a low growl of welcome.

'What's happening, Jack?' she asked. 'Will there be a fight?' Pink spots bloomed on her cheeks.

'I'll tell you on the way,' Jack replied, and stepped into the dusty main street. He rounded up the little Hatton kids as they too emerged from the schoolroom. Sometimes he thought they were worse to drive along than pigs. 'Get on home,' he said, sending them ahead, 'and tell Father we got the sale money and are coming directly.'

Echo and Charlotte, the older Hatton girls, stood with their brothers. The three Dunstans lined up along the verandah. Rags was dashing around in a wind blowing down from the mountain. Another rainstorm was on the way; there'd been a lot of rain this autumn. Arthur Dunstan stared at Echo and grinned when she met his eye.

Jack couldn't help but notice, and turned a suspicious face to Echo. 'You haven't been talking to that Arthur, have you, Eck?' he said. 'I don't know how those Dunstans know about that old lag Ben Walters. You didn't tell him, did you?'

'Of course not! You going to fight them, ain't you, Jack?'

'If I have to.' But he wasn't keen. His father wouldn't think it was worth it, fighting poor scum like the Dunstans over nothing but an insult. 'Where's Janie, anyway? Ain't she at school today?'

Janie Miller was Echo's best friend.

'Oh, she's coming out soon. But will you fight them Dunstans, Jack?'

Jack gave a sigh, shoved his hands in his pockets and looked around. They should be getting on, but he wanted to see Janie. On the verandah, Arthur Dunstan stood there grinning. Echo glanced up at him again and blushed faintly. But Jack didn't have time to think about that anymore, because Janie had appeared at the schoolroom door. She had her bag slung across her chest and her fair hair flew out around her peaked little face. Jack took a step towards her; he wanted to say something. But Janie saw everyone staring, ducked her head and hurried away, disappearing around the back of the inn.

'She's going to meet her mother,' Echo said, watching Jack watching Janie.

Ignoring a small fizz of disappointment, Jack turned back to his brother and sisters and raised his voice, gruffly commanding them to get going. The dog followed them out along the track lined with dead white tree trunks.

2

It was a five-mile walk from Sheffield to the Hatton farm, wedged on a hillside in Paradise. Leaving town, Jack led the way through the forest of ghostly ringbarked eucalypts. They kept to the centre of the track to avoid the canopy of white limbs; any one of them could fall unexpectedly. The shadows of the bare trunks striped the track as the sun lowered in the sky. Reaching thicker bush, they followed an old trail they knew, the quickest way home. The smaller children had run ahead and Charlotte hurried to follow them.

'Lottie don't want to see the fight,' Echo said.

The three older Hattons approached the big rock cautiously, expecting the Dunstans to be hiding nearby. Behind the rock they had a stash of river stones, brought down from the Gog mountain. These stones were one of the secrets Percy Coleman had let Jack in on. The Blacks had used them in the old times to grind their ochre up at the mine in the Gog range. Percy had taken Jack up there once, following a trail on the other side of the Dasher that ran up into the foothills. Pacing along quietly, as if listening for something, Percy had led the way along the eastern end of the range and up towards the brow of a conical hill. Jack had been surprised at how clear the trail seemed, though it'd been hard enough to find the start of it. Even Percy had hesitated, and pushed back and forth through the bush for a while.

'Can't you find the way, Perce?' Jack had asked.

Percy had replied with a finger to his lips. 'I'll find it. In the old days this country was well burned. The ancestors could travel through easy. Now I got to look careful.'

JACK

He cast about, looking from one rocky outcrop to another, and in the end he found the path. Jack wondered if badgers had made it, but it seemed broader and well-trodden, like plenty of people had been that way before.

Near the top of the hill, they'd found a shallow hole. Percy picked up a stick, sharpened at the end like a chisel, and began digging in the base of the hole. Jack could see several shallow diggings across the hillside. Percy grubbed out the reddish-coloured earth and stowed several big handfuls in his kangaroo-leather pouch. He said it was 'ochre', and he was taking it for his grannie.

He then showed Jack the stones, brought up from the Mersey to grind the ochre, left scattered around these abandoned mines. Pearly-grey, the stones had been worn smooth by the river and fitted neatly into one hand. Jack understood how useful they'd be as missiles. He took a few that first time, carrying them in his britches pockets, and Percy did the same. He said his grannie would grind the ochre and make paint. Jack couldn't think what you'd want that for, but there were things Percy's grannie did that only made sense to her. He'd seen her with Percy's baby brother tied on her back, going round the hills and lighting fires so her family could see where she was. Percy told him she was good at finding big grubs. They were tasty morsels, Percy said.

Jack went back for more river stones on later expeditions to the mine. He never told Percy he was collecting them; he felt like he might be taking something that wasn't his. Nevertheless, he'd amassed quite a collection in the hiding place behind the big rock, and now they'd come in handy in the fight with the Dunstans.

Rags pushed his nose under their arms as they pulled the camouflaging branches back and started to go through the smooth stones, selecting their weapons. Jack picked up a couple, shoved them in his pockets and began to climb the big rock. On top, he lay on his stomach and peered along the track, listening to the rustling in the undergrowth, sorting out the familiar sounds from any unusual activity.

Suddenly, he gave a low whistle, slithered down the rock and ran out onto the track, not caring that he might be in full sight of their enemies. The dog bounded after him, barking. Behind him, he heard Eddie hiss, 'What's he doing?'

Ahead, their little sister Charlotte lay on her side in the dust. As Jack bent over her, the others came running up. They stared in shock at the white-faced child. Rags paused beside them, panting. The little girl groaned. With Jack's arm around her shoulders, she sat up and pointed to her foot, moaning, 'It *hurts*, Jack.' Beside her lay a large smooth stone.

'What happened, Lottie?' Echo asked.

The child described how the other kids ran ahead but she couldn't catch up to them, and when she passed the big rock a stone came flying from nowhere and knocked her down and now her foot hurt so much she couldn't stand up, she'd tried, she had, Jack, but she just couldn't.

'Mongrels,' Eddie muttered.

'I reckon her ankle is broke,' Jack said, and he hoisted his little sister onto his shoulder. 'Better get her home.'

Revenge on the Dunstans would have to wait. They must look after the kiddie, so they set off, another two miles to go and the wind had picked up too. Eddie kept muttering that the Dunstans were cowards, and he paused now and then to yell into the bush, 'Mongrels!' Jack huffed at this waste of breath.

The small party turned a corner of the track. Arthur Dunstan and his brothers were standing there, presumably lured out of hiding by Eddie's taunts. Everyone stood stock-still; even Rags paused.

Arthur Dunstan stepped forwards, a tense-looking spokesman. His sandy hair stood awry, as if he'd been pushing his hands through it. A moment passed. Then he spoke, his voice low and gruff. 'You take the kiddie home,' he said, gesturing to Jack, carrying the child, 'while we deal with this here *convict*.' He pointed to Eddie and spat.

Jack hesitated, but Eddie's fists immediately lifted into a boxer's stance. Arthur squared up to him. One on one. The others stepped back a little.

'I don't know, Eddie,' Jack said. 'We got to get the little one home to Mother.'

But Eddie, ignoring this, took a step closer to Arthur Dunstan.

The fight was on.

The two boys dodged about a bit, sparring as their fathers had taught them. Then with a sharp jab Eddie moved in and the punches began to fly, fists connecting with shoulders and torsos and, with sickening thuds, jaws. The dog barked, dashing around in circles. Jumping and squealing, Echo urged her brother on, flailing her own little fists as if she were in the thick of the melee as well.

'Get him, Eddie! Get him!' she yelled.

Jack felt exasperated. This fighting when Lottie was hurt, it was wasting time. He lay the child, whimpering, on the ground at the edge of the track. There was no chance of stopping the fight now; he hoped Eddie would get it over with quick. He watched the boys closely, looking out for foul play, ready to intervene. When both fighters became bloodied, he stepped in to pull Eddie back. Arthur's brothers did the same for him. The two boys were panting and sweating. Eddie had blood running all over him but Jack thought it was only from his nose. Arthur's face was bleeding too and it looked like he might have a nasty split on his eyebrow.

'Good one, Eddie!' Echo said, elated.

Eddie gasped, trying to get his breath back. 'Why'd you hit the kid, you cowards?' he growled angrily.

One of the Dunstans looked across the churned-up track. 'We thought it were you lot, didn't we? You shouldn't have sent a kiddie along to the place.'

Tempers began to subside. Blood had been spilled, feelings eased in the physical clash of bodies. The Hattons turned their attention to the injured child, white-faced and still whimpering. Jack picked her up again and they carried on walking. With Arthur supported by his brothers, the Dunstans turned away in the other direction. The bush track returned to silence.

At Paradise their mother shrieked when the caravan of wounded arrived in the yard, the dog racing ahead. At first she rushed to Eddie, covered in blood. But he waved her away, told her it was nothing. He went to the bucket to douse his head with cold creek water.

'You better take a look at Lottie's ankle, Mother,' Jack said, and he carried the child inside to the sugar-bag mattress where she slept at night with her sisters. He set her down with care, then backed out of the kitchen to allow the women to do what they could. Grannie Eliza rose from her chair by the stove and began to warm a pan of water.

Out in the yard, the older Hattons conferred.

'You landed a few good ones, Eddie,' Echo said. 'I reckon you won that one.' She handed her brother a fresh-soaked rag for his nose.

'They won't try it on again for a while,' Jack said, 'not after breaking the little one's foot.'

'What do you reckon Father'll say about that?' asked Eddie, voice nasal through his bunged-up nose.

Jack spat thoughtfully into the dust. Their father wouldn't be happy about Charlotte's foot.

'He will surely be proud of Eddie,' Echo said.

'I don't know,' said Jack, kicking at the water bucket. The Dunstans had asked for trouble, but he wasn't sure they could explain this to their father.

'Good thing we got the sale money,' Eddie mumbled through the soaked rag.

'Yes,' Jack said. 'We should give it to him right away. Before he has time to get steamed up about the fight.'

Eddie reached into his britches pocket where he'd stowed the few shillings the pigs had brought at the sale. But his fingers came out empty. Same with the other pocket. Same with *all* his pockets. He tossed away the wet rag and searched frantically. 'Did *you* have it, Jack?'

Jack turned out his own pockets, protesting that he never had the money, Eddie had the money. He remembered Eddie paying for the ales at the inn. The money had been in Eddie's pocket – until it wasn't. Echo checked her own pinafore pocket, though the coins couldn't possibly have got in there.

'You must've lost it in the fight,' Jack said, 'when you were rolling around in the dust with that Arthur Dunstan.'

There was nothing for it but to go back along the track and look for it. Evening darkness wouldn't help things, Eddie argued, saying they should wait until the next day. But Jack didn't trust the Dunstans one inch; they might find the money and they'd take it for sure. He insisted on a search right away. Besides, their father would ask about it as soon as he got in from the bottom paddock.

The brothers took a kerosene lantern with them and retraced their steps, but all they found at the spot where the fight had taken place were patches of wet bloody mud, and a curious wallaby that hopped off into the bush. They came back without the sale money.

Father, standing stock-still in the yard, listened to Jack tell him of Charlotte's injury, of the taunts of the Dunstans and the fight, of the loss of the sale money. Jack watched warily as strong emotions chased across his father's face, Noah's beard twitching and his cheeks darkening. He waited, hands in pockets, boots shuffling. He wouldn't be surprised if Father gave Eddie a good thumping; he probably deserved it, losing the money like that. Mother stood watching, twisting her apron. Jack saw his father's fists clench; he wouldn't want to be Eddie right now.

'You should've been more careful,' Father said eventually. He drew his eyebrows together, and kept his fists clenched, but he didn't lose his temper. He just seemed awful worried. 'You want us to starve?'

This talk of 'starving' had been hanging around for weeks now.

'I'll find it, Father,' Eddie said, 'once it's daylight. If them Dunstans have not made off with it.'

'And I'll get some rabbits tomorrow,' Jack said. 'We won't starve.'

To Jack's surprise, their father didn't fire up. He merely grunted, turned, and walked slowly across the yard to finish stabling his bullocks.

Mother heaved a deep sigh. 'It's hard, Jack, losing the money like that,' she said quietly. 'Go and help him with the bullocks, will you?'

Reluctantly, Jack crossed the yard. Lion and Blue Boy were manoeuvred into their stalls, the yoke hung up, and straw heaved into the manger. The bullocks gave off a solid animal odour, shuffled in their stalls, oblivious to all but their feed and shelter. The sounds and smells and proximity of the animals helped soothe Jack's turbulent thoughts. He glanced over at his father, wondering if the bullocks calmed him too. Not that Father seemed agitated; the way he hung his head over his hands as he worked looked more like weariness than anger. Jack was used to his father's silences, though usually they were anything but tranquil. Those silences often seemed to Jack like an underground rumble that hadn't yet broken to the surface but might at any moment. He wondered if tonight would be one of those times. But his father's temper seemed to have gone off the boil.

'I can get some rabbits tomorrow,' Jack repeated.

Father pulled the bullock pen closed for the night. 'Make sure you go round the traps early, then.'

Jack wondered what his father was thinking, wondered if he should tell him about the tin lease out at Mount Claude that could make some *real* money, not like the sale money. But what would be the use? The Hattons didn't have any capital for mining, nor for anything else. Not even for one of the new steam threshers, a thing that could really make a difference when they finally got a crop of wheat in. What would Father do if those Dunstans taunted *him*, called *him* a convict? Did he come from convict blood like Mother? Grannie whispered that he did, that Grandfather Hatton had been a smuggler, but Jack wasn't sure; it might be one of Grannie's tall tales. Jack suspected many people in the district had an old lag in their family tree somewhere. People generally made sure to shut up about things like that – and so should those Dunstans.

Now that Jack considered the matter, watching his father's retreating back across the starlit yard, he wondered if his own anger at the Dunstan boys might have had something to do with Arthur making eyes at Echo. Jack didn't like that sort of thing. Echo was his sister; she should steer clear of those dirt-poor Dunstans. And why did Arthur Dunstan want to pick a fight with the Hatton boys anyway? Things could get confusing if you thought on them too much.

He shrugged, drawing up his shoulders against the cold and his father's silence. As he headed indoors he passed the byre and noticed Echo in the shadows. That girl, always lurking about, listening. Not that there'd been anything to hear tonight. Grabbing her by the arm, he took her into the house with him. 'You keep away from that Arthur Dunstan,' he hissed.

They left their father standing at the fence line of his yard, staring into the bush.

3

Having turned sixteen, it had been some years since Jack had spent his days in the schoolroom in Sheffield. Even when he was younger, he never went that often, since his father needed him on the farm. Jack had tried his best to learn his letters but somehow he never could get them straight. Outside of the schoolroom, this wasn't a problem, since Echo had turned out to be a natural at letters and willing to help him if asked. Not that there was much he wanted to read: maybe an old copy of *The Examiner* he picked up at the inn. Mother couldn't read, and it never worried her.

Echo borrowed a book from school, a story called *Robinson Crusoe*. She read it aloud to her little brothers and sisters every night. It took her most of the autumn to finish. Jack was too old to be listening to kiddies' stories but he liked the sound of Echo's voice when she read, slower and more deliberate than the way she usually spoke. She knew all the words, which impressed Jack. He found it something of a marvel. A couple of the little sisters were inspired by the story of Robinson Crusoe's fence, how he built it from sapling sticks to protect his cave house and how it sprouted and grew into a hedge.

'We will try that,' they said. 'Help us get some tea-tree sticks, Jack.'

'Tea tree won't sprout like that, you dills,' Jack told them. 'Or maybe that Crusoe fella made up that part of the story.'

But the little girls pestered, and so he helped them cut and strip tea-tree sticks and they planted them in rows surrounding the bean patch. They waited for the sticks to grow like Crusoe's fence but they never did. Jack wondered why they wanted a fence there. It wasn't going to keep the wallabies out, but the girls seemed to like this space of their own. They were playing house, that's what Jack decided. It was this incident that got him thinking about finding a hiding place for himself, like that Crusoe's cave. He'd fence off a secret place. Maybe even build his own hut someday.

While Echo read to the children, Jack usually pretended to be cleaning his shotgun or rubbing mutton fat into his boots, but he knew she knew he listened. Her eyes would flick up from the page now and then.

One night he asked her, 'Eck, where is this Crusoe's island, anyway?'

Echo showed him the map in the front of the book and they both pored over it but were none the wiser. The map didn't have any names they knew. They'd heard of Robbins Island near Circular Head, and Cape Barren Island where the mutton birds came from, and Flinders, near to Cape Barren. They knew of Launceston and Hobart, and Melbourne and Sydney, and England where London was, and Maidstone where Grannie came from, and France, where Napoleon was king. Jack decided to draw his own map. It would be good, he thought, to pinpoint their farm, to draw in the fence lines and the paths. It would be good to see it all laid out like a picture. Jack preferred pictures to words.

On a sheet of paper he found among Echo's writing things, he worked at his map in the evenings, by the light of the hurricane lamp. When she asked about it, he told her it was a map of the way to the old ochre mine, which was partly true. He didn't tell her it would also show the way to his own hiding place. It wouldn't be a secret if he told her.

Echo said his map was all wrong. 'It don't have any creeks on it, for one thing, and you have to cross creeks to get up there.'

He put in the creeks after that, the Dasher and the Minnow. Echo kept saying to him, 'But where's Mount Van Dyke? Where's Mount Roland? Where's the bridle track? Where's Paradise?' She kept pestering until he told her to get out of his hair. 'Why d'you need a map of the way to the mine anyway?' she asked him. 'Who are you going to show it to?'

'Nobody, you chump. It's a *secret* map. I'm going to hide it and one day, when I'm dead, someone'll find it and then they'll know the secret way.'

Echo seemed unimpressed by this. '*Everyone* knows the way to the mine,' she said, but Jack replied that wasn't true.

'Hardly anyone knows the way, unless they're Aborigines. If we died tomorrow, hardly anyone else would remember it, except the Colemans.'

'You ain't going to die, Jack, are you?'

'You never know,' he said darkly. 'People are always dying.'

Jack didn't name anyone in particular but he didn't need to. They knew about Mrs Martin who died of the consumption, and the Powletts who lost their father in a hut fire, and the farmer from Wilmot who fell off his horse, and all the babies lost before they had time to draw breath, and Uncle Edward who had the tree limb fall on him. And their own sister Caroline, who died before any of them had known her.

Echo left him to his drawing. Jack bent his head over the paper, carefully inking in the boundaries of his world. The map reassured him, a real picture of the farm at Paradise, of the district and where he fitted into it. When it was finished, he'd hide this map, as he'd told Echo he would. Percy Coleman had plenty of secrets, plenty of things he didn't tell Jack or anyone else, and Jack had picked up the idea that this was the way to make sure the important things weren't stolen. The way to the ochre mine, that was a secret to most people, one of the few that Percy had shared. Jack felt a responsibility. You didn't want every Tom, Dick and Harry going up there and wrecking the place. On the other hand, he didn't want to forget the way, either. He wanted to leave some record, for the future.

He scratched these confused thoughts into the paper with the nib of Echo's pen, sorting them into inky lines. When the map was finished to his satisfaction, he studied it carefully then marked a particular spot with a careful 'X'.

The old hands at the Sheffield Inn were predicting inclement weather. Jack and his father leaned on the verandah rail and listened. Gathered in a row, pint pots in hand, the men discussed the produce prices, the running of the school, who had died recently, the latest newspaper reports.

'G'day, Noah,' said one old fellow, waving his pot. 'What do you think – is there too much rain about for the wheat to go in?'

Jack knew these neighbours respected his father's opinion. And why shouldn't they? After all, Father had been farming in Paradise for fifteen years now. Some of the men argued there'd be too much rain. Others disagreed. Father announced he'd be planting anyway. He needed that crop and he'd almost got the paddock ploughed. Autumn had always proved an excellent time to plant in the past, he said, and he didn't believe this season would be any different.

Jack nodded. Father had carved the farm at Paradise out of scrubby bush. He'd ringbarked the big eucalypts and cleared space for his paddocks. He'd taken his axe to those trees he could manage to fell, and split timber from them, and built a house, and shifted thousands of rocks. He'd put up fences. Jack reckoned Father knew a thing or two about farming. To watch his father wielding an axe, to hear the crack of the blade in the trunk – Jack felt proud. You had to be good with an axe to keep the bush at bay, to keep it away from the fence lines, away from the farmstead. Yes, Jack reckoned his father knew a thing or two.

It was true, he admitted to himself, that you couldn't describe the Hatton farm as the best-producing in the district. They didn't have a big barn like Duggan, nor a flock of sheep like Percy, and they surely couldn't afford one of them new steam threshers. But they'd managed a pretty decent harvest of potatoes last season – it was only a pity the prices had slumped so much. Jack had faith in his father; he felt sure they'd have a fine wheat crop this year. All they needed was a turn of luck: enough rain to get it sprouting, but not too much so the wheat took the smut. The money from a good crop was sore needed at home, so he did hope Father had made the right decision.

A new group of men arrived, five or six of them, pushing through the door of the inn to order tankards at the bar. They were not farmers. The conversation on the verandah paused while heads turned to inspect the newcomers.

'It's them miners,' someone whispered, watching the group with sideways eyes. 'Them ones living in the shanties down at Beulah.'

The miners glanced towards the farmers, but didn't lock eyes. They turned their shoulders, took their ales and stood in a cluster at the other end of the verandah. Among them stood a tall, good-looking young fellow, well-built across the shoulders with high angular cheekbones. His linen shirt looked coarse and his britches, held up with suspenders, were old and patched; he wore a waistcoat, hanging open, but no jacket. The skin on his forearms pimpled with cold as he raised his pot. He stared across the street, avoiding the eyes watching him. Jack raised his own pot and pretended to drink while he took a good long look at this fellow. He thought he'd seen him about somewhere.

The miners murmured together in low voices. As far as Jack could make out, they were planning a trip to Waratah where the tin diggings offered possibilities. Since Philosopher Smith discovered tin out at Waratah a few years earlier, plenty of fortune hunters had tried their luck. Some had worked on the claim of the Mount Bischoff Tin Mining Company, where Jack had heard it'd been easy to get at the tin in sluices at the top of a waterfall. But the men gathered in the inn were planning to venture farther out, to travel through the bush, down into steep ravines, dodging the tigers, making camps out there, all in the hope of striking a rich new deposit. Like Philosopher Smith had done.

Though they whispered among themselves, Jack caught enough of the gist of the miners' conversation to feel a thrill at the thought of such an adventure. But he'd heard cautionary tales about these miners. People said there were desperate characters among them, blokes who stayed out in the bush because they had reasons not to be found. Maybe he'd ask Percy about them; Percy would know.

One old fellow with a wide moustache reaching out past his ears raised his voice a little, speaking to the young man with the angular cheeks. 'We'll make our fortune, Henry. I don't know why you don't want to come with us. You've been out at the mining camps before. We had some good pickings, didn't we?'

'Them camps is no place for a woman, Father,' replied the young man mildly, 'and you know I'm wishing to marry.' As he spoke, this Henry fellow stared across the road towards the school-room building.

His father brushed droplets of beer foam off his moustache then took another deep draught. 'You got small hope of marrying, lad. You don't even have a proper coat.'

'I'm going up the highlands after the winter,' Henry said. 'I can get good money for wallaby skins.'

'Ye'd make better money still from the tin!' another old miner interjected.

Henry glanced along the verandah and seemed to look right at Jack, still eavesdropping on this conversation. Embarrassed, Jack dipped his face into his pot. 'In any case, I prefer the high country,' said the young fellow called Henry, turning back to his father. 'Too many eyes and ears in town.'

Caught out, Jack turned away. But something bothered him.

This Henry fellow seemed familiar. Had he seen him when he was with Percy, down by the Minnow? Or somewhere else? Now that he thought about it, it may have been closer to home, closer to Paradise. The bloke gave him an uneasy feeling. The riff-raff down at the shanties in Beulah were well known to be a rough lot. Plenty of ex-convicts among them, for sure, maybe some of the worst ones.

'I've seen that fellow around somewhere,' he murmured to his father. 'I'm sure of it.'

4

When the preachers arrived in the district and Jack heard about it, he forgot that small moment when he'd imagined trying his luck at the tin diggings. So much began to happen. His restlessness turned into curiosity. He wished the preachers had ridden on a little farther and arrived first at the Hattons' place instead of the Clarkes'. That would've been something! As it was, the idea of the big revival planned for Duggan's barn was spine-tingling. From all the talk on the tracks and at the sale yards, Jack reckoned practically the whole district would be there.

Getting the family up to Duggan's place had been a right carry-on, bringing all those kiddies and even old Grannie. When they reached the lighted barn, Jack left them to sort themselves out and made his way through the crowd. Eddie might be content to stand back, but Jack didn't want to miss a thing. He spotted Janie with her mother, but he didn't think she noticed him. The Dunstan boys were there, worse luck, and Jack took the opportunity to give Arthur Dunstan a good shove under cover of pressing through the crowd. Finally he found himself a place close to the row of blue chairs lined up across the front (what were they for?) where he'd have a good view.

When the first preacher stepped onto the platform, the one with a white beard who looked like old God in heaven himself, Jack stood up straight. The elderly man had the air of a magician, come to show them some trick. He carried a Bible and Jack wondered if they had a Bible at home. He'd never seen such a thing about the house, never thought about it before. Then the younger preacher bounded up, raising his arms and his voice. As he spoke his first words, a silence came over the crowd.

Clutching his hat in his hands, Jack tried to follow the preacher's words – something about relief from back-breaking work, that seemed to be the gist – but even without fully understanding, the man's voice penetrated Jack's heart. He ran a hand over his forehead, sticky with sweat. The preachers began to sing a hymn, their voices surprisingly loud, and the people gradually joined in.

Jack was enthralled. He leaned towards the front, inched ever closer to the platform, and found his breath coming in heavy gasps. Butterflies tumbled in his stomach. Though he didn't know many of the words, Jack began humming, then joined his voice to the singers, feeling the sound reverberate inside his chest. He sang louder and louder into a cacophony of sound like a brass band, pierced by cries from the women who stood and swooned, stood and swayed, stood and pushed towards the row of blue chairs. The lights in the barn flickered in a breeze that came from somewhere, though the night outside had seemed still and expectant on the way over.

Jack heard shouts from the boys near the door, but he forgot about them when a neighbour – for a moment he thought it was Janie's mother but it wasn't – shoved her way past him. He couldn't make out what she was saying. At the sight of this distraught woman, Jack hung back for a moment, suddenly cautious. The preachers seemed exultant at the pandemonium they'd unleashed. They moved into the crowd, soothing the women on the blue chairs, calling reassuring words, and finally holding their outstretched palms over the heads of everyone and pronouncing a calm benediction.

The show was over. People gathered themselves and their families. Jack lingered, fingering his hat, twisting the brim around in his hands. It would be fine to have a chance to ask the preachers, to find out what a person should do next, how a person could partake of this *forgiveness for sins*. He moved closer to the platform. The preachers were passing along the row of women sitting on the blue chairs, bending and speaking low. Jack heard a few words – *only believe, sister!* Then, in a rush, he felt shy and he turned to find his family.

Eddie did nothing but laugh. Jack couldn't understand why his brother wasn't impressed, why he wasn't affected like everyone else. Even Grannie said the revival had been fine, and she was a hard old thing. Jack reckoned Eddie must have a good few things he could be repenting of, that he needed forgiving for. Everyone did, and his brother was no saint, that was certain.

Despite his attitude, Eddie said there was no way he was going to miss the baptisms down at the Dasher. 'It'll be another good show,' he said, laughing again.

But Jack had given some thought to these 'immersions'. He'd decided they were a serious thing, and so he told Echo.

'Ain't it too cold for swimming?' she asked.

Jack snorted. 'They ain't going *swimming*, you silly thing. They're going to be *immersed*. That's different.'

Eddie continued chuckling, like he'd heard a good joke. 'Not so different, I reckon. It'll give us a good laugh if they do it.'

Sitting on the hillside beside Echo, watching the creek below, Jack wondered if anyone would really wade in and be dunked fully-clothed. The water would be cold. It seemed so unlikely. And yet – in went their neighbour Mrs Mason! And a dozen other people after her. The idea was, as far as Jack could make out, if you got immersed you were converted and you could be sure of forgiveness and going to heaven when you died. They said you'd be 'born again'.

Quavery female voices rose up towards Jack and Echo on the hill. '*Shall we gather at the river, Where bright angel feet have trod, With its crystal tide forever, Flowing by the throne of God?*'

'Are they singing about *our* river, Jack?' Echo asked him.

Jack had been quiet during the immersions, not cat-calling like the boys in the trees. 'No, you chump,' he said. 'It's the river in *heaven*. The one you cross over when you die.'

He'd figured out that much.

5

Jack had faith in his father, but there were times when he wished Noah would trust him, consult with him – like this question of the weather. Jack understood the weather. Surely Father could ask him for advice. He was sixteen now, close to seventeen; he'd be going out on his own soon. A lot of his weather lore had been picked up from Perce Coleman. You could learn a lot listening to those Coleman boys, and keeping your eyes open too.

Father planted the wheat. He watched the sky and the clouds, checking for signs of rain, wondering out loud if he'd planted too early, or too late, or if frost would damage the flowers when the crop emerged. He wondered if he'd ploughed over the seedbed properly. If the seed, in which he'd invested his last funds, had been good quality, safe from the smut. Father chewed over these worries in the evenings, laying them out for Mother and his oldest sons in short, broken sentences, before he fell to dozing by the fire.

One cold evening after another day without rain, Father finally asked, 'What do you reckon, Jack?'

Jack straightened up and stood with his back to the fireplace. He was so tall now that his shoulders rose past the mantle shelf and he could rest his elbow on it. Jack thought the rain would come, but how could he convince Father? Jack had plenty to say, now he'd finally been asked. 'Well,' he began, 'it's a matter of signs.' He started with a sure one. 'If you hear black cockatoos calling, rain is on the way.'

He knew this was true: hadn't he seen it happen last year? But Father just grunted and pointed out there'd been no black cockatoos around lately. Jack said he'd heard them last week, when he was walking back from town. Father grunted again.

'Well, watch out for ants in the house,' Jack went on. 'They come in droves just before it rains.' Had there been any ants lately?

'You sure, Jack?' Mother asked.

Jack said he was, and thumped his fist into his palm to emphasise the point.

Mother turned to Grannie, sitting by the stove. 'What do you reckon, Ma?'

Grannie wriggled. 'If it rains on the new moon, it will rain again a week later.' She nodded with a sharp little jab of her chin.

'Oh Grannie, you don't know everything,' Jack said, though privately he thought she could be right. He thought back to the last new moon. Had it rained then? 'Watch for the signs, Father,' he said. 'I know what I'm talking about. It will certainly rain soon.'

'And I will try a prayer,' Mother said.

Jack smiled at this, but then he wondered if it might be a good idea. If those two preachers had still been in the district, he could've asked Mr Fenny about it, but they had moved on to the town for the winter. On the Kentish Plains, the farmers had to work things out for themselves, as they'd always done.

The following day Jack went out to the bullock stall and pulled his divining rod from where he'd hidden it under the straw. Echo came with him to the bottom paddock. Jack liked the way that she trusted him, that she had faith in him. Eddie used to – after all, Jack was the oldest. But Eddie had changed; Jack preferred to have Echo with him. They paced slowly along the edge of the ploughed and sown field. The forked stick in Jack's outstretched hands twitched;

he paused. Echo stood stock-still, watching. The stick trembled, then dipped towards the soil.

'Is it there, Jack? Is there water under there?' She was whispering, and the breeze almost carried her words away.

Jack screwed up his face, peering down at the patch of earth where his stick pointed. He waited for the fine hum of electricity along his arms. Then he gave a decisive nod. 'Yes, I reckon.'

'An underground river?'

'Yes, I reckon,' he said again, straightening.

The pair stood for a moment longer, contemplating the unremarkable patch of ground in the bottom paddock.

'D'you think Father will dig for it?' asked Echo, tugging at her bottom lip.

Jack cocked his head to one side. Did Father really respect his advice? He still wasn't sure. 'Maybe he will, if it don't rain soon. At least we know there's water down there, and we can come and dig a well if we need to.'

'Are you sure, Jack? How do you know for sure?'

Jack turned to his sister, puffing out an exasperated breath. She was supposed to trust him. 'Ain't I been right before? Ain't my stick found water before, when old Viney asked me? You never can tell what's underground, Eck. But my stick is always right.'

For a minute they stood staring at the chocolate soil at their feet. Then they turned to walk back to the house, Jack carrying his divining rod over his shoulder. He strode along in silence, thinking. He knew he wasn't too good at his letters, but he wasn't ashamed of that. Echo would always help him. He had talents for other things, like wood chopping, and using his divining rod. He was proud of that. But thinking about pride and shame led his thoughts to that old convict in the family, their grandfather

Benjamin Walters. Probably it was shameful to have a convict for a grandfather, though plenty did. Those rotten Dunstans and their stupid taunts – they made a bloke think there was something in them, repeated so often. Once, in a fight, Jack had punched Arthur Dunstan so hard he thought he broke his nose, though later Arthur's ugly mug looked the same as ever. Jack and Eddie were always getting into scraps with those Dunstan boys. At least, they were until Lottie's ankle was broken. The Dunstans had steered clear since then.

Echo's voice broke in on his thoughts. 'Where'd you get your stick, Jack? Did you get it from Percy Coleman?'

'No, I made it myself, from a tea-tree branch. I got the idea from a story I heard at the pub about an old bloke down on the west coast. He has a stick he uses to find gold.'

'Gold!'

'Yes. I want to try it myself, in the Dasher. The streams round here have gold in them, you know. There's certainly gold in the Minnow – there's dozens of blokes down there finding specks in the stream, and they're searching for the main reef too, all the way up into the Gog range. They've been burning off the bush and there's even a new town talked of. That Star of the West Mining Company is looking to buy machinery.' His voice had risen with the thought of it.

'But you only got your stick, Jack.'

He sighed. 'I know, Eck. And the Minnow is all taken up with leases and we've got no money. That's why I'm thinking of the Dasher. Near the place where the preachers did the immersions. There might be gold there, that's what I'm thinking.'

'If anyone can find it, Jack, you can!' Echo said. His heart swelled at this sign of her faith.

As they walked together across the paddocks towards the house, Jack's thoughts tumbled like a clutch of puppies. It got so he couldn't sort out the gold in the Dasher from the rain his father wanted from the singing at the riverside while the neighbours were *born again*. The strange excitement he'd felt in Duggan's barn became mixed up in his thoughts with Janie Miller and her beautiful hair, and his intense dislike of Arthur Dunstan grinning slyly at Echo, with the thrill of the preachers standing with their hands stretched over everyone in the yellow light of Duggan's barn, and Janie's hair and the gold and new machinery that would save them all from so much hard work.

He shouldn't have told Echo about the gold. Now she might rely on him, and what if he couldn't find it? He thought again about the hopefulness that had surged through him in Duggan's barn for no reason he could make out except the preachers were right and all you had to do was *only believe*.

Brother and sister tramped across the top paddock. Echo was still thinking about gold. 'Is that why you made that map, Jack? Not for the ochre mine, but for the gold?'

'That map is my own business, young Eck. You can keep your nose out of it.'

They reached the yard and Jack headed to the stalls where the bullocks snuffled, where he kept his stick hidden. The animals were his domain – he had become the bullocky of the family – and he greeted them with low, soothing noises. Sometimes he cracked his whip for the younger kiddies, who squealed with delight when the sharp thwack of the leather tip rang out down the hillside.

Below the yard Jack saw the dogs Rags and Tippet racing homewards. Eddie would be on his way back from the eastern paddock where he'd been clearing. Sure enough, his thin, rangy figure soon appeared, loping uphill. Jack saw him pause, push his hat back on his head, and look up at the house. What did Eddie think about these days? It used to seem to Jack that he and his brother were almost twins, with a kind of understanding between them. And Eddie had definitely looked up to Jack, as the oldest. Lately though, things had changed. They often got into arguments and Jack wasn't sure why.

When Eddie reached the yard with the dogs dashing about his legs, he saw Jack and called out angrily, 'Where you been?'

Jack raised his head and growled, 'What's eating you?'

'I been breaking my back with the scrub on the east boundary, that's my problem, while you were mucking about with that stick.'

'Jack found the underground river, Eddie,' said Echo.

Eddie looked at her, then back at his brother, his face reddening. 'Gawd, Jack, what are you doing wasting time with that rubbish, leaving me to do all the work?'

Jack turned his back and said nothing. He couldn't figure out what was eating Eddie.

'It ain't rubbish, Eddie,' Echo said. 'We can dig a well right there if we need to.'

Eddie stood, legs apart, hands on his hips, watching as Jack approached the bullock pen. 'You'll believe anything, you will,' he said, and kicked out at the dogs bothering his ankles. 'And give these blighters some food,' he told his sister. 'They're right pests.' With that, he stomped indoors.

Echo fetched some bits of rabbit offal from the shed and tossed it to the dogs. Their barking quietened and only the snuffling of the bullocks sounded in the yard.

6

The blows of Jack's axe rang out in the quiet of the bush. He'd come to the edge of the forest to split wood for the winter wood heap and the white limbs of a great peppermint gum, toppled months ago, lay splayed along the Hattons' western boundary. Jack hacked at the tree's topmost branches, cut them into manageable lengths, split the wood into logs, and piled them up against the fence line. Beyond, the bush flourished.

The season was cool. But even in the chill morning air, the hard work made him hot, so he took off his shirt. Braces dangled over his hips; sweat broke across his shoulders. Sometimes the sound of his axe, the sharp painful crack as the wood split, was answered by the call of a wattlebird, or an echo from the direction of the blue mountain.

As Jack worked, his mind turned over that incident last summer, that time he gave Arthur Dunstan a broken nose. He thought of the way his stomach always seemed to cave in like it'd been punched whenever the Dunstans yelled their taunts about his convict grandfather, Ben Walters. Though goodness knows how those Dunstans thought they could crow. Jack had seen their place. Father had once sent him over to get an axe sharpened on old Dunstan's grinding wheel. Jack couldn't say he'd actually seen old man Dunstan's face, completely hidden behind the thickest beard in the district, but those hairy features and big shoulders and the grunts the man gave – well, Jack reckoned the fellow had to be an ex-convict if ever he'd seen one, though he couldn't prove it.

The Dunstans' hut had a dirt floor, and not swept clean neither. Old mother Dunstan looked a dirty woman; all those grubby little kids who sat around staring at him as he showed the pitted axe blade to Mr Dunstan. He'd only come because their own whetstone couldn't do the job. The chooks weren't kept in a pen; they ran everywhere, in and out of the hut. Jack knew in his bones that Arthur Dunstan had no right to accuse the Hattons of convict blood, like he didn't have the stain himself!

He thwacked his axe down to get rid of the picture of Arthur Dunstan's broken nose. Instead, he thought of how Janie Miller's hair looked so soft when it escaped from the ribbon she tied around it. He thought of how he'd have his own farm one day, and *his* farm – *thwack* – would have one of those new steam threshers, and *his* farm – *thwack* – would thrive because he could find water with his divining rod, and maybe even gold. No-one on *his* farm – *thwack* – would go hungry.

Already, he'd saved a bit of money. He had a secret stash, hidden where no-one could find it. And now he had his map, so he'd never lose the hiding place himself. He'd begun taking loads of firewood around the district with his bullocks, earning a few extra shillings. He'd picked up a little here and there that his father didn't know about, nor anyone else neither. He was sure Eddie didn't suspect anything. They were *his* savings, for the time ahead, when he could lease his own place. He thwacked down the axe again, thinking of his map and the 'X' inked on it, of the place in the Gog range, which was secret.

The sun rose high in a cloudless sky. Now, as he sweated, Jack's mind flooded with memories of that night in Duggan's barn, the heady atmosphere of it. The preachers had said anyone could be saved and the Lord would forgive anyone's sins and shames. Jack wondered if he needed the Lord's forgiveness for breaking Arthur Dunstan's nose, even though that Arthur had asked for a good thump. He wondered too if he needed the Lord's forgiveness for that time, two years ago now, when he'd fibbed to his father about some spud money – he'd only needed a couple of shillings to start his savings – and his father had found out and thrashed him to within an inch. But Jack reckoned he'd already paid for that, so he probably didn't need forgiving.

But maybe he did, for keeping secrets. Not that he'd ever let on about his savings, not to anyone, not even Janie, though he had considered telling her. That money had to be kept safe until he could get his own place, until he could start out. But perhaps it would be best to start out washed clean and *born again*. Up at Duggan's barn the idea of salvation had sounded simple – the chanting and the songs and the rising voices of the preachers and everyone glowing and no-one taunting you or reminding you of things you'd rather forget. It had sure sounded grand.

The axe thwacked down yet again into the log, splitting the wood along the grain, dividing the yellow-white timber, sending splinters into the air. Jack barely concentrated on what he was doing, raising the axe high and bringing it down with all his skinny strength. The sound of the cuts rang out, underlining his skittering thoughts. Raise, descend, *thwack*. He wished he could end his childhood with a blow like that and step into manhood and all the adventures ahead. But was he worthy? Did he deserve Janie?

He recalled the strange sight of his neighbours wading into the Dasher, the vague sense of something forbidden now allowed. He felt as if he'd seen things he wasn't meant to see, a spectacle which had descended upon them all from another dimension, not from real life, not from the life of the farm and the paddocks and chopping wood. It had seemed like that in Duggan's barn too: as if the preachers had landed among them from the stars, bringing news they could never have found out for themselves. It seemed like good news too – that the Lord waited to love you, to forgive you, to help you through your troubles. *I will give you rest*, the preacher had said. It seemed that if you went converted, you'd always have the Lord to turn to. But how did you go converted? What did you have to do? Jack recalled his emotions that night, the strange, surging sense of gratitude, as if someone had offered him a precious gift. He recalled the physical tightening all over his skin, the way his thoughts had swum in the dusty air, the ringing between his ears almost like a blow to the head. But what did those preacher fellows *actually* say? What did they want him to *do*?

Sunshine beat down on his shoulders. He swung the axe again; his hat fell off his head. He stooped to pick it up, shoved it back on, looked to the sky, became blinded for a moment. His head spun. Unconsciously, he spoke his thoughts aloud.

'Lord, what must I do?'

An answer came to him – he heard it clearly, bell-like from the hot sky . . .

He that hears my word and believes on him that hath sent me, has everlasting life.

The preachers had spoken the same words, but to Jack they sounded like the words of the Lord himself. He fell to his knees, stunned.

'I am saved,' he said in an awestruck whisper.

He felt his heart squeeze in his chest, and something almost like a sob began to rise up his throat. He swallowed it, stood, and looked around him. The paddock and the bush and the white skeletons of the ringbarked trees all swam before his eyes. Strange tears, springing from nowhere, blurred his vision.

Jack pulled on his shirt, snapped his braces onto his shoulders, found his hat, and picked up his axe. He wanted to tell someone what had happened, he wanted to shout it out. But who would believe him?

7

In the yard that evening, Jack whispered to his bullock as he lifted off the heavy yoke: '*Only hear and believe*, Bluey, old fella. That's the whole truth.'

After the Lord had spoken to him, he'd thought all afternoon about who he could talk to, who would believe him about the voice from the sky. He decided to go over to the Clarke place after tea, where he'd heard they were holding a Bible reading.

Now the snorting bullocks had alerted Echo to his return and she'd slipped out to watch him unhitch Blue Boy and Lion. He supposed she wanted to find out where he'd been, such a nosey girl she was. The animals steamed with heat, but the air skittered cold and he saw Echo pull her shawl tighter around her shoulders. Jack began to whistle as he led the animals to their pen and dragged a half-bale of hay into their manger.

Echo stepped from the shadows. 'Hello, Jack. You back, then? You're pretty late. We wondered what become of you.'

Jack pushed his hat up on his forehead. 'Yes, here I am. What are you so interested for? Reckon I might've brought you something?' He grinned. His heart was feeling light, unburdened.

Echo smiled at him. Jack could never work out what his sister was thinking. 'You better come in and have some stew,' she said. 'There's some left. Eddie caught some rabbits in the snares today, so there'll be more tomorrow too.'

'Did he now? That sounds mighty tempting, young Eck.'

He finished his work at the bullock pen and strode over to his sister. She looked up at him, her features alert in the starlight. 'You sound cheerful, Jack. What has happened? Where did you go?'

Jack paused and put his hands on his hips. He supposed his sister could keep a secret, if anyone could. And maybe she could help him. 'I went to one of them Bible meetings over at the Clarke place ,' he said quietly. He leaned close, as if he had some secret and important news.

'All on your own? Was it good?'

Jack grinned from ear to ear. 'It certainly was. We had prayers and singing, and I found the answer.'

In his excitement, he'd raised his voice. Echo took her brother's arm and pulled him into the shadows. 'Keep it down, Jack. If you go shouting about it, Eddie'll be out here jeering. Tell me what happened.'

Jack put his mouth close to her ear. 'This morning, when I was out chopping the wood, the Lord himself spoke to me. "*Only believe!*"'

'No! While you were chopping wood?'

'Yes! Right there in the paddock. Only, you know I ain't too good with reading, Eck. It'd be no good me trying to read the Bible. But I wanted to find out what I'm supposed to do. So I went over to the Clarkes'.'

'And you found the answer?' Echo whispered. The moon had risen. Her face flickered a little in the silvery light.

'Over at the Clarkes' they sang this hymn about a fella who was *almost persuaded*, and he never made up his mind, and so he was *lost*. I don't want to be lost, Eck. I wondered if I should be reading in the Bible, and as you know, I don't read too well. So I asked them at the meeting what I should do. And they said the preachers had taught '*Only believe*'. That's all you have to do. And then – you are saved! Ain't it good news?'

In his excitement, he'd taken Echo by the shoulders and was shaking her. His face was close to hers – he *knew* it was good news, and wanted her to believe too.

But she only asked, 'Are you going to tell Father and Mother?'

He let her go and straightened up. 'Why? You reckon they might have a go at me? Laugh, like?'

'Eddie sure will,' she warned, 'but Mother might be glad of it.'

Jack scratched one ear. 'I might think on it a bit more. Could you help me with the Bible reading? We do have a Bible, don't we, Eck?'

'Yes, Mother had one as a gift from Mrs Stanton when she married. She asked me to write the names in the back.'

'What names?'

'Oh, all those born, and all those who died. I'll help you read it, if you like.'

Brother and sister stepped out of the shadows into the moonlit yard and walked towards the house and the smell of rabbit stew. A curious hum rippled in the air at Paradise, as if someone somewhere had strummed a great harp, but far away, so the sound became lost and only the vibrations remained.

The bush at night shivered alive with rustling. Walking the track from the Hatton place to the Miller place with a hurricane lamp throwing a circle of yellow light around them, Jack and Echo were quiet. Jack had persuaded her to come with him to one of the Bible meetings that were being held all over the district. Households with family Bibles had unearthed them from boxes, dusted them off, and were learning to read them. The converted had to find their own way without the preachers, so Jack said.

Echo carried the Hatton family Bible in a special bag sewn from a flour sack, to keep it safe. Jack, his hair slicked down, wore a clean shirt. He'd pestered his mother for it; it was two days until laundry day and she'd had to wash it specially.

Jack's reading had improved. Sometimes he even felt confident enough to read a verse or two aloud at a meeting. Echo had helped him choose one to offer this evening, her favourite, from the Psalms: *I will lift mine eyes unto the hills, from whence cometh my help. My help cometh from the Lord.*

'I reckon you can manage that one, Jack,' she'd said.

He'd chewed his lip, nervous, but he thought he could do it with her alongside him.

As they approached the Millers' farm, the hurricane lamp lit the muddy track into the yard. Like the Hattons, like all the farmers scratching out paddocks in the bush, the Millers had fenced off their yard from the tangle of ferns and scrub beyond. Jack and his sister hurried into the kitchen and joined those gathered around the rough table. Janie Miller smiled at them as they came in and Jack felt his neck flush. The sight of Janie, especially up close, always made him feel warm.

When it was his turn to read, he cleared his throat. Echo gave him an encouraging dig in the ribs. He pulled the kerosene lamp on the table closer to his Bible, and ran his finger along the lines. '*My help cometh from the Lord*,' he read slowly, '*which made heaven and earth.*'

Janie was following along in the Millers' family Bible with her finger. Jack noticed and wondered if she found her letters difficult too. He hoped she wouldn't judge him for his hesitations, for the way he stumbled over *'whence cometh my help'*.

When he finished and looked up from the page, his eyes met Janie's. In the lantern light, in the warmth of all the people crowded into the kitchen, he experienced a moment of dizziness, as if time had moved sideways. The tawny light, skittering like a visible magnetic current, flitted across the table, across the faces etched in shadows and glow, bent in concentration over their Bibles. Someone started on the next verse: *And whosoever liveth and believeth in me shall never die.*

They returned home late, Jack with a whistle on his lips. Before the meeting had closed, there'd been a singalong, everyone belting out the hymns with enthusiasm. Jack kept whistling one of them – 'Almost Persuaded' – his favourite.

'When will you tell Mother and Father about your believing, Jack?' Echo asked as they walked along in the dark. 'They must've noticed something, I reckon. You are a lot more cheerful these days.'

Jack chuckled. He thought he'd tell them soon. Probably they'd all go converted too. Except Eddie, of course. Jack had become wary of Eddie, who for some reason couldn't seem to see the promise of the Bible teachings – now as clear as day to Jack.

Worse still, Eddie couldn't hold back on the taunts. Penning up the bullocks one evening, he'd started in again.

'That Janie Miller is a corker,' he'd said, a jeer in his voice.

Jack had the impression Eddie was watching him from out of the corner of his eye, though it was hard to tell in the dusk. Eddie picked up the hurricane lamp and his Adam's apple bobbed. Jack kept quiet and pretended not to hear; if he thought about it he'd lose his temper. The bullocks shuffled and snorted.

'Well, if the attraction ain't Janie Miller,' Eddie went on, 'what is it? The entertainment as good as those fellas up at Duggan's barn? If it's that good, I might come meself.'

Jack guessed he was talking about the women, and the immersions at the river with thin wet clothes. Eddie got plenty of amusement from those things. Jack frowned. He said the meetings were serious, and the Believers didn't want any scoffers there.

'*I* better stay home, then,' jeered Eddie

Jack slapped the pen shut, looped the wire over the post, and loped off. His father had asked him to try to get along with Eddie, to keep the peace if he could, but it wasn't easy.

8

The rain came. At first Father greeted it as a blessing, but as it went on and on he called it a curse. Jack's spirits were dampened. He hadn't predicted *this* much rain. The deluge cut the family off from neighbours and slowed their work.

When a break in the weather finally came, Jack and Eddie took their little brother Amos out rabbiting. Apart from a bit of bacon, the family hadn't had meat for days. What's more, the boys could get threepence for a pair of rabbit skins in town on sale day. They had traps set along the bottom paddock where they knew there was a warren. Jack was anxious to get out as soon as the sky cleared. If they didn't go round the traps to check for any rabbits caught, the devils or the forest ravens would eat them first. He set aside his irritation with his brother, and hoped Eddie would keep his taunts to himself.

Rabbits were everywhere, and Jack could already taste the stew in his mouth. The brothers had their shotguns in case they saw a wallaby, or caught some extra rabbits on the run. Jack carried the setting-stick to reset any traps that had been sprung.

They strode through the bush, following trails they knew well. Jack, and Eddie too, had been along here plenty of times, it was a shortcut to the bottom paddock. Along the side tracks were entangling branches, clusters of native laurel, and batwing ferns wound as tightly as a ball of knitting wool. Sometimes a sudden opening to a glade of mossy tree roots revealed paths leading off into green byways. The bush, a moss-coloured world of possibilities, had been Jack's home since he could crawl.

Amos ran to keep up. He'd always been the runt of the family. Jack hadn't wanted to bring him along; he'd complained to his mother that Amos was too small to go rabbiting. But Mother had asked them to take the boy, to let him help. Amos, a small wiry child, pumped his short legs over the furrows of the paddock as hard as he could. He yelled at his brothers to wait.

'Get up here, then,' Eddie said, and stopped. 'We better wait for the little blighter.'

'You wait then. I'll get on with it,' replied Jack, and he walked on to the first snares, not far ahead along the fence line. Eddie waited for their little brother.

'You got to keep up if you want to be a good rabbitoh,' Eddie said when Amos reached him, his boots caked with sticky mud.

'I can skin 'em real good!' said Amos

'First you got to catch 'em,' said Eddie.

Farther on, Jack gave a cry as a trap snapped back. It had missed his thumb, but came close enough to scare a shout out of him. His curse split the morning air.

'Mind your bloody language,' Eddie said, coming up to him.

They both laughed at this, so Amos did too. The little boy looked down at the rabbit trap, now pulled open, set again for the next animal to cross it. The recent occupant lay beside Jack's boots, broken-necked. Jack picked it up, took his knife out of his belt, cut a slit in one leg and threaded the opposite foot through it, making a loop. He tossed the dead rabbit to Amos.

'First one of the day. I hope there'll be plenty more for you to carry home.'

Amos looped the rabbit on the stick he carried and put it over his shoulder like a swag. 'How many you reckon we'll get, Jack?'

'Not many at this rate, if we stand around gas-bagging,' said Eddie.

'Don't expect we'll get many in any case,' Jack said. 'Traps been set two days. Should've checked them yesterday. The devils will have got some of them by now.'

'But rabbits come out after a wet. Them traps'll be full. You want to look on the bright side, Jack.'

'There won't be many,' Jack repeated, his mouth set in a stubborn line. The weather had got him down, no doubt about that. They walked on to the next snare. The dead rabbit swayed on Amos's stick.

'We'll get at least twenty,' Eddie predicted.

'Yes! Twenty!' Amos said.

'Lucky if it's half-a-dozen,' Jack said. His hat, drawn low on his forehead, shaded his eyes. He rubbed his chin, blue with stubble. 'And half-a-dozen won't go far in the stew pot.'

'I can skin 'em for you, Jack,' Amos said. 'I can do it!'

Eddie laughed. 'You're a bit slow yet, nipper. I reckon you'll need some help. We're going to pick up heaps, remember.'

'Well, we better split up,' Jack said, 'or we'll never get any rabbit stew.'

Jack and Eddie each took a different boundary with a different row of snares to check. They both had their shotguns ready; wallabies rustled in the bush. Neither of them took any notice of Amos, hesitating between following one big brother or the other. As they set off, Jack made sure to stay within hailing distance, and occasionally he or Eddie called across the ploughed chocolate paddock. Soon, Eddie lifted his gun and fired at a scurry of rabbits breaking from the long grass at the bottom of the paddock.

'Reckon I got a couple!' he called to Jack.

Jack looked up, squinting. He'd seen the activity at the warren, but hadn't been quick enough. He shaded his eyes and peered towards the warren, then back over his shoulder, expecting to see Amos beside Eddie. 'Where's the little bloke?' he called.

'Ain't he with you?' Eddie asked.

'No, he ain't!'

Jack hurried over to Eddie, stumbling through the furrows and mud. The two brothers stared in the direction of the grassy bank into which Eddie had fired and yelled, 'Amos! Amos!' They ran to the warren. One dead rabbit lay on the muddy soil, warm and bleeding, limp as a wet rag.

'Amos! Where *is* that kid?'

They heard a reedy snivelling then, winding up out of the scrub behind the bank like a tendril of smoke. Jack couldn't make out words, only a sort of animal whine. For a minute, he wondered if one of the dogs had followed them to the traps.

They found their little brother lying by a rabbit trap in which a rabbit was caught by its foot, alive but weak and panting. Jack leaned down, took the animal out of the trap and wrung its neck in one quick movement. Then he noticed the blood stains blossoming across Amos's shoulder and back.

'You silly little blighter! What're you doing in front of me shotgun?' said Eddie, sweating and trembling.

'Bound to happen when you bring a nipper rabbiting!' Jack said.

Eddie looked a bit white, but Jack didn't think much harm was done. He'd had a sprinkle of shot in his own shoulder once and Mother had dug it out and patched him up. But Eddie said they'd better get the kiddie home. When they lifted their little brother, they noticed more blood starting to soak through his shirt. Eddie had to carry him slung over his shoulder.

Jack said he'd keep on and clear the rest of the traps. He tied the dead rabbit's feet in a loop. 'Won't be much stew today,' he added. The accident had worsened his mood.

Checking the traps took a couple of hours on his own, and he tried a few shots as well. By the time he returned to the yard he had two dozen rabbits in his bag and slung on the stick across his shoulder. He carried the load to the side yard to do the skinning, and found Eddie sitting on a log seat with his elbows on his knees. A thin strand of smoke wound upwards from his pipe and the acrid aroma of burning tobacco stained the air.

'There you are,' Jack said. 'You can help me skin this lot. I ended up getting a few. How's the kid?' Jack heaved his haul of rabbits onto the ground. Eddie grunted and took another suck of smoke from his pipe.

'Reckon I might have a pipe too,' Jack said, 'since I did all the work.'

Eddie looked up. 'The little blighter ain't too good.'

'What d'you mean? It was only a bit of shot. Mother'll dig it out.'

'Well, she's tried, and so has Grannie, and old biddy Clarke's in there too. Looks like he bled a bit too much maybe. Or a bit of shot hit something vital.'

'Argh, he'll be all right,' Jack said. He didn't understand Eddie's uneasiness. Mother would fix up the kid.

They skinned the rabbits together; they were quick at it, and silent. When the job was done, the skins stretched on wires in the shed for drying, the offal fed to the dogs, the meat chopped up for cooking, they went inside. They found their mother bending over Amos, who was stretched out on his parents' bed. The women had covered him with a sheet on which blood stains had already dried brown. The boy's eyes were closed. Mrs Clarke carried a bowl of grey water through the doorway and the brothers almost collided with her. She looked up at them, no reassurance in her expression.

'Mother,' Jack said, with a sticking sound in his throat like a cough coming out the wrong way. It was dawning on him that something bad had happened, that Eddie's unease had cause. Mother didn't look too good.

She turned to Jack and Eddie as they stood in the doorway. Her eyes were red-rimmed. The whimpering sounds she made reminded Jack of wallabies he'd shot, just before they died. It dawned on him that Amos was not going to recover, that in fact the still small body on the bed had passed beyond Mother's help, that he and Eddie had killed the boy.

Or Eddie had. It was his shot that had done it.

Eddie turned and strode from the room. He headed across the yard and into the bush. Jack heard Echo call to him, but she got no answer. They didn't see him again until late that evening, the dark night when Susannah wrapped another dead child in a blanket and Noah contemplated another shallow grave under the celery-top pine.

Sitting in the kitchen, Jack went over the story again. How neither he nor Eddie had noticed where Amos went, how they'd warned him to keep out of the way, how he was too small to go rabbiting in the first place. When his grannie piped up and asked who fired the shot, Jack stood and paced across the kitchen. He felt agitated, thinking of the moment. What should he tell them? What would they do if he said that Eddie had shot his little brother? He imagined the state Eddie must be in, still out there in the dark.

'I don't know,' he said at last. 'We both of us fired, rabbits were running about everywhere. I don't know which of us hit him.'

Grannie seemed to accept this. She pushed herself up from her chair. 'Ay, Susannah, we best wash the little body and get him ready for the burying.' Before the hideous fact of a dead child, she knew what was needed, knew what to do.

Jack was grateful, at least for this.

Jack helped his father dig the grave under the celery-top pine in the home paddock. Their shovels slid easily into the muddy ground, though shifting the wet soil made for heavy work. Father laboured in silence but Jack could see his features, behind his beard, crunched into grief.

'I'm sorry, Father.'

Noah lifted a shovel-load of wet soil and cast it onto the pile. 'Not your fault. Is it?'

A rush of heat flashed up Jack's cheeks. Did his father need someone to blame? 'No! I told you.'

'It's a hard thing to have the death of a child on your conscience,' Father said. 'I wouldn't wish it on you. Nor on anyone.'

Jack stuttered at this appalling idea. 'It was an accident. He was too little to go rabbiting.'

They finished the digging in silence, and Jack wondered if he should have told them that it was Eddie who had fired the shot. He decided he would, if he detected any more suspicion of himself. He wasn't going to take the blame. He would never have been so careless; he would never have shot the poor little blighter.

They buried Amos next to Caroline. Leafing through the family Bible and frowning, Echo found some verses to read. Jack thought she did a good job, though it wasn't enough to staunch their mother's tears.

'Amos has gone on before, Mother, to heaven,' Jack said, hoping that would comfort her. Turning away from the grave, he walked back up the yard. 'With a bit of help from Eddie,' he muttered under his breath.

9

Winter seemed to last forever at the Hatton farm that year. Jack had to shovel half-frozen cow dung. The milking still needed to be done every morning, and Echo had to trudge out into the thick frosts that coated the yard. As the weather in the highlands worsened and snow fell on Paradise, the snow-melt turned the tracks to mud. Jack wouldn't take the bullocks through it; they'd sink to their haunches, he said. The chooks stopped laying almost completely; they didn't like the cold any more than the family. The side of bacon that hung from the kitchen ceiling, salted and fatty, diminished quickly as Susannah cut away pieces to add to the turnips and other roots in the pot. She seemed to be always wringing out the water from her apron. The baby wasn't thriving as she should. The dogs whined. The bullocks shuffled, unexercised.

Spring approached in fits and starts. The Hattons had the biggest paddock of wheat in the district that season; everyone knew they were depending on it. Though the rain had eased, the soil remained soggy and there was always the risk of the smut. Jack watched Father grow anxious. As the grain came up in black patches, discoloured by mould, some of the new Christians offered to pray. The Lord, if merciful, could do something about the weather, they suggested, and Jack felt a surge of hope. They might be right! He tried including the wheat crop in his own prayers, but it wasn't clear to him if he was asking correctly. Was there some special formula? Would the Lord really bother Himself with one crop of wheat? He watched Father trudge around the muddy yard, worrying.

Preacher Fenny returned to Kentish with the warmer days. News travelling as it did through the district, it wasn't long before he heard about the plight of the Hattons' wheat. Declaring that prayer was indeed the answer, he turned up at the farm in Paradise. Jack watched him ride into the yard with a thrill. Father emerged from the lean-to where he'd been skinning rabbits, pushed his hat back on his forehead, and scratched his ear. Jack couldn't decide if Father was pleased to see Mr Fenny or not, but he hoped he'd at least listen to what the preacher had to say. Jack reckoned Mr Fenny was the one to help them – *the power of prayer*, that's what they needed. Jack felt sure of this. His spirits rose.

The black-coated preacher doffed his hat and shook Mother's hand at the kitchen door. He'd acquired a new waistcoat, striped in jaunty blue and green. Sitting in the Hattons' kitchen, discussing the weather and prices and the threat to the wheat, Mr Fenny agreed with Jack that prayer must be the answer – prayer and faith. He told the family that *believing* was the important thing.

'*For whosoever believeth in me shall not perish, said Christ,*' he intoned, his sandy whiskers twitching.

He encouraged them all to pray with him. He wanted them to kneel, right there in the kitchen. Jack watched Father chewing his beard and Mother twisting a corner of her apron. If only they weren't so doubtful! Jack squirmed with frustration at his family's hesitancy. He *knew* the preacher was right about this, they must pray for better weather, they had to trust the Lord!

'Come on, Father,' he said, as persuasively as he could. 'Let's do as Mr Fenny wants. Let's ask the Lord for his mercy on us.' Staring at his father, Jack willed him to give in, to accept, to move down onto his knees. He didn't dare touch him, but with his whole being he urged Father to accept the blessed offer.

'Trust in the Lord!' the preacher hissed, leaning close to Susannah.

'Oh, it can't hurt, Noah,' she said at last. 'It surely ain't never wrong to ask the Lord for something you sore need?'

Jack dropped to his knees to illustrate how easy it was, how natural, how obvious. Mother followed. Then – not to be left out – young Eck too. Finally, awkwardly, Father knelt, holding the edge of a chair. Jack took his mother's hand, and she took Echo's, and they listened to the preacher as he intoned his prayer. Preacher Fenny delivered the prayer in his best, most sonorous tones, reverberating and thrilling. He asked for better weather for their wheat, and he assured the Lord that they truly believed, they had faith that He would hear their prayer and save the crop.

After the *Amen*, when the family had risen and shaken their heads a little to bring themselves back to the reality of the kitchen, Mr Fenny stood to leave. Jack was elated that they had finally taken action, but Father looked sheepish. He shook hands with the preacher and walked out to the yard to see the visitor off. Mother sat in her chair by the fire, sniffling into her apron. Echo stood blinking for a few moments then went to put the kettle on. Jack, relieved and reassured, sat staring into the fire. He had been mightily moved by the preacher and felt an absolute certainty the Lord would hear their prayers for the crop, and answer them too.

'Ay, he's an eloquent one, that fella,' said Grannie Eliza, and Jack looked up.

He'd forgotten she was there.

Before he mounted his horse and rode away, Mr Fenny walked with Father along the fence line to inspect the wheat. Jack watched their heads bowed together; the preacher seemed to be talking earnestly, occasionally raising his hand with a gesture Jack couldn't interpret.

Afterwards, Father seemed a little more hopeful. Over the next few days, Jack watched him go out and pray over his crop, just as Preacher Fenny had taught him. Whenever Jack saw this, he raced across to join his father, raising his face silently to the damp sky and thinking of the generosity of the Lord. The weather turned kindly; the wheat flowers emerged and no severe frosts nipped them. New green shoots sprouted, and it rained just enough.

Jack had never doubted it would be so.

Now that the preachers were back in the district, Jack hurried to ask if he could be baptised. He'd been waiting all winter, but something inside had made him hesitant to talk to his family about this plan. He thought he might wait until after it was done. Keep it private, like. He imagined their comments and questions, and Eddie's snorts, and Grannie scratching her head and asking, 'What for, Jack?' Did he have to face all that? All he wanted was to be safe in the arms of the Lord.

But Mr Fenny explained: the whole point of getting baptised was to proclaim your faith to others, to be a witness for the Lord. So in the end Jack invited them all to come down to the creek behind Cable's flour mill one warm afternoon to witness him taking his immersion. He made sure to stare Eddie in the eye when he made this announcement, but Eddie only grunted and shuffled off to bring in more firewood.

Though spring had arrived, frost still sometimes lay on the grass in the mornings, and the paddocks were white at dawn. Down at the creek, Jack lined up with several ladies and two older men, farmers he knew from the inn in Sheffield. One of them was George Heyward, cheerful as always.

'Fine day we have for it,' remarked George.

'Bit of a chill in the air, though,' Jack replied, grinning at the older man. 'But that won't bother me!'

'That's the ticket, Jack.'

Jack hoped his parents would be proud of him. Mother had made oat stirabout for breakfast, insisting that he needed something to keep his insides warm. Father had helped her round up all the kiddies and get them down to the creek. Jack hadn't taken the least bit of notice of Eddie. The blighter could come or not. Jack intended to witness for the Lord whether his brother scoffed or no.

At the creek, Preacher Fenny stood in the water up to his coattails, his hat on his head. Jack's turn came. With an encouraging wave, Fenny beckoned him into the creek. Sucking in a deep breath, Jack plunged forwards into his future.

'I baptise you in the name of the Father!'

Down Jack went, the chilly creek water enveloping his neck and face and dousing his hair. In a second he leaped up again, washed clean and filled with an electric thrill. 'Hallelujah!' he cried, and he knew his whole family heard him, including Eddie loitering in the background.

Afterwards, Jack felt the warmth of contentment seep through him, as if he'd drunk warm honey. Now he wanted the rest of his family to see the light: Father and Mother, and young Eck. They would soon feel the Lord's blessing, he was sure of it.

When the preachers held another revival meeting, this time out at Wilmot, the Hattons went over in the wagon. Jack reckoned it was almost as good as the first one in Duggan's barn. Jack could see Echo thinking hard on it all, and he tried to instruct her as well as he could. He felt a thrill to think they'd all be baptised soon. Except that dill Eddie, of course. He was a lost cause.

The optimism of spring suited Jack's new mood. He even began to get along better with his brother. It wasn't Eddie's fault his shot had killed Amos; it had just been a terrible accident. When he thought about it, Jack decided it was understandable the whole matter had turned Eddie a bit sour. If only the silly git would listen to the stories of forgiveness that were in the Bible. How about that one about the prodigal son? Even a wastrel like that son could be welcomed back to his family. It remained a mystery to Jack why Eddie didn't seek forgiveness in prayer. Sometimes he suspected his brother might not even be *repentant* about shooting Amos – though he shied away from such a hard conclusion.

By the spring afternoon when the Colemans organised a cricket match at Dawson's paddock, the brothers were more or less talking to each other as usual. Jack had shrugged off the problem of how to convince Eddie to listen to the word of the Lord. The bloke was on his own. Tom Coleman had promised to demonstrate the new overarm bowling and both Hatton boys put up their hands to play in the 'friendly'. It might've been better if the captains had picked them for the same team. But when Percy chose Jack – they were mates, after all – Tom grabbed Eddie. The next thing Jack knew, his brother was rollicking down the pitch like a tiger was chasing him. He flung the leather ball with a great swipe of his arm. It sprang up and clobbered Jack in the knee and put him out of the rest of the match.

Jack was angry, for sure, but once he calmed down he supposed it'd just been another accident. Eddie and his accidents. Lucky for him Jack's knee wasn't broke, only bruised. If it'd been broke, Eddie would've been doing all the farm work himself for the rest of the spring.

10

The wheat, harvested safely, brought in some decent money at last. In the summer, Father bought a second-hand cart and a young cart horse from George Heyward out at Wilmot. Jack's spirits rose at this improvement to the farm, though they still used the wagon to carry any heavy loads. The horse couldn't take some of the really rough tracks. One sale day, Jack and his father loaded a few pigs in the wagon and drove into Sheffield. They unloaded the animals and herded them up the muddy street and into the sale yards, their barking dogs dashing alongside. Though the weather was warm, the street never seemed to dry out; it always had a layer of mud on the surface, and plenty of unseen holes too. A few blokes standing outside the inn called to them, 'Noah! Jack! When you get them pigs stowed, come on back for a yarn.'

With the pigs penned up, Jack and his father joined the men standing at ease along the verandah of the inn. Farmers had come in from the back-blocks for sale day, and were lined up in their dusty jackets along the verandah rail. Janie's father, William Miller, stood there with flecks of ale foam in his beard. George Heyward was there too. The inn was the meeting place for the district, and it looked to Jack like everyone who mattered was there.

'Season ahead be wet again,' said Miller. 'We need this road metalled, I reckon.'

'What about that petition to the government?' someone else said. 'Something's got to be done. I don't know how I'm going to get the spuds through to the coast this year. You can hardly get bullocks along that track. And what about that tramway to Don we heard spoken of? Where's that, then?'

Like the others, Jack looked to George Heyward. Someone urged George to write to the Road Trust. They'd sign a petition, they said. Jack agreed with this plan; he added his voice to the others – a petition, that'd be the thing. The roads around the district were a disgrace.

Miller took a long drink of his beer. 'Don't know it will do much good,' he said.

'We got to look after ourselves. We got the Union chapel built,' said someone else.

There was a moment of quiet while the drinkers remembered how they'd all banded together and put up the Union chapel, so useful to the town, as a schoolhouse and everything else. Though it was nowhere near big enough for the revivals. The preachers had been urging the converted to erect a larger building for Assemblies.

'We could build a Gospel Hall,' suggested George Heyward.

Some of the men sniffed; a few raised their eyebrows. The scale of the idea filled Jack with energy; his old restlessness began to stir, ready to take on a new project, to imagine something big. The farmers trusted Heyward with their letters and their business deals. Could they trust this big idea of his? George sipped his beer, pushed his hat back on his forehead, and repeated, yes, certainly they should build a Gospel Hall, like the preachers had talked of.

'Now *that* would be a project!' Jack cried. Enthusiasm bubbled up inside him like the froth in his ale.

The men, a little beery perhaps, declared themselves ready to meet the challenge. 'Progress is up to us, I reckon,' declared Miller, and everyone agreed.

Among a babble of talk, planning got underway. They refilled their pots and discussed where they might find the land for this new building. Sheffield had the inn and sale yards but West Kentish, everyone agreed, was the geographic heart of the farmlands. At the crossroads there, a blacksmith and a wheelwright kept up a busy trade. The row of conifers planted along the creek had already grown respectably tall.

'And the creek would be good for immersions!' Jack pointed out. That was a great benefit, he thought.

Discussion followed, then argument. Joe Martin, who had been among the earliest to be baptised, said he would give half an acre off his property at the West Kentish corner. They slapped his back and paid for his beer. Jack saw that Joe Martin earned a lot of respect by this gesture, by his generosity. But Joe had land, and he could afford it. Jack thought of his own savings, hidden safe at the spot marked 'X' on his map. He itched to get started: to get his own lease, and bring in decent crops, and put aside enough to buy a place, to put money into the tin mining maybe! To raise a family and get a steam thresher. It was overwhelming, sometimes, all the possibilities. He needed a plan. As soon as the Gospel Hall is built, he thought, *that's* when I'll move out.

He stood with his father at the verandah rail, as the drinkers around them went back to complaining about the muddy tracks.

'D'you reckon we'll ever see better roads, Father?' Jack asked.

Noah sighed. In his view, there would never be any help from the settled areas, nor from the government far away in Hobart Town, and he and Jack and everyone else better just get on with things themselves. 'There ain't been any change since I come here,' he said, 'and that's more than fifteen years now. Meanwhile, Jack, you and me has got to get that wagonload of spuds down to the docks next week.'

'It'll take the full team,' said Jack. 'Lucky we got a couple of good leaders now. Snowy and Tiger are fine ones.'

Father sipped his pot of beer, then cleared his throat. He seemed to make a decision. 'We'll not be taking Lark and Linnet this trip, Jack,' he said. 'Nor Eddie.'

'Ay?'

'Your brother is going to take up a lease out at Staverton and I agreed to lend him two of the bullocks for a bit.'

'Eddie is going out on his own?' Jack said, dumbstruck. 'And with two of my bullocks?' He scratched his head. 'But we need the whole team.'

'We'll be right. It ain't forever. Just till Eddie gets his fences up and the first spuds in.'

Jack's jaw dropped. His beer pot rested forgotten on the verandah rail. His brother was a year younger than him and here he was starting out on his own. With his – Jack's – best bullocks to boot. 'Well, I'll be darned,' he said eventually.

'There's another thing too, son,' said Father, speaking slowly. 'He's got a girl going with him. Janie Miller.'

Jack knocked his pot to the packed dirt floor, where it cracked open, spilling frothy ale across his boots and turning the dust to mud.

'Listen, son. I know you got your own hopes,' Father said. 'I know what it is to think of your own house and your own paddocks. My advice is to bide your time. Your day will come.'

Blank-faced, Jack stared at his father. For the first time, he was offering advice about how to live his life. For the first time, Noah was offering advice about how his son should live his life. Every fibre of Jack's stringy adolescent body rebelled against the idea of *waiting*. Though he hadn't formulated it clearly before, in this moment he knew *exactly* what he wanted. He wanted what Eddie had apparently just grabbed for himself.

'Maybe you could pray on it,' suggested Father

Eddie moved out to Staverton early in the new year. Jack watched the preparations but he was hanged if he was going to lift a finger to help load the wagon, or give the bastard a load of wood to get him started. Out in the yard, he stood in the lee of the bullock pen while Eddie got Lark and Linnet hitched. All the family came out to see him off, to wave him on his way to the Miller place to collect Janie. Though Jack had tried to pray about the swirling stink in his gut that started up whenever he thought of Eddie with Janie, it hadn't been any use. He supposed he wasn't a good enough Christian yet.

Eddie finished loading the wagon and kissed and hugged the women, and shook his father's hand, and then, after a brief hesitation, he crossed the yard to where Jack stood fuming.

'I'm off, then,' Eddie said, holding out his hand.

Jack couldn't take it. 'You bastard,' he growled.

Eddie dropped his hand, but stood his ground. 'I don't know what your problem is, Jack. I reckoned you'd be glad to see the back of me. You can get on with your God-bothering in peace.'

Though this was a jeer, Eddie's tone was mild. He didn't seem to understand that he was a thieving mongrel.

'You're still a bastard,' Jack said. 'Taking Janie out to the sticks. And you ain't even married her! I don't know what you did to convince her to go with you.'

As he spoke, all kinds of lurid ideas flooded his mind, about how Eddie might've tricked Janie, or bribed her, or – who knew what?

Eddie turned and spat into the dirt, then faced Jack again. 'No more from you about my wife,' he said quietly.

Jack's fists came up in a split second and he punched Eddie square in the jaw. Eddie doubled over, but he was up again quickly, and then the two of them were trading wild, inflamed punches before anyone knew what was happening. Father raced across the yard and broke them apart; the horrified scream had barely left Mother's lips.

Echo came running over too. 'Cut it out, Jack!' she yelled.

As Eddie shook his head, wiped his face and led the bullocks away, Jack eventually did calm down. But he felt better for having landed a good punch on that mongrel.

11

The Launceston Examiner, *Monday 12 April 1875*

A new chapel has been erected at Kentishbury by the Believers; the building is quite an ornament to the place. The Gospel Hall was opened for divine service a few Sundays since by Messrs Fenny and Braithwaite, Evangelists, who have been labouring in the district for some time past, with great success.

Early on Sunday morning a woman dressed in her best black marocain began setting a table in the centre of the new West Kentish Gospel Hall. The Hall had been built in record time by the

Believers. A reporter from *The Examiner* had even travelled from Launceston and written about the achievement. Nothing like it had happened in the district before.

Dew still glistened on wet grass; the Sister had arrived with the sunrise. She threw a white cloth over the table and set out the emblematic meal, the makings of which she'd carried here in a canvas bag on the handlebars of her bicycle. As she finished arranging the loaf and a cup of Kentish cherry wine, the sound of cart wheels drifted in through the open door. A young man strode into the hall, called, 'Morning, Sister!' and began helping her with the last few benches.

'Thank you, Brother. Fine morning.'

With the benches arranged in a rough circle, the young man sat down near the central table. Pulling a dog-eared Bible from his bag, he skimmed through the filmy pages looking for a passage. He bent his head to read. People began to arrive, dressed in their best clothes, greeting each other at the door but not pausing to gossip. 'Brother, Sister', they nodded to each other. The bare wooden Hall slowly filled; all the benches were soon occupied.

Silence descended; the people waited in quiet contemplation. There was a palpable air of release; everyone seemed relieved to sit down after a week of work in the paddocks and kitchens and bullock yards. They sat quietly in the still centre of their week. A line of young Hattons filled two benches. The little girls wore white pinafores over their thin dresses; the boys had clean linen shirts. Susannah's Sunday hat was wide-brimmed with a navy blue ribbon. Echo wore a hat too, now she'd turned fifteen and had become a woman. It was made of straw and trimmed with a bunch of bush berries she'd found herself. A few quiet minutes passed and the only sounds were the rustling of Bible pages, the call of a wattlebird beyond the open door, and the soft breathing of the gathered people.

The service had no leader, no signal. It simply began when a Brother near the front was moved to stand – it was the early arrival who'd helped shift the benches. Jack Hatton. He proposed a hymn, one they all knew, and explained why he'd chosen it. He said he'd thought of it, and sung it too, on Thursday last week when those high winds came through and took the roof clean off his father's barn. People murmured; that wind had been destructive, they all remembered that day.

The singing began, led by Jack in his strong baritone. The voices were ragged at first but soon found their rhythm. They sang without organ music, without hymn books, without a cantor. The song left the hall through the open door and wound across the paddocks. Sheep lifted dull eyes, currawongs sat still in the branches of the conifers that Joe Martin had planted down at the corner. '*Oh Jesus is a Rock in a weary land, A weary land, a weary land; Oh Jesus is a Rock in a weary land, A shelter in the time of storm.*'

Outside, the mountain sat in the landscape, benign and solid, visible from everywhere in the paddocks and farms, along the forest tracks and in the town. Its rocky face remained unchanging except for its moods and colours, never deserting them, never abandoning them.

In the quiet pause that followed the singing, a man sitting near the back of the Hall rose to his feet, a closed Bible pressed against his worn waistcoat. Faces turned and took in his young, weather-beaten features, his wiry hair askew, his eyes glistening. Jack recognised Arthur Dunstan's oldest brother, who leased a place out at Promised Land. The fellow gave a small cough, then said he wanted to ask a question, a question that weighed heavy on his heart. 'Why? Why did the Lord take her, only twenty-five years old and leaving four young ones, and the newborn too? What could be His purpose?'

Even before he'd finished speaking, several women had risen and moved to him, putting their arms around his shoulders, pulling him gently back to his seat. He hung his head, his face in his palms. This Brother needed an answer, that was clear.

There was no official leader here, but a certain authority seemed to fall naturally on some. George Heyward was among those natural leaders; Percy Coleman too. Both now rose one after the other and offered a prayer for the soul of the young mother and a line of verse from the Bible that might comfort and explain. The Dunstan fellow sat quietly, his shoulders shaking.

Lately, the Believers had begun to look also to Jack Hatton. He'd become accustomed to speaking up, and adept at giving his opinion. Though he was still young and still living with his family at Paradise, his neighbours had started to turn to him when a word of leadership was required. Jack expected to go out on his own soon, though he'd told his parents he was waiting for a better place than Staverton.

As Percy finished his reading, Jack stood. He looked around the Gospel Hall and saw Father sitting beside Mother, with his beard combed and his black coat brushed, wearing an expression that looked something like pride. Jack straightened to his full height, threw his shoulders back, then led the congregation in a prayer for the soul of the dead young wife and for the heart of the widower, so near to broken. Though the bloke was a Dunstan, you couldn't help but feel for him.

There was not a person in the Hall who had not been touched by death; many had laid children in graves. As he spoke, Jack remembered the day Amos was shot, how the boy had died on the bed with the bloody sheet covering him, and how Mother had been inconsolable. He opened his Bible and read, '*And God shall wipe away all tears from their eyes; and there shall be no more death, neither sorrow, nor crying, neither shall there be any more pain: for the former things are passed away.*'

Jack knew he had come a long way since he'd struggled to read, since he'd needed his finger to trace the text. As he exhorted the congregation, he copied the tones of the preachers, 'Remember, Brothers and Sisters, the hope of better things to come. And all the more a paradise for us, because we know our loved ones are there now, awaiting us.'

'She's there, Brother,' the women murmured to the grieving man. 'She's in the wonderful Kingdom of God!'

The man, Arthur Dunstan's brother, sat up and wiped his eyes, gulped, and pushed a hand through his dishevelled hair.

'I'll come over and see what I can do for the children,' said the Sister sitting next to him. She had six of her own.

Jack spoke again, suggesting a moment of quiet contemplation. Calm descended on the gathering. They were silent. After a few minutes, as people began to raise their heads, someone else began a hymn, a favourite from Sankey's hymnal, '*Just beyond the silent river, Over on the farther shore, Many loved ones there shall greet us, Where the many mansions are.*'

As the congregation returned its thoughts to the Hall, attention focused on the centre of the circle, on the presence that had been with them throughout the morning. They shuffled forwards to the Lord's table one by one, broke the bread together, and sipped the wine. His body and His blood. It was the only ritual they practised, apart from baptism.

ON A BRIGHT HILLSIDE IN PARADISE

Communion over, Brother Jack stood, lifting his Bible in one hand. Heads turned; people listened to Jack nowadays. Everyone became quiet as he proclaimed, 'Always there is the hope, nay, the absolute assurance, of eternal fellowship with Jesus in heaven, and joyous reunion with the loved ones who have gone before! Let us all sing "The Glory Song"!'

Susannah

1

Two years after the Hatton family arrived in Paradise – by which time Susannah Hatton had two small boys – she was expecting again. Puffing a little, she waddled around the yard at the end of the day, making sure she'd forgotten nothing, that all the evening jobs were done. Yes, the chooks were fed, those ratty dogs locked up for the night, the pig quiet. In the mild air, the fading light of dusk turned the mountain a deep purple. Leaning on the top rail of the split timber fence enclosing the yard, Susannah gazed upwards at the violet flanks of the mountain. She listened. There were times, such as this one, when it seemed closer than usual.

'Ho!' she cried. 'What are *you* looking at, old mountain?'

Its broody presence seemed a bulwark against outside trouble.

'Ho!' A faint sound drifted back to her.

She wondered what to make of the mountain's reply, but felt grateful that at least it was listening. Susannah was short and her elbows only just reached the top of the fence rail. Her hair had started the day wrapped in a linen kerchief but now chestnut tendrils escaped in an untidy halo and she pushed stray hairs back into place. It was a blessing she carried her babies so easily, she thought. She was nineteen.

Spreading both forearms along the rail, dropping her chin onto her hands, she dreamed into the tangled forest beyond. Rustling noises reached her. There were all kinds of creatures out there. Not only the wallabies that Noah shot for meat but devils too, out to scavenge after dark. Once, she'd glimpsed a tiger sneaking off with one of their best chooks – those tigers were a fearful sight. They could open their jaws wider than a man's head.

Warily, she stared into the forest in case another chose this evening to come sniffing around. Noah would surely shoot it if he saw one. Though he must take care with a shot in the dark, because people often came up through the forest; there were many paths. Most certainly he would not want to shoot a neighbour. She smiled a little at this absurd thought, then her smile faded as she again contemplated the rustling bush. Susannah was fond of the protective mountain, but she wasn't so keen on the bush beyond the fence. Stepping back inside her yard, she returned to her house and her children. This would be her fourth birth.

Two small, grubby bodies lay asleep on a sugar-bag mattress stuffed with dried fern: Susannah's boys, Jack and Eddie. They curled together as if they were young, spiralling fern fronds. Noah dozed as he often did at this time of the evening. He looked exhausted. Through half-closed eyes, Susannah watched the rise and fall of his chest and listened for his light snore. It always roused an affectionate contentment in her. Noah had built their hut of split timbers and stuffed the gaps between the planks with tree fern. Then he'd papered the walls with pages from newspapers he'd picked up from neighbours. The print had faded to almost nothing, not that Susannah could read. Noah knew a little of his letters and sometimes looked through *The Launceston Examiner* if he came across a copy when he went into town.

The hut had a wooden chimney with a hearth of bush stones where a fire always crackled. Noah kept a bucket of water handy in case of accident. Many a hut was lost to fire in this district, so he told Susannah, but still they must have a fire *day and night* or they would die of the cold. Under the mountain, the frosts could be fierce. If this baby didn't come soon, Susannah thought, it could be born in the winter snow. The packed dirt floor never would stop shedding grit and dust into everything, though she swept it every day. A hessian sack hung in the place of a door.

Beside the fireplace, Susannah leaned back in a broad, comfortable chair that Noah had built from split timbers and padded with kangaroo skin. She shifted her big, distorted body and let out a groan as the familiar pangs began. At this sound, her husband's chin went up and he woke, alert.

'Should I be getting Mrs Clarke, love?' he asked.

'Yes, I reckon you should. I hope it ain't too dark to go over there. The track is that muddy.' She shifted again and drew in a steadying breath, letting the air out slowly. Her lips felt dry.

Her husband stoked the fire with extra kindling, took his hat, and went out to hitch his bullock, Blue Boy, to the wagon. Walking over to the Clarkes' place would be quicker, Susannah thought. It was only about three miles and the track such an awful bog for the bullock. But he had to bring the old girl back to help with the birth, and Mrs C. would prefer the wagon. She watched as he left, a hurricane lamp swinging from the driving bench, casting a swaying circle of light as Blue Boy gamely pulled out into the dark.

Susannah lay down on her sugar-bag mattress and waited.

Alone on the floor of the bush hut, with her two sleeping toddlers beside her, the sounds of the bush night drifting in through the doorway, she sucked in deep, slow breaths and rode the waves of pain. Help would come. Noah never let her down. She had confidence in him; he was a determined man. But as an hour passed, she began to groan, and then wail.

'Oh, hurry, Noah!' she hissed between clenched teeth.

She found it hard to tell how much time had elapsed. The pains came more often. The baby must surely be close.

Rolling awkwardly onto her side, she watched the fire as she recovered from each wave of pain. Staring into the flames helped calm her thoughts, gave her something to concentrate on. As she watched, a log rolled forwards onto the hearth, flaming as it hit the stones. Susannah stared at it dreamily, her cheek flat against the hessian – would it roll out? Twigs and curled dried leaves were sprinkled across the stones, and a corner of her rough wool blanket had strayed onto the hearth. Sensing, as always, the danger of fire, Susannah reached out to pull it back. Just at that moment, another fierce pain squeezed her belly. Closing her eyes and riding the wave, she barely noticed the acrid smell of burning wool.

When the pain eased, she saw that the blanket was alight, blackening. Tendrils of smoke curled up and the sharp smell frightened her. Her fear of a hut fire drowned out her fear of giving birth alone. With one arm across her belly, she shifted her position, rolling to face the hearth. Dragging the blanket towards her, she closed her palm around the hot burning wool. She forgot the hurt of it as another fierce contraction squeezed her.

By the time Noah returned, bearing his neighbour's wife next to him in the wagon, night had long since fallen. When Mrs Clarke pushed aside the hessian sacking over the doorway, the smell of dung hurried in from the yard with her, mixing with the wet odours of childbirth, the metallic tang of blood, the smell of burned wool, and the ashy fireplace. Out in the yard, Noah began unharnessing the bullock. Through the rush of relief at their arrival, through the next wave of pain, Susannah heard Mrs Clarke calling him in to help. Within a few minutes the new baby's weak cries drifted out into the dark. A boobook owl hooted a reply from the bush and its vivid yellow eyes watched from the night outside the door.

Susannah wanted to name her new daughter 'Echo'. 'For the mountain,' she said.

Noah grunted. 'What about Eliza, for your mother? Or Mary?'

'She was born under the mountain,' Susannah said. 'And it's like Caroline has come back to us – like an echo.' She cradled the baby to her breast and gazed at the scrunched little face. She knew her husband wouldn't argue with her.

Mrs Clarke, whose name was Emmeline though few called her that, was an older woman with her own brood of children. She stayed overnight and rose early to build up the fire and boil the billy.

'How are you doing, dear?' she asked the new mother, sticking her long nose into the billy to check for tea dregs. Susannah had helped with Mrs Clarke's last baby, the one she lost. It had lived only a few hours.

'I'm fine, Mrs C.,' Susannah said, pushing herself up on her elbow to gaze at the baby beside her. 'She is an awful good baby, I would say. Look at her. So quiet.'

Mrs Clarke bent over to squint at the newborn. 'Not *too* quiet, is she?'

Baby Echo opened her eyes and bawled into the fuggy breath that puffed from the woman bending over her.

Susannah suppressed a chuckle. 'Has Noah gone out?' she asked.

'Yes, but he'll be back for breakfast when I've got it ready.'

'Thank you for coming, Mrs C.'

'No trouble, dear. Your husband brought me in the wagon. Better than walking, ay? But I'll be walking back.'

'Oh, it's a terrible walk at the moment, after that rain last week. The track is such a struggle when it's muddy, the way your boots stick. You have to be careful not to pull your foot right out, especially if your laces is worn.'

'Broken bootlaces! Terrible when that happens. And the muddy boots like bricks when you take them off.' Mrs Clarke poked the fire, cleared away a pan of bloody water and collected the soiled cloths. 'I'll soak these in a tub before I go. Good thing you had the mattress on the floor. Always a lot of cleaning up after a birth.'

'Bless you, Mrs C.,' Susannah said, sitting up and putting the baby to her breast. 'You got here in the nick of time.'

'I did. Baby's head was pushing out as I walked in the door! Though heaven knows why babies are so keen to arrive.' She let out a low cackle at the ignorance of babies, at all they had to learn. The two women watched the suckling child for a few minutes.

'Your husband was a great help, Mrs H., I must say, getting behind to hold you. More comfortable to push that way.'

'Oh yes, me husband's pretty used to it. Had to catch one or two on his own.' Susannah smiled at this thought. The new baby helped her forget, for the moment, about the accident when they crossed the Mersey. As she put her forefinger up to stroke the child's cheek, she noticed blistering on her hand. Better get some lanolin for that. 'Good thing you got here when you did,' she said. 'I thought the fire was going to escape. The blanket caught, though I managed to crush it out. I have such a fear of a hut fire. The stories you hear.' She glanced at the hearth. Red coals were now banked up into a hot pyramid with the billy hanging on an iron tripod.

'You can't be too careful,' agreed Mrs Clarke, prodding the coals. 'I heard the Powlett place went up because a log rolled out while they slept.'

'Oh, it's a worry.' Susannah sucked in her breath and gazed down at her new baby.

'Doesn't look like she's going to die on you, Mrs H.,' the bush midwife said, leaning over the baby for another close inspection. 'Not like mine.'

Susannah looked at her neighbour, at her greying hair and long nose. It was easy to laugh at horse-faced Emmeline Clarke but Susannah didn't feel like laughing at that moment. She wondered what she could say about the lost baby. 'Oh, it's a sad thought, Mrs C. He looked all right when he come out. His skin was a bit blueish, it's true, but he gave a yell – or a gurgle sound, anyway. And you put him straight to the breast, I recall. That's the best way.' Her own new daughter whimpered, detaching from one drained nipple, anxious for the other.

'He was certainly breathing when I passed him to you.'

'Ah well,' sighed Emmeline Clarke. It had been her eighth birth. 'He didn't survive more than a day.'

'What was wrong with him?'

'Oh, just weakness. Bert buried him in the paddock near the house. He planted a Kentish cherry in that spot and it's coming along well.'

The women looked up as the two young boys began to stir. They'd want food soon. The lid of the billy clattered as the water came to a boil. Mrs Clarke threw in a handful of tea leaves and sat beside the fire, stirring the brew with a stick.

2

Afternoon, a year before Echo's birth. Shadows growing longer, the day cooling. Susannah sometimes told her children of this day – as a warning. The baby, one of her boys, had been colicky all day and the men were late back. It was close to sunset when she heard the bullocks coming up the hill at last. The Hattons had been on the lease at Paradise for barely a year. Five miles it was into town, and three miles to their closest neighbours, the Clarkes. This was long before the Millers took up their lease, or the Vineys. Noah, still trying to clear the big bottom paddock, had asked his brother Edward to come over from Sassafras to lend a hand. They'd been down working all day on the lower boundary.

The wagon creaked up the hill. Susannah watched Noah plodding beside the great horns of the bullocks, his whip dangling unused. As he approached, she noticed his shoulders hunched and thought she could see tears on his face. She ran to him. 'Oh, what has happened?'

Noah's brother Edward lay on the wagon, stretched out stone cold.

'A dead tree limb fell right on him. From one of them ringbarked gums,' Noah said.

This was the lesson, the lesson of the ringbarked trees that surrounded them, waiting to die and sometimes to kill. Susannah had wailed, but what could be done?

Noah had taken his brother's body back to his wife in Sassafras. He had driven the bullock wagon through the ford with his brother wrapped in a horse blanket. At Sassafras, he dug a trench and lowered in his brother's body. A preacher came; Edward's widow had a Wesleyan fellow over from Latrobe.

'Lead us to a place of peace and refreshment,' the preacher said. 'Guide us to springs of life-giving water; wipe away the tears from our eyes and bring us to heaven where there is no more death, no more grief or crying or pain.'

'Amen,' Noah had said to that, putting his hat back on.

When he returned to Paradise he told Susannah how it had been. Such a blessing they'd named their second son after Edward; she liked to think of this remembrance.

In the early years at Paradise the Hattons had all slept together at one end of the kitchen, keeping warm; parents and babies and little children. As time passed, Noah added more rooms and the hut grew into a proper house. But the kitchen remained the place where everyone gathered. Such a great thing it had been when Noah found a bricklayer, and a brick chimney and hearth were built. You had to get a man who knew his business if you wanted a proper chimney that didn't smoke.

Susannah liked to pace around her house, queen of all she surveyed, checking no gaps had appeared in the plank walls, making sure the new doors still moved freely on their real metal hinges, polishing the glass they now had in the front windows. Where one wall had been an outside wall, it became an inside wall, though timbered with weatherboard planks. Inside, the rooms were still papered with old newspapers.

When they first came to the lease, and for some years afterwards, Susannah had cooked on an open fire. Oh, she remembered that blessed day when Noah brought home the big cast-iron stove he'd got off Jim Sharman. Jim had it spare and wanted only two piglets for it. When the stove came, Noah replaced the original timber chimney with corrugated iron and he and Jim ran the stove pipe up it. With a fire built under the stove, everything became less trouble. The soup pot could be kept warm, and bread-making was so much easier. They could keep the stove alight *day and night* with less risk of a hut fire – thank the Lord! When Susannah's mother Eliza came to live with them, Susannah set a special chair next to the stove for the old lady. No-one else ever sat there: this was observed as an unspoken rule. Susannah liked to tell the story of the stove coming.

'It's fair amazing, the stories you have, Susannah,' remarked Ma, 'for a woman who never left the district after she come to Paradise.'

The kitchen was Susannah's court, the place she lived out her life. The sense of safety, the embracing warmth of home, the fact that here she was the one who made the decisions, and here she could keep her brood around her – she loved that kitchen, though it was still a rough old place. Here she cooked, fed her family, sat to nurse her babies, and mended clothes by lamplight. In the kitchen she bathed the children in a tin tub, and watched them struggle with their writing at the table, and received visitors, and squabbled with her mother.

In an alcove used as a larder she kept fruit preserves, and ropes of dried onions, and sometimes a barrel of mutton birds. She spent long days on her feet, often standing at the stove, but she loved to see her own chair always ready beside the open fire – the old wooden chair Noah had built and padded with kangaroo skins. Not that she sat down often, except to nurse an infant. Babies arrived every year until she could hardly keep track of how many she had borne, though she could reel off their names well enough.

A woollen blanket, dark red like a plum, lay draped over the back of the nursing chair. The colour changed to a bluish hue in the evenings when the only light came from the glow of the fire and from the kerosene lamp that sat on a shelf. Cradling a baby, framed by the kitchen pots and jugs, the preserves and dishes, all the bits and pieces of a large household, there Susannah sat in the evenings.

Ma, installed in her own chair beside the stove, would pipe up with advice, but Susannah rarely answered. She'd listened to plenty of Ma's instructions over the years: how to make the praties go further, how to deal with cuts and bruises, how to spin out the flour with potato meal, what to do about mice invading the larder. These days, with children everywhere, Susannah was often too distracted to listen. Her mother's low sing-song prattle floated, but didn't settle in her mind. Now the family were so many. Susannah fell often to worrying – how to feed them all? Sometimes she thought her suckling infants did better than the weaned children, who had to make do, many a time, on thin broth and a bit of bacon.

If anyone would listen, Eliza poured out stories, some heard from her own mother in the Maidstone days, poorly remembered and often embroidered. Some were from the time of her own marriage and the trouble she had with her husband, Susannah's rough father. Susannah liked the faerie stories Ma told, and the little songs from her childhood, but she always shushed her when the tales got onto her father. Ben Walters, his criminal career, his rough handling of his own children – Susannah had no wish to recall the drunken shouts, nor his fists. Those things came back often enough in her dreams: the bush hut on the edge of the forest, the crowd of her brothers and sisters, Eliza taking the brunt of his fists when he'd got hold of liquor, they never knew how, Eliza poaching sometimes or stealing a little flour to start her potato bread. How much it hurt a young girl to take the full force of a big man's fist to the side of the head. Susannah hadn't been able to hear too well on that side ever since.

'Don't tell anyone about that old convict,' Susannah would caution her own children. 'There's no need for anyone to know.' She spoke in a husky, musical brogue, her own bush dialect softened by the echo of a faint inherited Irish burr.

She was pleased to have her mother living with them, despite Noah grumbling about it. Though the gossip about the convict years was not to Susannah's liking, Ma's bushcraft came in useful – yes, most welcome sometimes. When the Dunstan boys broke Charlotte's ankle, she'd been mighty glad of Ma's skills. The shocking sight of the poor little white-faced child had sent memories shooting into Susannah's mind, befuddling her – memories of that other small white body, the one they had to bury under the celery-top pine when they first arrived.

Broken bones were a terrible thing in the bush. Pulling and setting the child's ankle was a torture, but necessary, of course. She accomplished it as swiftly as she could, holding back her tears for later. When Ma had taken a handful of sheep's wool from her basket, placed it on a dustpan full of hot coals and sprinkled it with sugar, Susannah had watched closely. She hadn't known of this remedy but she'd remember it for the future. The smoke had the odour of sweet lanolin. Susannah held her child's broken ankle in the fumes, watching Lottie's face to see if the remedy had a soothing effect. After a time the child's breathing settled.

Charlotte eventually recovered from the injury. Her bones knitted back together somehow or other, but she was left lame for the rest of her life and had to wear a metal brace fashioned by the blacksmith.

3

It was wash day and Susannah stepped out into the morning light to fill the tub. Noah was hitching his bullocks, Lion and Blue Boy, to the wagon. He always had a pair he called Lion and Blue Boy. There were four more bullocks in the farm stalls these days – Lark and Linnet, Turk and Tiger – a small team. All six were needed. Taking a full load of potatoes to the Rocky Cape jetty was a dreadful tough job, heaving the load along the muddy tracks that passed for roads.

Noah had enclosed their yard, their home space, with strong split-timber fences. Within these boundaries children and animals grew and worked and played and had accidents and recovered, squabbled and fought and argued and reconciled. Susannah stood for a moment and gazed around, checking that everyone was where they should be.

Charlotte's injury, the fight with the Dunstans and the loss of the sale money: Susannah had tried to consign these troubles to the past. What could be done? She poured a bucket of creek water into her tin wash tub, the splash mingling with the snorts of the bullocks.

Only Eddie's resentment of the Dunstans seemed to linger. As the boy helped his father hitch the bullocks, Susannah could hear him muttering yet again about confronting the Dunstans over the lost shillings. She worried about Eddie. He'd been staying out all night recently, fishing, and though she was surely grateful for the catch of blackfish he brought home for breakfast, she was not so keen on him being away from the house in the dark. She didn't worry so much about her eldest, Jack – he seemed to be turning out like his father, reliable and predictable. But that Eddie was another question altogether.

He often seemed discontented, ready to take issue at any small thing and get into an argument over it. She was relieved to hear Noah tell the boy he wanted no more fighting. The sight of Lottie with the broken ankle, lying white-faced on her bed, seemed to have changed her husband somehow. He'd been even more quiet than usual. It occurred to Susannah that he'd been reminded of Caroline, but she turned away from that thought as soon as it intruded.

If Jack still resented the Dunstans, if he was still angry over what had happened to Lottie, he seemed to be taking out such feelings on the woodpile, thwacking his axe down with more force than necessary for a bit of kindling. The muscles rippled in his skinny bare arms. Susannah felt a tremble of pride in her chest. Her Jack was good with the axe.

Then, with a spurt of annoyance, she noticed Echo crouched on the other side of the yard. Her pinafore was already grubby and it had been clean the day before. Her cheeks were no better. She was poking and digging around in the vegetable patch.

'Give over that digging, Eck,' Susannah called. 'Where is Amos? Where are your little brothers? You are supposed to be looking after them while I get the washing done.'

Echo looked up from the trench she'd dug. 'I'm looking for worms, Mother. If I get some bait, I can catch eels in the creek. Or some jollytails down in the Minnow.'

'Oh, give over, Eck, and get the eggs collected, will you?'

Susannah tipped another bucket of creek water into the tub and set the washboard in the water. Bending to scrub the clothes, she glanced across her yard and her family, the fence enclosing them all and the mountain standing sentinel above. Noah had the bullocks hitched and the wagon loaded with the sacks of potatoes. He'd likely need to go on the jetty so she went into the house to fetch his tucker bag, packed with bread and cold mutton and a bottle of tea. Noah pulled his hat lower on his forehead, did up the top button of his worn vest, and told her he'd be back by dusk. He called to the bullocks and the loaded wagon creaked off.

Bending low to shove her arms deep into the sudsy water, Susannah thrashed the children's clothes on the washboard and scrubbed at the dirty stains. Noah would manage to feed them all, one way or another. She could be sure of that, couldn't she? He came from a big bush family like hers, though she didn't know whether old father Hatton had been free. Some said he was transported for smuggling rum, and that could be true. Noah had a number of brothers.

'Lawd!' she said aloud, trying to remember. 'I forget how many now!' There was Edward, who helped with the clearing at Paradise and was killed by the tree. And others, whose names she'd forgotten.

Noah's family had lived and worked on a farm out past Deloraine, east of the Mersey. Susannah's family's hut stood on the edge of the same district, too close to town according to Eliza. Ben Walters could get there too easily and would come home drunk and angry. Why did he go where they taunted him? It was best to stay in the bush, that's what Ma always said. But Ben would go to town, and he would drink and come home on the edge of some terrible, unhappy place in his mind, and quick to anger with it. At those times, if they were fast enough, Susannah and her sisters would head into the bush to a place they knew under the man-ferns and wait it out. But they couldn't always escape the back of his hand.

Susannah sighed, as she remembered. Childhood was not all

terrible. She and her sisters once captured a young quoll and raised it as a pet. She'd loved that little animal, cradling it like a baby. You wouldn't think you could tame a quoll, but she'd managed it.

She first saw Noah during harvest time. When she recalled that moment, the scent of new-cut hay came back to her as if it were yesterday. At reaping time, everyone in the district assisted around the farms. They cut it all by hand, with sharp curved sickles. The drays were piled higher than a house. Everyone helped bring in the harvest, as quick as ever they could, while the weather held. Daydreaming of the old harvest, Susannah stood and stretched. She pressed the back of her hip as she recalled the work in the fields. It fair broke your back, reaping with a sickle.

When she'd first noticed Noah, she'd seen a tall, thin boy with leathery hands and his beard just coming in. Muscles knotted his forearms as if he had ropes instead of arms. He always pulled his hat down over his eyes, so it was hard to know what he was thinking. 'It's still the same,' Susannah mused, feeling a surge of affection. On that warm golden harvest day, she'd been attempting to tie a bundle of hay into a sheaf. There she stood, in her old working dress and pinny, struggling with the twine, trying to get it around the sheaf and not doing a good job of it.

A low voice said, 'I'll help you with that.' Ropey brown arms pulled the twine tight; the sheaf was made and tossed onto the dray in a minute.

'Thank you kindly,' Susannah said.

'You are welcome.'

He said nothing else, just stood there next to her with his hands in his pockets, looking at his boots. The two of them were still, despite the activity around them, in the shade of the dray piled high with the harvest. Susannah waited, sure this fellow wanted to say something more, but he never did. So after a while she said, 'My name's Susannah.'

He untied his tongue and said, 'My name's Noah Hatton.'

'I know your farm. Ain't it over to Quamby Brook?'

'Yes.'

'I live near to Elizabeth Town.'

'I know. Can I come over and see you Sunday afternoon?'

'That would be fine.'

And he did come over, and it wasn't too long after that they were married.

At that time, Noah worked on Paterson's farm with his father. He then got work over at Chudleigh at Mr Stanton's place and it came with a cottage for a married man. It was the dearest little place, and Susannah loved it, though it had only a dirt floor and was built of split timbers. The cookhouse stood separate, safer for fire, and Mr Stanton had a water tank in the yard so she didn't have to fetch from the creek. She had two babies while they were living in that cottage.

There were milk cows on the farm and chickens for eggs. Noah trapped rabbits. The night cold seeped in through the timbers, despite the newspaper lining the walls, and they huddled under the blankets. Noah liked to take his comfort of her often. When he rolled on top of her, Susannah wrapped herself around him and breathed into his neck. The babies, the dirt floor, the wind through the gaps in the timbers – they entwined themselves together and it felt good. It was certainly something fine to have a husband, to have warmth and satisfaction in the cold night. To have escaped from her father.

Her own mother came to help with the first child, but the second arrived too quick and Noah had to catch him. Now, settled in Paradise, they had their own place, not working for anyone else.

She knew how much this meant to Noah. He hadn't wished to work his whole life for Mr Stanton, for nothing more than their board and keep, no different to being a convict like her father, and maybe his. It was slavery, Noah said, and she could see that. Having their own place was a grand thing.

Straightening from the wash tub, she looked out again over her yard, surveying her domain. She would not mind some flowers by the door, like Mrs Stanton had, but she'd heard those came from England, as cuttings. Roses, Mrs Stanton had. A boronia bush would do as well. Perhaps she could ask Eddie to find one in the bush and plant it by the door. Whatever you might say about Eddie, he'd always been a good boy to her.

Her wedding had been simple. The biggest annoyance had been having to wait until a travelling preacher passed through – though some people didn't wait, starting married life without the preacher, then fixing things official later. Susannah thought she and Noah would have to do that too. They even moved into the hut at the Stanton place, because it was an opportunity not to be lost. It was months before a preacher arrived – almost too long. She hadn't reckoned on expecting so soon, but it turned out she'd always have her babies quick, one after another.

On the day the preacher arrived in the district, she saw his horse approaching and ran all the way over to find Noah in the paddocks. She cried, panting and puffing, 'Preacher's come!' and he said, 'Hallelujah!' And they were married the next day in Mrs Stanton's parlour. Baby Caroline arrived soon after.

As this memory emerged, Susannah looked across to the celery-top pine and the small wooden cross. Noah had gone off and made that cross in the days after they buried her. Susannah had wondered at the attention he'd put into it, with so much else to be done.

What had he been thinking? Perhaps he wanted Caroline's grave to be like those in a real churchyard. They had to look after themselves now, out in the bush on their own place. That's what Noah had said when she asked if they'd done the right thing, burying the child like that, in their own yard.

Susannah often told her other children about Caroline, so they'd remember their sister, just as she told the story of what happened to their Uncle Edward, killed when the tree limb fell on him. She warned them of the danger of the ringbarked trees, to avoid walking beneath them, to keep away from those rattling skeletons when the winds blew. And she warned them to be careful down at the creek, never to wade into the Dasher.

4

Susannah finished the laundry, pegged it out to dry, then went back into the kitchen and began chopping the root vegetables for the pot. She called the names of her children to make sure they were all accounted for. By evening Noah hadn't returned, so it seemed he did have to go on to the jetty to sell the spuds. The thought twisted in Susannah's stomach. Would the price be good enough? They needed flour or there'd soon be no bread.

When the sun shone and the mountain stood over the farm, blue and protective, and all her children were safe, Susannah found it easy to be in good spirits. But the constant grubbing for food wore her down. Though the last season had been plentiful for spuds, the prices had dropped so low it had hardly seemed worth digging them up, and the lease money still had to be paid. When the worries became too much she'd let herself cry quiet tears. Ma would call from her chair by the stove, 'Tears don't help nothing, Susannah.' On the contrary, she found that tears helped ease her anxieties. She added the wrinkled parsnips and a couple of yellow turnips to the pot. From the sour smell, the children would know there was cabbage too. Eddie, in response to her call, clanged open the cast-iron stove door and shoved in more kindling. Susannah bent over the pot. The steam turned to water rivulets on her cheeks and ran down her face until her apron became soaking wet. The children clustered around the table waiting for her to ladle out their share. She took a little herself and passed a bowl to Ma, who held it against her breast as if the warmth satisfied her just as well as the food.

The small girls all slept on a big sugar-bag mattress, and the boys on another. That night, as the little ones huddled under their blankets, Susannah watched from her high bed opposite, resting her cheek on her curled fingers. The light of the candle showed a widening damp spot on her pillow.

'Don't fret, Mother,' Echo whispered to her in the dark.

'Hush now, Eck.'

'But what's the matter?'

Susannah sniffed and whispered to Echo to come and climb in beside her. She held her close. 'The news from town ain't good, love. William Miller says the whole colony is in a bad way. He says that was why we couldn't get much for that last lot of spuds.'

Echo tightened her arms around her mother. 'But Father got the mutton birds, from that carter down in Emu Bay.'

Susannah dabbed at her eyes with the blanket. It was true. A cask of mutton birds sat in the larder, still half full. How could she have forgotten them, with their stink filling the house? 'You're right, Eck,' she said. 'They're a bit whiffy, but we are surely lucky to have them.'

Tomorrow she'd make some potato bread with the last of the flour. Potato, a little flour, salt, a spoonful of sugar, some hops. Leave it to prove overnight by the stove and that would give them a few loaves. This thought cheered her up. She could almost smell the fresh bread. Susannah drifted off to sleep, soothed by the thought of the lucky mutton birds and the comfort of hugging her favourite daughter.

Noah returned the next day. The potatoes had sold, though not for the price he'd hoped. There was a terrible glut on the market, he said. But his return cheered Susannah; it always did.

It was evening, and Susannah sat with Echo at the kitchen table mending clothes. Ma dozed in her usual chair; the fire in the stove burned warm. The light from the hurricane lamp was low for stitching but if the work didn't get done the little ones wouldn't have shirts and britches to wear.

Echo shifted restlessly and scrunched up little Rosie's pinafore. 'I don't know how that girl gets her pinny in such a state.'

'Oh, give over with your grumpiness, Eck,' said Susannah. 'Leave that now if you want to be doing your writing.' She never had any trouble indulging Echo, who always seemed happy to leave the housework for her books. Susannah bent her head and smiled her secret pride. It was not a right thing to favour one child over the others, but she marvelled at Echo's learning.

Echo happily tossed aside her share of the mending. She set out pen and ink and opened a book on the table. At school they all used slates, but the teacher Mr Pullen had given her a proper book to write in. Susannah's eyes remained lowered over her needle and thimble, but she raised them now and then to observe her daughter. Echo fixed a new nib in her pen, unscrewed the ink pot, and frowned over her page, a little vertical line forming between her eyebrows.

'Tell what you are writing, Eck,' asked Susannah. She knew all about the project and had heartswell every time she thought of it, and wanted to hear her daughter tell of it again.

'You know I am writing about you, Mother,' Echo replied. 'You're the heroine. I told you before.'

'I know that, Eck.' The idea of being *the heroine* made her warm. 'But what things are you telling *about*?'

'Oh, the way you cradle Baby when you nurse, the way you sing, the way you cry in the night.'

'Goodness me!' Susannah paused in her stitching. That described family life well enough, she supposed. As the sounds in the house settled, the younger children already asleep, the scratching of Echo's pen joined the crackle of the low fire and Ma's light snoring.

Later, as they were making their beds ready for the night, Echo whispered to her mother that Jack was drawing himself a map. 'Boys do like that story about Robinson Crusoe,' she said, sounding like an expert on boys. 'They like the idea of exploring, and building a house to live in, like Crusoe did. I reckon Jack wants to find a cave in the Gog range and hide out there and build his own place.'

So that's what Echo had learned, watching her brother. Susannah rolled out the boys' bedrolls and flapped a blanket to make sure no spiders had got into it. She wondered what she would do when her big boys moved out to their own places. Who would chop the kindling then? Who would catch rabbits and fish to help feed them all? Anticipating the loss of Jack and Eddie, she forgot for a moment about the bevy of younger sons, growing up quickly to take their big brothers' place.

'It ain't that easy to make a home,' she said. 'It is awful hard work. Like when we first come here. Have I told you about that time, Eck?'

Of course she had, plenty of times, the story of how they came to Paradise. Certainly it had been a hard start, but the telling of it helped to settle her heart.

5

Noah had obtained the farm on a twenty-year lease. The rent was sixpence an acre in the first two years, a shilling an acre for the next five, and by ten years it would be two shillings. Payment didn't take account of bad years; he had to make the land produce. By the time he'd heard of the surveying and opening up in the Kentish district, all the blocks had been snapped up by speculators, by those with money to invest. But when bush lots began to be offered, he said to Susannah that it would be a fine thing to take one, an opportunity to have a place of their own. He was a quiet young man, her husband, not often roused to excitement, but his fervour over this plan became infectious.

Some, it was said around Chudleigh, had paid many pounds for a block on the Kentish Plains then found the soil to be heavy clay. Mr Stanton warned Noah to be cautious. It took a big team of bullocks to plough land like that. Noah had decided to take a scrub block. It was offered as a heavily timbered place, and the lessee was obliged to clear and improve it, but his brother Edward promised to help. Edward had a lease of his own, and a family, at Sassafras.

Noah had already signed his mark on the lease when he went the first time with Edward to find the lot. They crossed the Mersey River at the ford on borrowed horses and started up Stoodley Hill along the rough bridle track. To find the place, they had a description of the major bends in the track, and of a big fallen log that marked the start of the lot. Noah told Susannah how he'd sat up in the saddle, peering along the bridle track for the fallen log. When he saw it, he said, he knew it for *his* place immediately. He'd raised his crumpled rabbit-fur hat, waved it high in the air as he stood in the stirrups, and yelled to his brother, 'Here she is! Home!'

'Yes, that'll be it,' Edward had replied. 'But it'll be a while before it's home.'

Though the country before and beyond the fallen log looked identical, what lay beyond the log seemed different somehow. That's what Noah had said to Susannah, and she couldn't help but share the wonder of it. *Their* place. She saw that the idea of it gave him the heart to cross the Mersey again and again, and to get on with the back-breaking work of clearing the land.

Noah finished building their first hut with its timber chimney and temporary canvas roof, and Susannah and the children were finally able to travel to Paradise. With the wagon loaded, the family set out north-west from Chudleigh. On the second day of the journey they approached the Mersey River. The weather hadn't been kind;

there'd been rain at night and frost in the morning. As they neared the riverbank, Susannah could see the water flowing fast and high. There was only one place to cross, Kimberley's Ford, where the cattlemen of the Van Diemen's Land Company had driven their herds through when white men first penetrated the back country. Though the district had been surveyed for nearly two years and settlers had rushed to take up leases, the river still had no bridge, only the natural ford – accessible enough if the river was running low. But a thundering herd of cattle with stockmen on horseback was a different proposition to a frail wagon loaded with household furniture, chickens trussed in sugar bags, a wife, a small child, and a babe in arms. Noah drew up on the south-eastern bank, scratched his beard, and climbed down for a closer look.

'We cannot go through, Noah,' Susannah called from the wagon bench. 'We must wait until it goes down a bit.'

She did not like the look of the rushing water, not at all. The air was cold. She wrapped the blanket closer around the baby. A wind bit through her shawl. Two-year-old Caroline tugged at her skirt, repeating, 'Mama! Mama!'

She watched her husband walk across the round smooth stones that formed a shingle on the riverbank. She saw him scratch his beard again. They'd already camped out one night on the journey from Chudleigh. He surveyed the river with his hands on his hips, impatient to get to his land. Another night camping out would be hard, but she feared the high water.

'We will have to camp again,' she called, shifting the whimpering baby to her shoulder.

Noah remained, assessing the river. Susannah pressed down her fear and tried to trust his judgement. He and his brother Edward had crossed the Mersey plenty of times, sometimes when it was flowing high. She could sense the strong pull of the home he'd begun to make, as he raised his eyes to the hills on the other side.

'I reckon we can get through,' he called at last, turning back to the wagon.

Clutching the baby, trusting her husband, Susannah pulled Caroline closer to her. She was a good child, giving no cause for worry, but today she squirmed and squealed and pointed at the swirling water. She was too young to have the words, but seemed excited by the prospect of the crossing.

'Sit still, Caroline!' Susannah scolded, and searched for her own courage.

Noah's whip cracked, he called to his leaders, and the bullocks heaved forwards into the river, dragging the laden wagon behind them. The water dashed turbulent. Susannah had expected that. She hadn't expected it to be so deep. Halfway across, the water was almost lapping their feet. She feared that Noah had misjudged. The bullocks, the first Blue Boy and Lion, pulled well – but Blue Boy lost his footing in a hidden dip beneath the churning water. The wagon tipped.

'Hang on!' Noah yelled.

She let out a jolted cry; the boards of the wagon and the ropes holding its load creaked like the rigging of a sailing ship. Caroline squealed delightedly.

The straining bullocks and the swirling river took all Noah's attention. As the wagon listed to one side Susannah clutched her baby with a frantic grip, her other hand clenched to the side of the wagon. Suddenly without her mother's restraining arm Caroline slipped from the bench into the water. She made no sound as she went, none that her mother heard above the roaring and urging and creaking and snorting. As Susannah realised Caroline had slid into the river, an unearthly wail escaped her. The child's white pinafore flashed for a moment then disappeared. Noah urged the animals onwards, screaming above the roar of the water and the cries of his wife, and the wagon emerged from the Mersey on the other side, the side of the promised land.

With Susannah shocked and silent, holding the bawling baby, Noah scrambled back along the riverbank. A shingle of river stones edged that side too. She watched him climb a jutting bank crowded with twisted myrtle and tall sassafras trees, and heard him calling his daughter's name. He called and called.

He found her just beyond the bank, tangled in tree roots where a deep waterhole caused the river to curl into a ferocious eddy. When Susannah saw him pull the child from the river, hope surged. Clutching the baby, she climbed down and hurried towards him. He staggered back to the wagon carrying his daughter, but neither of them could coax a breath from her.

'Oh, we should not have gone through!' Susannah wailed, through gulping sobs.

Noah cradled the soaking wet child. It was as if she'd fallen asleep, tired from the long journey. He muttered something, over and over, but Susannah couldn't make out his words; she could hardly think. Her baby squalled; the river in spate laid a coverlet of noise over the scene. When Noah looked up and she saw his expression, Susannah understood that he would always carry the blame of this.

They wrapped Caroline in an old horse rug and put her on the wagon, lying her across their feet, and that was the way they came down the track into Paradise.

As they reached the little hut of which Noah was so proud, Susannah sat dazed, unaware they had even arrived. He'd had to pull her from her bench and push her inside. The first thing he did was start a fire in the bush-stone hearth.

'We should not have gone through,' Susannah said again, her voice dull. She tried not to think about the fatal riverbank. Her baby boy whimpered. She sat on a stump, pulled open her damp dress and offered him her breast. She didn't raise her head when Noah carried in the small bundle wrapped in the horse blanket.

'I best bury her right away, love,' he said. The new fire crackled and flared.

Susannah nodded, closed her dress, and put the baby down on a bed of hessian bags. She unwrapped her daughter, straightened the child's wet clothes, kissed her cold face. Her tears kept flowing.

Noah found more hessian bags to wrap the small body. He went out into the dusk and dug a shallow trench. Evening shadows crawled across the rough yard and a wind began to sough in the bush as he leaned on his shovel. Susannah stood beside him as he lowered the little body into the earth. They both wanted to say something, to say the right words, to send her up to heaven from Paradise, but neither could recall the right phrases, though they'd been to enough burials in their time. As they turned back towards the hut Noah said softly, 'I'm sorry, love.'

Susannah didn't reply, though she heard him.

Susannah roused herself from her grief to tend to the baby. Just six months old, it seemed he wanted to be fed around the clock. Susannah was a young woman, only seventeen years old, but to bury a child and feed a child at the same time seemed to her a hard thing. 'It would try anyone,' she'd say, years later, telling the story, weeping anew in the telling.

On that first night Noah kept adding logs to the fire, trying to bring some warmth into their new home. Sitting on the low stump, the baby guzzling at her breast yet again, strands of chestnut hair fell about Susannah's face. She felt so grubby from the journey, and the grim task of burying.

'You'll have to keep a fire going *day and night*, or we'll die of the cold,' Noah said. 'But be careful to watch it, now. Hut fires are deadly.'

He told her of the Powletts over at West Kentish whose place had burned down, twice. He'd heard the story at the inn at Sheffield. She would meet the neighbours soon, Noah said. For the time being, in the dark clearing, it was just her, her husband and her baby.

'We have to have a fire going,' Noah repeated. 'Or die of the cold.'

Susannah nodded and held her baby close. She sensed Noah watching her and understood that he didn't want her to keep weeping, but she didn't know how to stop. The water kept running down from her eyes. He ventured a remark.

'It was hard to lose the little one,' he said, 'but more will come.'

'I'll see her in heaven, won't I, Noah?' She turned her damp eyes to him.

Her husband, bent over the fire, replied, 'So the preachers tell.'

'We did right to bury her without a preacher, didn't we?'

'Yes. There was no choice. We have to look after ourselves now we're out here on our own place.' Noah's mouth turned down. 'We can do without preachers.'

6

The year Echo turned fifteen, life at Paradise seemed to change. Susannah became more involved with the goings-on in the district, more enmeshed in her neighbours' lives. There were more visits, more outings, more long talks around kitchen tables. Everyone seemed to think something momentous was about to happen, and Susannah agreed. With the arrival of the preachers, a crackling energy spread through the Kentish Plains. It affected Susannah as much as anyone, right from the first time she saw them.

Susannah could see the entrance to the yard from her kitchen window. Breathless with excitement, she watched the two strangers hitch their horses to the fence rail and approach her kitchen door. She shouted for Echo, and invited the visitors in. Her kitchen gleamed tidy and scrubbed; she'd been looking out for this visit ever since Emmeline Clarke had told her of the arrival of the strangers. She called for Echo again, shouting more brusquely than usual, and the girl hurried in from the ferns with Amos trailing behind her. The baby coughed, a rasp like an unoiled hinge; Susannah picked her up from the cradle.

'The little one isn't well?' inquired the older, white-bearded gentleman politely. He offered Susannah the latest remedy for the baby's cough, even wrote the ingredients down for her. She was that pleased! Echo would read it for her later. He spoke of news from other districts, and encouraged Eck to recite her psalm, which she did with no mistakes. In a flurry of nerves, Susannah fussed about, refilling the teapot and offering the gentlemen griddle cakes.

The visit filled her with a physical warmth, whether from pride or excitement or friendship brought to her door, she could not say.

'It was fair amazing,' she said to Noah afterwards in a voice still full of the wonder of it.

That gentlemen like them should sit in her kitchen and converse with her! Susannah sensed something magical about these strangers, though she couldn't say exactly what this meant.

After the big revival meeting in Duggan's barn, Susannah decided that this idea of magic was most likely right. What a night that had been, what a show! When she thought back on it, as she so often did as she worked about her house and yard, chopping the roots, filling the washtub, brushing the floors, sweeping the hearth, she'd sing under her breath, '*O what peace we often forfeit, O what needless pain we bear, All because we do not carry, everything to God in prayer!*' If it hadn't been for Echo, she might've fainted right away that night. Some women had. Susannah remembered her head swimming. She'd felt woozy and thought angels might have come down into Duggan's barn – that would have been real magic!

Surely something like that could not happen in a barn in Paradise? But she had almost expected it; she would not have been surprised. As the preachers spoke in their rising voices, their arms outstretched, stepping forwards as if they would walk right down among the people, their eyes flashing, their shoulders swaying, Susannah had felt a tremendous urge to rise up and go to them. 'Oh,' she said to herself when she recalled the moment, 'I heard voices inside me head. I saw heavenly angels. I wonder if I cried out?'

But when she asked Echo about it, Echo said she had not, though she *had* looked a little strange. 'Like you were asleep, but sitting up.'

When the revival meeting ended, Noah had taken her arm and led her out into the night air. She couldn't find words for her feelings. She left with her family and sat silent all the way home with the music of the hymns swimming in her head. Jack had started singing one of them: *'Blest be the tie that binds.'* That was a good one, she thought, and true enough besides.

Then came the first baptisms – in their own creek, the Dasher. By that time, the whole district was roused. All the kiddies clamoured to go down to watch. Susannah often felt nervous when her children romped near the creek; of course she couldn't help but think of Caroline. But they would be safe enough, she would be there with them.

Mrs Mason from the next-door farm was going to be the first immersed, that's what Susannah had heard, and she could hardly believe it. Mrs Mason had the reputation of a sensible woman. As they watched from the hillside and she saw it was true – Mrs Mason dunked under the water! – she felt the whole revival had intoxicated everyone.

What would happen now? If she could only hear those magical preachers again. Perhaps they'd hold another meeting. She would pester Noah to take her if they did.

That winter, when Amos was shot out rabbiting, Susannah feared she would never get over the shock of it. Her sorrow enveloped her and she cried floods; she could barely stop, though Ma advised again that tears would do no good. The frantic working over his little back, picking out the shot with Ma beside her, Emmeline Clarke bringing clean water and murmuring advice, the child becoming paler and paler as his blood kept flowing until at last it stopped flowing and that was not a good thing, it was not. Where had the fatal shot hit? What had they missed? Should they have tried the sassafras tea? Should they have turned him over and searched again across his baby white skin?

Ma said it was no good, the boy had lost too much blood.

They laid Amos in the ground under the celery-top pine next to Caroline, though they could have put him in the new community burial place in Sheffield. But Susannah told her husband she wanted him at home, she wanted him nearby. Echo found the verses in the family Bible and read beside the grave. '*Yea, though I walk through the valley of the shadow of death, I will fear no evil: for thou art with me; thy rod and thy staff they comfort me.*'

'Can you find the one about being together again someday, Eck?' Susannah asked, and Echo leafed through the old Bible. She'd marked some places with gum leaves.

'I have this one, Mother. *We which are alive and remain shall be caught up together with them in the clouds, to meet the Lord in the air: and so shall we ever be with the Lord. Wherefore comfort one another with these words.*'

Susannah touched the end of her shawl to her red eyes. She found comfort in the sing-song cadences of the verses, in the Biblical promises.

'Amos has gone before, Mother,' Jack said, and put his hand on her shoulder.

She supposed that Jack wanted to comfort her. He said this was the good news the preachers had spoken of – that you would meet your loved ones again, if you believed and went converted. Jack was keen on his Bible reading these days. She certainly hoped he was right, but she couldn't really draw comfort from this idea – it seemed too far off, too unlikely. Oh, she should have gone up to the front at the revival! The preachers might have revealed more, given her something she could hang onto now.

Hoisting one of the small children onto her hip, she returned to her house, back to the work of the family.

For a long while she cried in secret corners and her tears flooded the house, soaked her apron and her pillow, as if trying to wash away the pain of the loss. Oh, that death hit her hard. Though she knew others suffered too – Mrs Clarke, for example, losing her baby, and neighbours lost to accidents, and little children carried off by the diphtheria.

'Nothing you can do,' advised Eliza from her chair by the stove, 'except go on.'

'Oh, Ma, leave me be to cry as I like.'

'You had better give over sometime or we will all be damp 'til Christmas.'

Susannah threw her apron over her head and sat like that for a while.

As the winter dragged on, her grief eventually eased. She recalled how it had been after they'd lost Caroline. Then, too, she'd thought she could never go on. But she had to feed Baby, and look after her husband and tend to her house and children, so she did go on.

It was a hard winter, that one. Jack and Eddie began to argue and it drew the winter out like a long, sad song. Echo came in from taking their crib down to them in the lower paddock and said they'd come to blows. Their father had to split up the fight. It was Jack as started it, so Eck reported, though it was Eddie who landed the first punch. Oh, her own boys fighting! Susannah hugged her elbows and blinked away more tears. When she asked Noah about the fight, he told her to leave them be. Susannah wondered again which one of them had fired the shot that killed Amos, and wondered if the fight was about that.

7

When the weather warmed the preachers returned, and the district came to life again. Sunday after Sunday, Mr Fenny would wade into the creek and preach, 'Immersion is the Biblical way of baptism!' He urged his listeners to heed only what the Bible said, and not to listen to those other clergymen, those of the established churches, who claimed to *interpret* the Bible.

The Hattons often went to see the show. Susannah wondered if Mr Fenny would say something about how she could see Amos again, if he would be able to reassure her that her little boy was happy and safe with the Lord, if the Lord would come again soon. The teachings were hard to follow, but sometimes Mr Fenny would say something clear and shining, and it was worth going to hear him, oh yes it was certainly worth it.

'You can read for yourselves!' he said, forgetting the many among his audience who were not readers. He opened his Bible to Acts, to the story of Philip baptising the man he met on the road. '*And they went down both into the water,*' Mr Fenny read, '*both Philip and the eunuch; and he baptised him.*' Without pausing to discuss eunuchs, he dunked the new Kentish Christians in the same way. The 'new Saints', as they began to call each other, seemed to revel in the physical thrill, and the neighbours adored the spectacle, turning out by the dozens. Creeks were dug out or dammed up in Barrington and Nook, at Sheffield and West Kentish. Some of the boys still ridiculed the immersions, scoffing from the trees, and coming just to see the matrons doused, and there were shenanigans along the riverbank when they shoved each other into the water.

'Just hurrying things up!' they'd yell, cackling with laughter.

But these larrikins were outnumbered by the converts.

On Sunday mornings the new Saints met to worship at different houses. The preachers rode to isolated farms, down to Beulah, and out to Wilmot. People were converted everywhere: 'getting saved', they called it. Susannah felt these meetings were only for those who had been immersed, even though Jack went all the time.

Sitting around the fire in the evening, Noah and Jack discussed the craze for the revival and the baptisms. Susannah wondered if they all should get saved too, though she wasn't sure what it meant, beyond being doused in the creek. Her thoughts turned to Preacher Fenny, her favourite of the two. He had come and prayed for their wheat crop – in her very own kitchen. It was a moment Susannah would never forget.

'That Mr Fenny saved our wheat,' she said.

'Give over, Mother,' Eddie said, rubbing mutton fat into his boots. 'The crop would've come good without all that carry-on.'

'Don't say that, Eddie! If we had lost it, we'd have been in a terrible bad way.'

'It's the power of prayer,' Jack said, nodding. 'If you believe, you can use it for good.' He had the Bible open on the table and was running his finger along a line of the text, frowning in concentration.

'Sing us that hymn, Jack,' suggested Susannah. 'You know the one I like.'

Eddie gave an elaborate sigh and shook his head. He went on tending to his boots.

Jack turned away from his brother. 'All right, Mother. Is this the one?' His voice had matured to a tuneful baritone. '*When all my labours and trials are o'er, And I am safe on that beautiful shore, Just to be near the dear Lord I adore, Will through the ages be glory for me.*'

Susannah beamed. '"The Glory Song",' she said with a sigh. 'Oh Jack, I wish I could be sure of going to heaven, when it's me time. To see Caroline and Amos there.' The thought nearly brought on her ready tears again.

Jack left the Bible on the table and went to his mother. He squeezed her shoulder. 'You can, Mother. If you believe, you can have the Lord as your saviour, like me. I'll ask Preacher Fenny to talk to you, if you want.'

He spoke softly but with a strange urgency. Susannah felt he was trying to save her from something she didn't fully understand. What would she have to do? Noah was awake now, listening. Susannah didn't know what to think, didn't know what was required of her. But if it meant being sure of seeing her lost babies again, why not go converted? It would be a fine thing to have that comfort.

Little by little, Jack persuaded his father too. In the end, Noah said Jack could ask Fenny to come out to Paradise again. 'We can have a chinwag with him,' he agreed, and Jack looked that pleased with himself.

It seemed to Susannah that most of their neighbours found something in this conversion business and, as Noah pointed out, those who had embraced it seemed right cheered up. Susannah had noticed this herself. When it came to Emmeline Clarke, or Janie Miller's mother, you had to admit it looked like a good thing.

When the preacher rode up to their yard on his borrowed horse a few days later she had made up her mind, and couldn't help a broad smile. Noah saw the horseman arrive and came in from the paddock. He shook the preacher's hand. Together, they ushered the visitor into the kitchen and Mr Fenny sat with them over a pot of tea. The discussions went on for some time. Eliza, in her corner, remained silent and Susannah almost forgot to introduce her. Echo hovered by the kettle.

With a cup of tea in front of him, the Scotsman spoke of salvation, of the Promised Land, of Christian living and its rewards. He suggested a prayer, and over their bent heads he made ambitious requests for the Hatton family: health, safety, prosperity, peace. To Susannah, they seemed magical words; the preacher bewitched her. With his prayer done, he congratulated them both on their conversion.

Is that what had happened? Susannah experienced an inner thrill – now she was included in the magic. Happy shivers ran down her arms and hands, across her breasts and down through her belly and thighs. It was a feeling she couldn't remember ever experiencing before – unless in bed with Noah. She put that thought from her mind as soon as it popped in.

Afterwards, when the visitor had ridden off triumphantly down the bush track, Echo asked if she could be converted too. Susannah hugged her daughter, cried a little.

'Most certainly, I want for us all to be together in heaven!'

'Except Eddie,' Echo said. 'He don't want to.'

'Oh, that Eddie.' Susannah sighed. He was a worry.

Echo read some of the Bible passages that Jack suggested. He told his mother she needed to be ready for her baptism, ready to answer the questioning of the preachers, to prove she truly believed. He pointed out a verse in the Gospel of John. Echo read it aloud, '*Whosoever liveth and believeth in me shall never die. Believest thou this?*'

Do Christians never die? Was that what it meant? Susannah puffed at the miraculous thought. It was a marvel.

Now they could go to the Bible readings and the Sunday meetings at the other farms, and have the Christian neighbours to their place too. Socialising and praying filled the spring days. With this fellowship, and the certain knowledge that she'd see her lost children again, Susannah was able to stop weeping, most of the time.

8

Down at Dawson's paddock, Susannah settled herself beside Emmeline Clarke. They had a blanket spread on an old log and it made a fine enough seat to watch the play. Cricket was certainly a good game for a warm afternoon.

'I do like to watch a cricket match,' she said, feeling happier than she had in ages.

Everything seemed better when spring came. Down at John Dawson's paddock, green shoots were pushing through the soil and all the boys of the district were getting together for a cricket match. Her own sons had convinced Susannah to come and watch. Jack in particular wanted her to see the game, so he said. Percy Coleman's brother Tom was going to show them all the 'overarm', the new way of bowling. The English team bowled this way; they were touring on the mainland and everyone had read of it in the newspapers.

Ma had wanted to come too, but it was too troublesome to load her into the wagon. The kiddies were growing, they were awful boisterous; there was not so much room as before. That's what Susannah had told her mother, who'd grunted and agreed to stay home with Baby.

Emmeline Clarke had a bag of apples from her store. Susannah bit into the crispy skin of a stone pippin; good eating, heart-shaped. Her teeth, not the best since she'd lost quite a few last year, were still strong enough to crunch a crescent from the pippin.

'These are good apples, Mrs C. Last year's?'

Emmeline Clarke paused in her survey of the paddock to consider her own apple. 'Yes, they've kept well,' she said with a satisfied air, her jaws working on the apple flesh. Turning her attention to the ground, she added, 'Your boys are both out there, I see.'

Jack and Eddie were lined up with the other young men of the district watching Tom Coleman demonstrate the new bowling technique. Tom raised his arm high, flung a wide arc in the air, and brought his forearm down with vigour. As the two women watched, he expanded his demonstration to include a long run-in from one end of the makeshift pitch before letting the ball go with all the force he could muster. It slammed into the pitch and bounced high.

'It's a funny way to bowl,' remarked Susannah. 'Not like we seen before.'

''Tis the new way, Mrs H. They calls it "overarm", I believe.'

'That Tom Coleman sure is up with all the new ways.'

'He's a good cricketer. One of the best around here.'

When the demonstration was nearly finished, a ruffle through the onlookers indicated a new arrival. A cart drew up at the side of the paddock. Susannah stood, stretched her legs and threw her second apple core into the bush. The preachers had arrived, Mr Braithwaite and Mr Fenny, lately returned to the district with the spring warmth. The women strolled over for a better view, and saw Preacher Fenny greeting Percy Coleman. Several of the Colemans had been baptised last autumn.

'That family is most caught up in the Bible studying,' Mrs Clarke remarked.

They heard the preacher offering to pronounce a blessing on the match. At this suggestion, a few jeers floated from the branches of a spreading gum tree at the fence line. Several boys had climbed the tree for a better view. 'We don't need no God-botherers at the cricket,' they called. 'Pipe down if you want to stay!'

Ignoring these scoffers, Percy Coleman led Mr Fenny onto the pitch. With the players gathered around, Percy waved his arms towards the onlookers and called out, 'Ladies and gents! Attention please! We are about to begin the match. Here is Mr Fenny, a gent you all know well, come to give a blessing. Quiet down for Mr Fenny!'

Percy Coleman had a streak of authority; he could get people to pay attention if he wanted. Susannah noticed Jack, entrusted with one of the bats, standing behind Percy like his second-in-command.

The preacher raised his arms, his black coat-tails flapping behind him, and pronounced a sonorous prayer. He asked the Lord's blessing on the players and on everyone in the paddock. 'For Thine is the glory!' he bellowed.

Two teams then formed up, their members chosen by the two best players, the Coleman brothers, the ones who knew something about the new overarm bowling technique. Susannah saw that Jack and Eddie had been picked and she nudged Emmeline Clarke.

'My boys are both going to play.' At last those boys had stopped arguing and fighting.

Mrs Clarke peered out on to the pitch. 'On different teams,' she observed.

Susannah hadn't noticed, but she didn't worry about it. The main thing was that the boys were both out there playing together. Much better than fighting. She and Mrs Clarke moved back to their seat on the log. Echo waited there for them, having rounded up her younger brothers and sisters and seated them in a row along the paddock fence.

'I got the little blighters rounded up, Mother,' she said. 'Any apples left?'

Mrs Clarke chuckled and pointed to the bag placed by the log. 'Your brothers are both going to play, Eck, on *different* teams.'

'That don't matter, Mrs C. It's just a "friendly".'

'But who will you barrack for?'

Echo squinted and considered this. 'It don't matter,' said Echo, 'so long as they play fair.'

The match began. Tom Coleman ran in and tossed the ball with his dashing overarm. When the batsman managed to connect – and that didn't always happen, the ball flew so fast – a loud crack sounded. The fielders raced all over the paddock. Echo had called it a 'friendly' but there were times when it didn't look too friendly. Susannah heard howls when the umpire disallowed a ball, or when someone was caught out, or a batsman hit the ball right over the paddock fence and into the bush. Plenty of name-calling went on too if a fielder missed a catch or a bowler didn't manage to take a wicket as his teammates thought he should.

'I don't know what an "unfriendly" would look like,' Emmeline Clarke said at one point.

Susannah lost track of the scoring. Noah had been standing with a group of men who were smoking and watching proceedings. When he came over, she asked him which team was winning. Was it Tom's team or Percy's? Play had paused for the tea break and all over the field players were meeting with their families. Women were spreading out refreshments on the grass.

'Percy's team is ahead,' Noah said. 'They have a strong lead, despite Tom's new-fangled way of bowling. I reckon they should stick to the round-arm. It's good enough for W. G. Grace.'

Susannah unpacked the pottery tea bottles, the cold meat sandwiches and the apple cake, and Jack and Eddie walked over to join them. Oh, it was better now spring had come. Susannah felt contentment spreading through her like warm tea.

The break over, the teams returned to the field. It came Jack's turn to bat. They were playing with a hard red leather cricket ball that the Colemans had got from somewhere, but the bats were old homemade things. Susannah wondered how the fast, overarm balls didn't split those bats. 'That ball do go at some speed,' Susannah said, watching the play with a little trepidation.

Jack took a crack at a ball and hit it right to the boundary. She and Noah and Echo and the little Hattons gave out a cheer.

Then Eddie stepped up to bowl. This quietened everyone. Two Hattons playing against each other – who should they cheer for? Susannah felt her happiness dim a little. Eddie walked back twenty paces as Tom Coleman had taught, then turned and faced his brother at the far end of the pitch. Susannah remembered that Eddie's team was well behind in the scoring, and had a long way to go to catch up. His teammates were urging him to take the wicket. 'Get him, Eddie! Give him the overarm!' Eddie responded with a determined scowl and rubbed the ball on his trouser leg.

Jack hunched over his homemade bat, rounded his shoulders, and eyed the flash of red leather in his brother's hand. Eddie began his run-up, the first few steps rather slow. Then he accelerated. His right arm went up in a high arc and came slamming down as the ball left his grip. It speared into the rough grass of the pitch, shot up and hit Jack in his right knee, as quick and sudden as a bullet.

The bat in Jack's hand flew up then dropped as he let it go.

He fell, clutching his knee. Play stopped.

The umpire and players rushed over to Jack. Eddie had halted at the end of his run, just beyond the bowler's crease. With his hands on his hips, he watched as the crowd clustered around his brother.

Noah rushed onto the pitch with the other men. He helped Jack limp off, their arms twined around each other's shoulders.

'Oh, Jack!' Susannah cried, and the tears started as they always did. She pulled the blanket from the log and insisted he lie upon it, though he drew the line at letting her strip off his britches. 'So I can see the hurt,' she said. 'It might be broke! It'll need a compress, at least.'

'When we get home, Mother, not here!' He glared at the pitch where discussions were underway between the two team captains and the umpire, Mr Pullen. Eddie stood back, his arms folded. The umpire disqualified his bowl as a 'no ball'. Eddie took exception to this – Susannah could see him arguing. It looked all wrong, a young fellow like Eddie arguing with a white-bearded gentleman like the umpire. It unsettled Susannah and she tingled a little with shame for her boy. Tom Coleman, the captain of Eddie's team, tried reasoning with him and seemed to calm him down. He was sent out to deep mid-wicket to field. 'To keep him out of trouble,' Noah said.

After some careful prodding, Jack declared that his knee wasn't broke, only bruised. Susannah, not satisfied, wondered what kind of compress would be best. She'd ask Ma's advice when they got home. She would have preferred to leave for the farm right away, but the match wasn't over, and Eddie was still playing. Jack – he seemed all right – began to explain to his father the difference between throwing and bowling, and why Eddie's bowl had been a no ball. None of it made sense to Susannah. It was all just tossing the ball, after all. She couldn't decide if she'd wanted Eddie to win or lose his argument with the umpire. She supposed the ball hitting Jack so hard and hurting him – he might have trouble walking for some days, even if it wasn't broke – had been an accident. It could not have been deliberate.

The match was more or less over for the Hatton boys. Jack's knee kept him from returning to the wicket and Eddie was stuck out at the boundary, but the remaining sportsmen played the match to a conclusion. They'd changed the rules to play a short game; the spring light was fading when the umpire called time. People began to pack up. The players gathered around their captains, clapping them on the back. Someone started a round of three cheers, and Jack joined in. He stood, propped against the Hatton wagon, ready to head home. Eddie slouched over and reached for his jacket. With his chin lowered, he glanced at his brother. 'How's your knee?' he said, rather gruff.

Jack shifted his leg a little and spat. 'I'll live, I reckon.'

In the wagon on the way home, Susannah asked Echo which side had won the match, Jack's or Eddie's? Echo said she didn't know, but it didn't matter because it was just a 'friendly'. Jack, propped in the back of the wagon, called, '*We* won, of course! Better and fairer!'

Eddie walked home. Everyone had seen the bad blood between the brothers, and Emmeline Clarke had said it was 'hardly surprising'. Susannah wondered what Mrs C. had meant by that.

9

Out in the yard, Susannah watched Echo as she plucked a rooster. She wondered if her daughter might soon be thinking of courting. There were signs – some moodiness, plenty of distraction. The girl had turned fifteen, so it wouldn't be surprising. Several girls in the district, not much older than Eck, had married recently. She herself had married at fifteen – or had she been fourteen? It seemed years ago now, that day during the hay harvest when she'd first seen Noah.

'What do you reckon about going on a picnic, Eck?' she suggested.

'Oh, I don't know, Mother,' Echo replied. 'We could if you want.'

Her daughter's lack of interest seemed feigned to Susannah. 'Them picnics are fine times for young people.' Ma was in her yard chair, listening, and Susannah noticed the old woman's face crinkle into a smile. Ma understood what she was getting at.

'Not only us young people, Mother,' Echo said. 'You love picnics too. Sitting there gossiping with the ladies, calling out to the kiddies: *come away from the bush! Watch out for the creek!* As if them little ones didn't run free over the farm all week anyway.'

'Oh, but down at Dunn's Swamp is different, Eck. The back country behind ain't surveyed yet. It's still wild down there. There might be tigers and all in that country.'

'Not at the picnic place, Mother.'

'No need to laugh, Eck. There's other things to watch out for at them picnics too, as I believe you well know.'

'What do you mean?'

Susannah chuckled, sounding like one of her hens. 'No need to be coy, my girl. There's quite a bit of courting goes on, as I recall.'

Echo looked down at the half-plucked rooster. 'Not me.'

Susannah thought before answering. 'Perhaps, Eck. But your friend, Janie . . .'

'What? Did you see Janie with someone?'

'Sure enough, the last time down at Dunn's. I thought you did too.'

'I saw her and Eddie. They went for a walk. But Mother, you don't think – ?'

A funny little laugh emerged from Susannah. She watched Echo's face turn red.

'Oh, don't talk about that, Mother. Let's talk about what we could take, the cold meat sandwiches and the apples.'

'We could eat as well at home,' Susannah said. 'We don't go on picnics for the food.'

'Oh, Mother. Stop laughing.'

That spring, the two preachers sometimes asked for the use of a farm kitchen for an afternoon where they could pray together and have a discussion. About the best way forward for the new Christians, that's what they said. Susannah offered hers – after all, she was part of the Christian community now. She chased the children out and moved Ma to her chair in the yard.

Susannah had taken a shine to Mr Fenny in particular. It gave her pleasure to provide a pot of tea and leave the two gentlemen – in *her* kitchen! – to have their discussion. Naturally she listened in, as she reported to Emmeline Clarke the next day.

'Mr Fenny has a wife and two kiddies in Melbourne,' reported Susannah, with Mrs C. hanging on every word. 'But Mr Braithwaite is alone in the world.'

'Did they say anything about us?'

'Mr Fenny declared we had "true salvation" here in Kentish,' Susannah said, smiling at the thought.

'That we do!' Emmeline Clarke agreed, equally pleased.

'Then,' said Susannah a little breathlessly, 'Mr Fenny announced he had another issue he wished to discuss. He mentioned my own family!' she cried. 'He maybe forgot I were in the next room.'

Emmeline Clarke laughed. 'He didn't know you were listening, I expect. What did he say?'

'He said Noah and me will soon be on the list for baptism.'

'Lawd!' Emmeline Clarke cried. 'And are you going to do it, Mrs H.?'

'I certainly am,' Susannah said, beaming.

10

Jack drove his mother and sister to Sheffield in the wagon to the creek on Hubbard's farm. Sunshine lit a blue afternoon sky.

'We are that lucky with the weather, Eck,' Susannah said, as the wagon lurched along the track. 'Thank goodness it's a warm day.'

They wore three layers of dress: their chemises, then house dresses, then thick woollen dresses on top, so their clothes wouldn't stick too closely when they climbed out of the water.

'You silly things,' Jack had said. 'Those heavy dresses you have on top will get too weighed down when they get wet. If the preacher don't keep a tight hold, you could drown. You better take them off before you go in.'

'I ain't undressing in front of everyone!' Susannah cried, shocked.

But Jack told his mother there would be a shelter set up for the ladies, for taking off heavy clothes and getting dry afterwards.

When they got to Hubbard's farm, they found dozens of people gathered on the grassy banks of the creek, some sitting in good viewing positions, others standing about in small groups, talking. It turned out to be true, what Jack had said about the tent arrangement. Susannah declared she felt better because Mrs Clarke, Mrs Miller and Janie too were all there to help.

Echo hung back at first, but did well when her turn came. Jack helped haul her, dripping, from the creek, calling out, 'Look after her, Janie!' Janie smiled back at him as she threw a blanket around his wet sister.

Susannah couldn't remember ever feeling as nervous as she did standing on the edge of the creek, putting one foot into the water and feeling the chill of it. Mr Fenny, in his hat and coat, his teeth beginning to chatter, held his hand towards her and smiled. She gathered her courage and stepped into the water, giving out a squeaky 'oh!' as the cold hit. Then before she knew it, the preacher had taken her by one arm and the nape of the neck and plunged her backwards into the water, talking all the time, though she couldn't make out the words. She rose, spluttering, and Jack hauled her onto the riverbank where Mrs Miller wrapped her in a blanket. A group of women were singing, '*Gather with the Saints at the river...*' It was over almost as soon as it began.

Jack said he was proud of her. Noah said he was too, and he was dunked himself the next Sunday. Eddie refused to watch these family baptisms, and Susannah's heart clenched a little over this. He still called it all 'rubbish', but she kept hoping he would one day *see the light*. Hadn't all their friends and neighbours come to the Lord? Still Eddie held back, and she wasn't sure why. He'd been born right here in Kentish and grew up here too. It was not a good idea to cut himself off from his neighbours.

After the Christians built the Gospel Hall at West Kentish, the Hattons would load their children into their new cart and drive over there for Assembly on Sundays. The gathering became the central event of Susannah's week. She felt special pride in the way Jack had become one of the leaders. By the time the Hall was built, Eddie had moved out to Staverton to grow potatoes. Though she missed him, and often wondered how he was doing, she had to admit that the peace made a good change. No more fighting, no more scoffing. And Jack grown into a man, so good with the bullocks, and working on his Bible reading. Emmeline Clarke often remarked how he was becoming quite a figure in the community. Susannah had heartswell at the thought.

After the service each Sunday, the Christians gathered outside their new Gospel Hall for a gossip. Children ran amok. A man chased two small boys – they were Hattons – out of the gum tree that hung over the creek. The bullocks and horses stamped restlessly. The assembled Saints, blinking in the morning sun after the dim indoor light, shook hands, exchanged greetings, passed on news.

'It's not my favourite hymn,' Mrs Miller said to her neighbour, Mrs Clarke. 'I prefer "What a Friend", myself.'

'You ask William, then, to propose yours next Sunday,' suggested Mrs Clarke.

'I tell him, but he is too blooming slow. You got to get in quick, I tell him.'

'It is true, dear, you do. The Brothers are all keen to get in their word.' Emmeline Clarke laughed her horsey neigh. She seemed full of energy. Her own husband rarely got a word in, but today he had managed to suggest 'Blessed Assurance', her own favourite.

'I'll take something over to that young fella after dinner,' Mrs Miller said, referring to the new young widower who had raised his troubles during Assembly. 'I think his eldest girl can manage the little ones with a bit of help.'

'The Lord be praised,' whinnied Mrs Clarke.

Noah hitched his horse to the new cart and Echo tried to round up the children with shouts they ignored. Susannah stepped over for a last word with her neighbours. 'That young fella,' she asked, 'has anyone taken in the newborn?'

'A wet nurse over at Barrington has him, temporary,' Mrs Miller said. 'A boy, I believe.'

Susannah had thought of offering to take in the baby – she still had her milk from Baby Alice – but it sounded like the newborn was safe at Barrington.

'Have you been out to Staverton yet, Susannah?' asked Mrs Miller. It was rare to hear anyone speak of the couple out at Staverton. Susannah thought Mrs M. must worry about her Janie.

'No, not yet I haven't, Mrs M. Have you news?'

'The baby has been born,' announced Mrs Miller, and Susannah gave a low gasp. 'Janie's sister is staying with her. You are a grandmother now, Mrs H.'

Susannah could not reply at first, she felt so overcome. Her first thought was that Noah must take her out to Staverton as soon as he could. *A grandmother.* She felt her skin flash warm then cool in a cycle of confused emotions. *A grandmother.* Then a thought occurred to her. 'And you too, Mrs M,' she said.

They smiled at each other, but warily.

Susannah wasn't sure how Mrs M. felt about her Eddie.

11

It had been a mild summer, and a cool autumn was approaching. The wheat had been safely gathered in and threshed over at Hubbard's, and the Hattons had made enough money to invest in a cart horse. It seemed to Susannah that things in Paradise were so much better since the preachers came, since she had got herself immersed and all the neighbours had taken to Bible reading and Christian living. Sitting by the fire, the late summer dusk fading outside, her protective mountain still standing where it always had, she felt a softening in her limbs, a contentment.

'Come over here, Eck, and write some more for me,' she called to her daughter. 'The kiddies are all asleep, we have a little time.'

'They ain't asleep, Mother, but at least they're abed. Has Jack brought in some more wood for the fire?'

'Yes, yes. All's done. I want you to write a bit more of the story. Write about yourself now.'

'I ain't writing that. Anyway, I thought we finished with that old story.' She tossed a small log onto the fire.

'No, no, I want you in it. Please, Echo, my dear girl, always such a help to me, write this for me now. It won't take long.'

'No need to wheedle, Mother. I'll do it for you, but be quick. I'm that weary tonight,' said Echo, leaning back in her chair.

'Sit up at the table. Write about how you met Henry at the picnic and he come hanging around here, though he had nothing but shanks' pony for transport.'

Sighing, Echo pushed herself up out of the chair by the fire and went to the dresser, rustling around until she found her journal and the pen and ink. She settled at the table to write. 'Shall I write that you weren't so welcoming?' she asked.

She sounded irritated, but Susannah was unbothered. Echo had always been a bit prickly. 'Of course I was not exactly welcoming,' Susannah said, but with a smile in her voice. 'He was not good enough for my girl. Though it was obvious what you saw in him. A better-looking bloke I ain't never clapped eyes on. Now wipe away that grin, Eck. We both know that much is true.'

'I ain't arguing the point, Mother.' In the quiet, Echo's pen scratched.

Susannah stared into the fire. 'After a time of hanging around and taking you out on long walks, leaving your work to your sisters—'

'About time they did more around here.'

'. . . after a lot of this courting, Henry asks me husband if he can marry you.'

'He didn't receive a kind reception.'

'Now don't sulk about it, Eck. You were married in the end.'

'But only after – Mother, I ain't writing all that.'

'Echo, my lovely, this is a story of family life, and that's a bittersweet thing, as you'll find out, if you don't know already. Please, just write the story up to now and then we'll have finished the book. Write how you came to me some months ago and told me your secret, and how worried you were about missing your bleeding. I took one look at your beautiful worried face and knew I was going to be a grandmother. And I told Noah we better get you married to that Henry real quick. Oh, why are you crying, Eck?'

Echo sniffed into her apron. 'Mother, I was that scared!'

'Ah well, Father's come round now, and we got you married.'

'Oh, I wasn't scared of Father. Many's the time my temper has bested his.'

'That's true!'

'I was scared of what was happening to me. I still am. Look at this great belly! Some nights I'm so afraid of the time when the baby comes.'

'Now, it will all be fine, Eck, don't you worry. I should know. I had . . . how many have I had, Eck? What are you laughing for?'

A rueful chuckle had replaced Echo's sniffles. 'You can never remember how many.'

'Well, they do seem to be everywhere, and I was never too good at me numbers. You'll have your own soon.'

Echo left her journal and came to perch beside Susannah on a wide wooden stool. She lowered her voice. 'I was that scared when I knew I was making a baby. I won't ever forget those mornings. Another day, and another day, and no bleeding, and I knew I had to tell you.'

Susannah stroked Echo's hair. 'Why were you scared of me? Your own mother. You should not have been scared.'

'But you never liked Henry, and – well, we weren't proper married, no matter what he said.' Echo pressed her face into her mother's arm.

'That Henry!' exclaimed Susannah, indulgently. She knew about good-looking young men and their importuning.

'And, well, it ain't what the Bible teaching says, I don't think,' Echo whispered. 'Mother, are you listening?'

Susannah stared into the fire and said nothing for a while. In the red coals, she saw a vision of her own life with her babies, each one both a trial and a blessing. 'Maybe we should pray, Eck.'

'Praying might be good, but I don't know what to say.'

'Tell you what, I reckon we should thank the Lord for the baby that is on the way. Every baby is a blessing.' She felt she had never said anything more true. Susannah knew she had become stout and big-bosomed, though she was still less than forty years old. Sometimes she felt her age, but the babies were indeed a blessing, and worth it all.

'All right, Mother,' Echo said. 'We can pray if you want.'

They sat by the fire and bent their heads over their hands as the Saints did at Assembly. Susannah thought of how it felt to be a mother, the responsibility of a baby, the blessing of a baby, the work a baby can be. She tried to remember some Bible teachings on the subject, but in the end she could only recall the lessons of her own life.

When a few minutes had ticked by, Echo stood again. 'Have we finished writing, Mother?'

Susannah looked up, remembering. 'Write how beautiful you looked when the preacher came to the house and married you, how we put boronia flowers in your hair and we all sang. Though it might have been a bit out of tune.'

Echo lifted her pen and wrote the last few lines. 'It was eleven o'clock in the morning and yellow sunshine came through the window and everyone crowded into this room together, and you cried – as you love to do – and Father finally shook Henry's hand and said we should stay here until the baby comes. And Grannie told me how handsome she thought Henry . . .'

'It was a lovely wedding, Eck.'

'Eddie was none too pleased, when he first found out. I reckoned he was going to fight Henry.'

'Don't joke about that, Eck. Eddie ain't always straight in his head. I hope he don't get into any more trouble.'

'Let's not talk about Eddie. Let's write how you'll be a grandmother again soon. Then I'm finished with this story. I expect I'll be too busy for writing when Baby comes.'

'Please stay awhile after he comes. I hope you don't leave me right away.'

'Now don't get teary-eyed, Mother. You know Henry has a job waiting, up at that farm at Lorinna. We have to start our own family life. I hope the birthing goes all right. Will I have to have old Mrs Clarke?'

'No, no, Echo. You got me. You don't need anyone else.'

The fire died down as the women sat together in its afterglow. Eventually Susannah roused herself, knocked out the last embers with the poker, and they each climbed into their beds beside their snoring husbands.

12

The mountain looked over the town with a steely face as the burial service at Sheffield commenced. Keen winds blew across the square of earth. It didn't rain that day, though the soil clumped damp and heavy from a week of showers. The men had such a time digging the pit. Eddie and Henry did it between them. The soil seemed sticky, as if it didn't want to give, didn't want to open.

No preacher was available that day; Mr Fenny had gone to the south of the island and Mr Braithwaite to New Zealand, last anyone heard. The Christians in Kentish had to look after themselves. They had to make their own burial services, just as they made their own Sunday Assemblies. Jack said the funeral service reading from dear old Psalm 23, which everyone seemed to find a comfort. His sonorous voice was now that of a grown man: '*Yea, though I walk through the valley of the shadow of death, I will fear no evil: for thou art with me.*'

Susannah wrapped her old coat more closely against her chest and listened to her son intoning the Bible words.

'*Surely goodness and mercy shall follow me all the days of my life; and I will dwell in the house of the Lord for ever.*'

A trickle of singing arose from the group around the pit as the men lowered the coffinbox. The family clustered in a circle and tried to find some comfort in the old hymn, though their voices were thin and the sound carried off in the cold air.

'*When all my labours and trials are o'er, And I am safe on that beautiful shore, Just to be near the dear Lord I adore, Will through the ages be glory for me.*'

With so many growing children in the house, Susannah lived in a tangled web of other lives, some she could see and some she could only remember. Perhaps she wouldn't miss the baby so much, but she would miss her oldest girl and her favourite, that was sure.

With the burial over, she returned to her home in the bush and went back to work.

Eddie

1

A fallen log made a good enough seat, Eddie reckoned. He sat with his elbows on his knees and watched smoke rise from his pipe. He was almost sixteen and had recently taken up smoking like his older brother Jack. Father smoked too; all the men in the district did. They got the tobacco from a carter that came down from the coast now and then. Sometimes it was the good stuff off the ships, and sometimes it was the local weed grown up the north-east by them Chinamen. Eddie had learned to tell the difference. He sucked in another lung-full and enjoyed the buzz inside his head.

Beneath his skinny shanks, the old log felt soft and mossy with time. He wondered how long ago the tree had fallen; it had a thick trunk, though not the biggest he'd seen. Sometimes he thought about these things: the passing of time in the bush, how quiet it became in the middle of the day when the creatures were asleep or hiding, and the almighty crash that must have sounded when a giant like this one came down.

If he sat for long enough, he might think of the people who lived here back then, them Aborigines. The ones he knew in Sheffield really liked their smokes and Eddie wondered how they had got on for tobacco. Jack said they had their own leaf and that Percy Coleman would tell him about it one day. But Eddie wasn't thinking about them old Aborigines today; he had plenty else to think about, sitting on a fallen log in the quiet bush. He was waiting for Janie Miller. His girl.

He heard her coming from the direction of the picnic. Summer picnics were popular and Eddie knew why. Those who wanted could sit around yakking with their neighbours by Dunn's Swamp, while others could get away beyond the boundaries for the afternoon. Down here, ferns clustered thick and a canopy of tall trees grew overhead, sassafras and celery-tops and peppermint gums. Not like the rattling white skeletons of the ringbarked ghosts that surrounded every farmhouse.

Janie's white pinafore came flashing through the bush. He could see her glancing about, looking for him. He stood and gave a low whistle. It was easy enough to get lost in this scrub in the foothills of the mountain. *Phweet!* he whistled again. 'Over here, Janie!'

A relieved grin lit her face as she spotted him. 'Oh, Eddie! I nearly missed you!'

She stumbled as she pressed forwards through the bracken. He lay his pipe on the log and flung out his arms to steady her. Oh, his Janie was a pretty girl, she was remarkable.

Eddie felt a physical rush when she pressed against him, much better than he got from the tobacco, deeper and more disturbing, more pleasurable. Sometimes, he wondered why she'd picked him. His arms were only thin and hard, though he supposed he might grow more yet. Now that he had a girl, he'd learned you had to watch that some other fellow didn't try to take her away, even a fellow who might be your own brother. You had to mind what was yours, secure your advantage.

He crushed out his pipe with a piece of damp moss and shoved it in his pocket. 'Come in here, Janie.'

He'd found a place where the lofty ferns stood in a cluster, their fronds forming a canopy like a ceiling. A rough pavement of dry fallen ferns crunched underfoot but they were soft, soft enough to lie down upon. They lay together. Eddie pulled his girl close and kissed her hair and her face. The unnameable joy of it threatened to overwhelm him but that didn't stop him from instinctively knowing what to do, nor Janie from responding. The quiet swallowed their soft moans. Something rustled outside the ferny enclosure but if any animal looked in and saw them, they were not disturbed.

Janie sat up, picking bits of dry fern out of her hair and straightening her dress. Eddie lay on his back, spent, and watched the sunlight flicker in and out above the green canopy.

'We better be getting back to the others,' Janie said, looking down at him.

'What's the rush?' He reached up and circled her elbow with his fingers.

Janie giggled. 'Mother will be looking for me before long. And some of the boys were planning to have a go at catching some jollytails. We could too.'

'What d'you want with all them others? Ain't you happy enough here with me?'

Janie giggled again, flipped over and lay on top of him. 'I love being with you, Eddie,' she said, then blushed.

He flushed with pleasure and surprise to hear her use such words and tightened his arms around her. A great need to secure Janie for himself alone threatened to overwhelm him. He'd try to keep her back from that crowd beside the creek for as long as he could.

But she soon sat up again. 'Don't you want to go back? Mother brought some cherry pie.' She brushed her fingers through her long hair. 'Did you hear about them Colemans going to look for tin out at Mount Claude? D'you reckon they'll get rich?'

Eddie sighed. His Janie was like a little girl sometimes, and she could be a bit of a gossip.

2

At the Sheffield sale yards, Jack sat perched on the rail, waiting for the auctioneer to get around to the Hatton pigs. Eddie couldn't help noticing how he kept glancing towards the schoolroom door.

'Got a match?' Jack asked Percy Coleman. Percy obliged.

'We going to get these pigs sold, Jack?' Eddie asked. 'I'd rather be gone before them Dunstans get here.' Them bloody Dunstans better keep away or Eddie'd knock their blocks off.

With the pigs sold and the sale money in Eddie's pocket, he and Jack sauntered over to the inn. As was the custom on sale day, men stood around in front of the inn and exchanged gossip. Percy Coleman yakked on and on about tin mining. Him and his brothers were always speculating, going on about those mining ventures of theirs. In Eddie's view, prospecting was a terrible poor life, camping out in the damp forest, sluicing in the creeks, always wet, and never finding much to speak of. That's how Eddie saw it. Better to get on with planting and getting in the crops in due time and selling for a good profit if you could; that was the surest way.

Just as Eddie raised his pot of ale to his lips, Arthur Dunstan walked right up behind him and jogged his elbow. Deliberately. A real coward, Arthur Dunstan. And what's more, he made eyes at Janie; Eddie had seen him at it. *And* he brought up that old convict story, as if half the people in the district didn't have convicts somewhere in their blood.

With a surge of aggression, he grabbed Arthur by the armholes of his waistcoat and would've thumped him right there in the inn if Percy hadn't stepped between them. Then Jack took his arm. Jack always wanted to map out a plan before he acted. Eddie would have preferred to do what he had to do right there and then. But this time he got hold of himself, and listened to his brother, older than him by a year. He told Arthur what he thought of him and pushed him aside.

When they'd finished their ales and stepped out into the road, Eddie saw his sister Echo appear at the schoolroom with her bag slung across her chest. Immediately he looked past her for Janie. Echo crossed the road towards the inn and Rags ran up to her, barking. Eddie kept concentrating on the schoolroom door.

Then he glanced at the boys standing along the verandah. Jack was still watching the schoolroom door too. And so was Arthur Dunstan. That Arthur had a sly grin all over his ugly dial. Eddie's fingers clenched in his pockets and his muscles tensed as he watched for Janie.

At last, out she came into the sun, wearing a blue ribbon in her hair. Janie always had something like that. She looked across the road and saw the row of boys at the inn staring at her. Eddie thought she smiled at him – he was sure he felt her eyes looking right into his – but it was obvious she didn't like all those blokes gawping. She ran off, to find her mother, Echo said.

'We better get going,' Eddie told the Hatton kids, and called Rags to heel.

More than ever he wanted to deal with them Dunstans.

3

As they walked the track homewards, Eddie reminded Jack what needed to be done. The Dunstans never stepped away from a fight, and Eddie insisted he had no intention of doing that either. Cautious as always, Jack sent the little kids on ahead. Echo, who liked to watch a fight, stayed with her brothers.

When they reached the big rock, Jack hoisted himself up on it while Eddie and Echo delved into their stash of stones. Rags turned out to be a terrible bother, and Eddie swore at the dog under his breath as it shoved its snout into the hiding place.

'D'you think one of these could *kill* someone, Eddie, if you hit him square on the head?' Echo whispered.

Eddie glanced at his sister. She was a rum one sometimes. Why think of killing anyone? 'Maybe.' He paused, hefting one of the stones in his hand. 'Yes, I reckon.' Though he was looking at Echo, he didn't see her face; all he saw was Arthur Dunstan grinning at Janie.

'Probably we don't want to *kill* anyone, Eddie.'

He came back to himself and laughed. ''Course not! We'll

give them a scare, though. They deserve it.' As he knelt to pull the stones from the hiding place, he thought something was different. Someone had been in it. 'Hey Eck, we had more than this, I'm sure of it. I reckon they got into our stash.'

Then they heard a whistle from Jack, and the next minute he came sliding down the rock and dashed onto the track, the barking dog racing after him.

'What's he doing?' Eddie said, annoyed. 'Some ambush this is!' He wondered if Jack had gone bonkers, running out onto the track like that when their enemies were up ahead. He emerged cautiously.

A short distance away, Jack was bent over their little sister Charlotte. The sight started Eddie running. When he reached Lottie and spotted the round river stone lying beside her, and she began pointing to her foot and crying, the turbulence inside him bubbled up into a shout. Red-faced, he raised his head and yelled into the bush, 'You mongrels! Come out here!'

No-one emerged.

'What happened, Lottie?' Echo asked, running up.

The child described how the other kids had gone on ahead and she'd tried to catch them, but when she got to the big rock a stone came out of nowhere and knocked her down, and now her foot hurt so much and she couldn't stand up.

'Mongrels,' Eddie kept muttering.

'I reckon her ankle is broke,' Jack said matter-of-factly. He hoisted his little sister onto his shoulder. 'Better get her home.'

They started along the track, Jack carrying the child. Eddie clenched and unclenched his fists. He glared around, looking for the villains, anger pressing painfully inside his chest. He kept pausing to yell into the bush, 'Cowards! Mongrels!'

Suddenly, as they rounded a bend, the Dunstans were there in front of them. Everyone stopped, even the dog. Quiet descended. Then Eddie stepped towards Arthur Dunstan with his fists raised as his father had taught him. Oh, how grateful he felt for those lessons. Father always said a man had to defend himself, always said you had to be prepared to look after yourself out in the bush, and now by God Eddie was going to do just that.

Arthur stepped up too. He didn't appear frightened. He looked eager. His sandy hair stood on end like a scarecrow. 'You take the kid home,' he said, nodding towards Jack without taking his eyes off Eddie. He spat.

Jack ignored him and set Lottie down by the side of the track. But he didn't step in to stop his brother this time.

It was one on one and the others stood back. Eddie had to remind himself that a good boxer dodged about a bit to assess his enemy's weaknesses; he had to remind himself not to go in too quick, as his temper urged him. They sparred a little, bouncing on the balls of their feet. Eddie was aware of sweat beginning to prickle. Then he could stand it no longer and in he moved. The punches flew, the rules of boxing went out the door. There were sickening thuds as blows connected, and Eddie took a fist on the nose. Blood spurted everywhere, covering both fighters, but the scent of it only fired up Eddie the more. He went after Arthur as if he would not just punch him but beat him senseless. His right fist connected with Arthur's left eyebrow. Arthur went down. Eddie leaped on him, pulling him up to have another go. That sneer on Arthur's face when he looked at Janie, her blush as she turned away. Eddie hit him again. It felt deeply and viscerally satisfying. The dog barked like a mad thing, dashing around in circles.

Echo was squealing. 'Get him, Eddie! Get him!'

Both combatants were bloodied. It was hard to tell where all the blood came from, or which of them was worst injured. Finally Jack stepped in and pulled Eddie back; Arthur's brothers did the same for him. The reek of sweat and blood seemed to draw a primitive growl from Rags, down on his haunches now. Both the fighters panted for breath. Though Eddie's nose had soaked his shirt with blood, Arthur looked the worst for wear. Eddie gasped, trying to get his breath back. He saw his opponent doubled over and holding his head, and he felt it was a job well done.

'Good one, Eddie!' Echo cried.

'Why d'you hit the kid, you cowards?' Eddie growled.

Arthur, sitting on the ground, held his head between his hands. One of the other Dunstans answered, sounding more sheepish than angry. 'We thought it were you lot, didn't we? You shouldn't have sent a kiddie along to the place.'

4

The blood that soaked Eddie's shirtfront came only from his nose, and he didn't think it was broke. That's what he told his mother when they got back to the farm. He staunched the flow with a wet rag and sat out in the yard, watching his family coming and going from the kitchen. After a time, Lottie's scream told him Mother had pulled and straightened the bone. He wondered if Grannie had any remedies for pain like that; he hoped so. At least he'd avenged his little sister. There was some satisfaction in that.

Echo handed him a fresh soaked rag for his nose and congratulated him on the fight, telling him he'd won for sure. She seemed mighty excited. Sometimes he wondered about young Eck, her strange enthusiasms. The blood flow from his nose began to dry up at last.

Jack was pacing restlessly across the yard. 'They won't try it on again for a while,' he said, 'not after breaking the little one's foot.'

'What d'you reckon Father will say about that?' Eddie asked, his voice muffled by the rag at his nose.

None of them spoke for a moment.

'He'll surely be proud of you,' Echo said.

Eddie wondered if she might be right. He'd fought as Father had taught him, hadn't he? *And* won, fixing those mongrels who broke Lottie's foot. He felt proud of himself, so maybe Father would see it that way too.

'I ain't so sure,' Jack said. 'Father don't like trouble with the neighbours.'

Eddie thought about this. His sense of being a hero returned from the fray faded a bit and an image of Father, riled up, rose in its place. 'Good thing we got the sale money, then,' he said. The money would ease Father's mind.

Jack agreed and said they should give the sale money to Father right away, before he had time to get too steamed up. That was when they discovered the coins had been lost. Eddie felt sick. He knew they'd have to tell Father the truth, their father couldn't abide fibs. They'd have to tell him all about the fight, *and* losing the money. Unless they could find it.

Dusk had begun to fall as Eddie and Jack walked back along the track. Neither spoke. The place where the fight had occurred proved easy to find because of the wet mud where all the blood had spilt. The eyes of a wallaby glittered in the lantern light. Eddie felt a lift of hope when they found the spot. Swinging the lantern about, he searched everywhere, but he couldn't find a thing. His hopes rose again when he noticed his brother bending over and reaching for something near the bracken at the edge of the track.

'You found it?'

'Nah,' said Jack, straightening up. 'Thought I saw something, but nah.'

Eddie spat. 'Bugger it.'

Jack had placed the lantern on the ground. He stood with his hands in his pockets and seemed to be taking one last look around. Eddie had felt certain Jack picked up something from under the ferns, but maybe he was imagining things in the dark. 'Bloody stupid to go into a fight with the money loose in your pocket,' Jack said to the dark bush.

Eddie forgot his imaginings and fired up. 'All my fault is it? Whose idea was the ambush anyway? The bright idea that got Lottie's foot broke?'

Eddie was easily irritated by Jack lately. The way he made eyes at Janie. Now some sixth sense whispered to him that Jack had seen the money, and he searched in the bracken himself, but could find nothing. He kicked at a loose stone. They'd have to go home empty-handed.

'You shouldn't let that Arthur get your goat,' Jack said.

'Look who's talking. Didn't you break his nose that time, in the fight last summer?'

'I don't reckon it were broke. Arthur's nose looks as ugly as ever to me. Did until today, anyway.'

Eddie snorted. He wished he'd had a chance to punch that Arthur Dunstan even harder. Next time he would, for sure.

5

Though he was pleased enough to have avenged Lottie's injury, Eddie couldn't shake off his resentment. He found himself hoping he'd broken Arthur Dunstan's face. Luckily Father hadn't blown up when they told him about the sale money, though he'd called it a 'terrible loss'. Now they'd be short of tobacco, for one thing.

Autumn advanced; the Hattons harvested cherries from their two trees, and pulled up onions to dry in bunches in the larder. Eddie kept daydreaming about how to get a hold of Arthur Dunstan and make him give the money back. Jack had convinced him that the Dunstans must have found it after the fight. Otherwise, he and Eddie surely would've found it.

Mother cried in the night and Eddie found it unnerving. He couldn't settle. The weather was no good for picnics and he hardly ever saw Janie. Out clearing rocks from the paddock to be sown with late wheat, a rubbishy job if ever there was one, he told Father he wanted to go over to the Dunstan place and confront them. But Father said he wanted no more fighting. The sight of Lottie lying white-faced on the bed, and now hobbling in the brace, seemed to have sobered Father.

But still, Eddie could not stand to see Mother so upset, so distressed about losing that damned sale money, about Lottie with her busted foot, about whether they had enough food to get through the winter. He wondered how a family ever managed to go on when the mother died, as they sometimes did, of the consumption, or in birthing a child. It had happened in their district, more than once. One of Janie's older sisters, married and moved to Barrington, had died having her second baby.

To give Mother some cheer, he came up with the idea of catching blackfish in the Dasher. The extra food might stop her talk about 'starvation'. His rod, a pliant myrtle stick, had given him good service in the past. It was a mighty fine rod, though homemade. He went out at night because the fish bit better in the dark, and came home with a dozen of them. Mother's face lit up, thank goodness, when he presented them to her in the morning. She fried them up for breakfast and not a skerrick was left. Eddie decided he'd go out as often as he could. The only trouble was blackfish had a lot of bones; you had to pick them out for the younger kiddies.

In his heart, Eddie still wanted to confront the Dunstans. His logic – he explained it to Jack – was this: the Dunstans were feeling guilty about injuring Charlotte. They'd apologised for that, hadn't they? So if he accused them of taking the sale money, they'd likely feel they were in the wrong and give it back. And if they didn't, Eddie would offer to fight them again. He became pretty steamed up about it. But Jack threw cold water on the idea. For one thing, he pointed out, Father didn't want more fighting. And – this was Jack's clinching argument – Eddie had never seen old Dunstan. He was a real rum bloke and no-one should try him on, especially not at his own place.

Eddie turned his head and spat. 'I ain't afraid of none of them Dunstans.'

'They will have spent it all by now anyway,' he said. 'They're awful poor.'

6

The stony bridle track which came up from the ford at Kimberley was not much of a road. In wet weather you had to jump from stone to stone to keep out of the deep puddles, but it was the only route up onto the Kentish Plains from the river. Travellers from that direction always came across the ford and up the bridle track – though Eddie could not recall many such travellers. But that autumn, after the fight and the injury and the loss of the money and the worry about winter hunger ahead, he heard news of two strangers who had ridden up the track on horseback and stopped at the Clarke place. They were preachers, so Eddie heard from the Clarke boys, strangers who planned to hold a big revival meeting.

The Clarkes' property was the first place you come to along the bridle track, and it was a better proposition than Hattons'. The house had more rooms and a good shingle roof and a proper verandah. Pumpkins and beans grew down the slope in front.

'Those two must've thought they were onto a good thing when they walked up through them vegetables,' Eddie said.

'They come at teatime,' Mother said. A pot on the stove came to the boil and she peered into it. 'Mrs C. told me all about it. She's right pleased to have them.'

'What are they doing now?' Jack asked.

'You can ask Mrs C. yourself,' Mother said. 'Clarkes is coming over here for a game of cards tonight.'

'For a good gossip, you mean,' said Eddie.

'Mrs C. says they're going to hold a revival meeting,' said

Mother, sounding a little breathless. 'I would certainly like to see a revival.'

'I fancy meeting them fellas,' Grannie said from her chair by the stove. 'Is they Anglican?'

Eddie lifted his head. He often forgot about his grannie, sitting there listening. But she knew a lot, more than you might think. He had a fondness for the old biddy; sometimes she told him things she never told the others, mostly about the old days when she lived in the bush. Sometimes it was useful information. She knew a lot about crops, Grannie did, though Father never consulted her.

The rumour turned out to be true – the preachers *did* hold a revival meeting in Duggan's barn, and it had everyone in the district going as crazy as a devil with a carcass. What a carry-on! Still, they didn't often get a good show in the bush so Eddie was as keen as the rest to see what it would be like, up in Duggan's barn at night, with some real performers. Grannie asked him to carry her up the hill so she could see the revival like everyone else. She weighed no more than a feather. The old girl seemed to enjoy herself, and Eddie certainly did. The preachers turned out to be great showmen, waving their hands like magicians performing tricks, talking as if they were offering treasures to all. And the singing – there was plenty of that, it went on and on. Eddie thought the night had turned out mighty entertaining. Nearly as good as the dances for which Duggan sometimes cleared his barn, when the fiddler played. There was singing then too, the old songs about Blighty and coming over the waves and all that.

With the preachers' show concluded and all the men trying to convince their wives to leave – and having a hard time of it, too – Eddie stepped outside to have a smoke. A tall fellow stood a few feet away, idling with his hands in his pockets. The bloke seemed a quiet type, not going off his rocker at the shenanigans in the barn like the rest of them. Eddie offered his tobacco pouch. 'What d'you reckon about all that?' Eddie asked, as the two of them stood smoking in the starlight.

The tall fellow sucked in a lungful of smoke, then exhaled slowly. When he spoke, his soft voice drawled. 'Wouldn't surprise me if they was all drunk,' he said. 'Acted like it, didn't they?'

Eddie snorted. 'You might be right.' He wasn't sure if his companion was referring to the preachers or their audience. He agreed either way.

The tall fellow sucked in another mouthful of smoke. He seemed thoughtful. 'They acted like drunks,' he said. 'There was a definite smell of liquor in that lean-to Duggan has out the back.'

'You don't say?'

'I do say.'

'Well,' said Eddie, 'I guess those fellas have to get a bit of courage from somewhere, if they're going to harangue everyone like that. And send all the women crazy.' He laughed.

Grannie was keen to see the baptisms too and so Eddie carried her from the house and down to the hillside near the Dasher and set her on a comfortable stump. Then he looked for a better vantage point. Boys around him were saying that women were going to wade into the creek in their dresses. Eddie didn't want to miss that. He found a crooked old gum and hoisted himself onto a low branch. The tree was already festooned with young fellows Eddie's age whom he'd known since they were little, when they walked to school in Sheffield. They all worked for their fathers now, like Eddie, clearing and digging, butchering and skinning, bagging potatoes and herding pigs.

From his perch he scanned the crowd. There must be more than a hundred people, he thought with some astonishment – half the district or more. He looked first for the Millers and spotted Janie standing with her family close to the riverbank. He knew, because Janie had told him with bright-eyed excitement, that the preachers had already visited the Miller place. They'd been to the Hattons' too, and Echo had said her psalm for them – which Eddie thought was going a bit far. These preachers, it seemed, had been to almost everyone's place. Janie said they returned to the Miller place several times and her mother and father were right keen on it all. Eddie couldn't see the Dunstans anywhere.

Eddie watched from his tree. As all the pairs of eyes gazed from the hillside, a group of neighbours began to wade into the river, beginning with old Mrs Mason from the next-door farm. Sure enough, as the rumours had predicted, the preacher did dunk them right into the creek water and brought them up spluttering and screeching – not only the women, but some men too. Eddie couldn't understand why anyone would do that, but he'd heard that God-botherers liked putting on a good show. He watched Janie watching her mother, who joined with a group of women singing their lungs out as the soaking wet converts climbed out of the creek: *'Shall we gather at the river, where bright angel feet have trod.'*

Eddie couldn't be sure – he was too far away to see clearly – but he thought Janie might be singing too.

7

As the autumn days grew cooler the preachers still rode out, criss-crossing the district, urging conversion on anyone who'd listen, promising who knew what. Eddie was amazed that so many seemed to be taken in by it all.

One day he was driving some pigs into town with Echo, headed for the sale yards. Eck chattered on, pestering, asking about the preachers and the revivals and the baptisms. He wished the kid would knock it off; it was a tedious walk at the best of times, especially with pigs.

'D'you think they'll come back to our place, Eddie?' She meant the preachers.

'Might do. They're always looking for a free feed,' he said, trying to put her off the subject.

Echo was reflective for a moment. 'Mother liked the Bible reading they did for her. And they were quite kindly to me, and gave us that remedy for Baby's chest.'

Eddie flicked his stick against the rump of a straggling boarlet. 'They put on a good show, I'll say that for them, but I reckon they're a bad influence. Look at the way everyone is so late with the hay gathering – too busy holding them Bible meetings and sitting around praying. Praying never got a crop harvested, Eck.'

As the track flattened out at the top of a hill and the pigs scattered down the other side, they noticed two figures on horseback in the distance. When they reached the base of the rise and rounded a curve in the track, they came upon Braithwaite and Fenny, mounted on borrowed horses. Eddie recognised their horses as belonging to that fellow out at Barrington, the one who owned his land and had made a good thing of it. The horsemen were headed towards a hut that stood beside the track, the Harrison place. It looked like they were going to visit.

'They won't be too popular there,' remarked Eddie flicking his stick at the pigs. 'It's harvest time, like I said. Old Harrison won't want no time-wasting.'

A woman with grey hair flying came running from the hut as soon as the two preachers rode up. Mrs Harrison dashed out in her pinny, waving joyfully as if the men were bringing her a bag of flour and a side of bacon. Soon old Harrison came round from behind the hut where he'd been tending their cow. The beast wandered after him, big and clumsy; the white patches on her flanks rippled.

'What are you fellas doing here?' Harrison yelled. 'Get off! We got work to do!'

'Oh no!' his wife cried. 'Stay and talk awhile, do. I so want to speak with you. I was left so anxious after the last meeting. Please tell me what I must do to be saved!'

The old woman was almost sobbing. Echo asked Eddie in a whisper if she ought to go and see if the old lady was all right.

'Let's just watch,' he said. 'Ought to be a bit of fun.'

Old Harrison snorted and picked up his pitchfork; it wasn't clear if he planned to chase the cow back to her shed or chase off the unwelcome visitors. Fenny leaned down towards Mrs Harrison and held out one hand to her. She clutched at it.

'Well,' Eddie said, 'this is a fine thing, to see preaching in the morning right beside the road and them never even getting off their horses.'

Old Harrison carried on abusing the preachers. Echo and Eddie sidled closer.

'Them preachers might feel the end of his pitchfork if they don't watch out,' Eddie whispered. 'Maybe that's why they stay on their horses.' He grinned and spat.

'Mr Fenny has a lovely silky voice,' Echo whispered back.

The preacher's coat had seen better days and his hat sat askew, but he leaned towards Mrs Harrison and spoke to her as if she were the only woman in the world. He had a close-cropped beard and long-fingered hands. Mrs Harrison gazed up at him, transfixed. Eddie and Echo stood eavesdropping among the ferns at the side of the road.

As the pigs trotted off down the track without them, old Harrison suddenly noticed that they had an audience. He shifted his attention away from the preachers for a moment. 'What you kids gawping at?' he growled. 'Your pigs is gone!'

Eddie put his hand on Echo's arm to indicate that she should stay where she was. They ignored the old farmer.

Preacher Fenny meanwhile was speaking in the musical, mesmerising tone he'd used up at Duggan's barn. 'The Lord helps those who believe in Him,' said Fenny, still mounted on his horse.

'Oh, what must I believe?' cried Mrs Harrison.

'That He is your saviour who died to redeem your soul!'

'Me *soul?*'

'Just for you, missus,' Fenny said, still smiling as if he had brought her good news. 'For you personally, though you might have lived a destitute life 'til now.' Fenny glanced at the poor hut for a moment. 'He will forgive all, if you take Him to your heart.'

'Oh, I do believe!' she cried. 'I see it all now. It's so clear when you explain it! I am *saved*!'

Old Harrison stood rigid in the doorway of his hut. He had one hand on his hip, one hand gripping the pitchfork, and his hat was pushed back. 'Take your flaming rubbish talk off my place!'

Sitting astride the other horse, Braithwaite responded loudly, 'And do you feel confident about where your own soul will end, sir?'

'You are all crazy with your immersions and praying and singing,' old Harrison said, flapping his arm and taking a step forward. He even waved his pitchfork. Fenny continued talking to the woman, who remained standing by his stirrup, gazing up into his face. His horse chose this moment to drop a dollop of dung. No-one took any notice.

'Scoffer!' cried Braithwaite, looking across at the penitent's husband. 'I'll pray for you to see the light too. The Lord welcomes even scoffers if they are willing to repent their ways.'

'I seen the light!' Mrs Harrison shrieked, clutching her apron to her chin with both hands.

The two preachers still hadn't dismounted, which seemed to astonish Echo. 'They must be in such a hurry,' she whispered to Eddie. 'They must have many houses to visit, saving people, you know.'

After a few more words with the scoffer, and some earnest talk bending over Mrs Harrison, Preacher Fenny clasped her hands. Then both preachers wheeled their horses around and trotted off down the track, leaving Mrs Harrison standing outside her hut sobbing her heart out. Old Harrison, still growling and grumbling, turned back to his cow. The preachers burst into song as they rode off, the sound of it receding as the horses trotted away, *'Bringing in the sheaves, bringing in the sheaves, we shall come rejoicing, bringing in the sheaves.'*

The wattlebirds in the treetops squawked; the cow gave a great, long low. Eddie and Echo set about gathering their pigs, long scattered downhill.

'Well, that was something to see,' Eddie said.

'Something to tell Mother.'

Eddie was silent for a moment. 'I don't know. Maybe we don't want them fellas up at our place again.'

The sound of the hymn drifted back to them along the track – *bringing in the sheaves*. The two preachers were singing into the morning. Only Eddie and Echo and the bush were listening.

When they finally got the pigs to the sale yards, the neighbours were all yakking about the preachers. People wondered at the way they visited everywhere, uninvited; how they just rode up, sometimes not even dismounting, and spoke – just as Eddie and Echo had seen at the Harrison place. The gossips reported that in some houses there were scoffers like old Harrison, but most people came running out, begging for the preachers to talk and pray.

'I reckon it won't be long before they get to our place again, Eddie,' Echo said. 'I expect Mother will go converted. Maybe Father too.'

Eddie considered this, his stomach squeezing slightly. He had noticed that his parents seemed mesmerised by the preachers and their promises. He wondered if it was because all the neighbours were going in for it. The way everyone talked, the way they followed each other like sheep – well, you were the odd man out if you didn't go along. Not that Eddie worried about that, but he did have a gripe about Jack, who had begun paying more attention to the preachers than to his work. Which left Eddie to take up the slack. That was not to be stood.

Eddie shook his head as they waited for the sale auctioneer, wondering what had got into his neighbours, wondering when the preachers would move on and leave them all in peace. He thought about his brother. He thought about the Dunstans. But mostly he thought about where Janie had got to; he hadn't seen her for more than a week.

'Janie ain't coming to school anymore,' Echo said when he asked her. 'She helps her mother now. She's turning sixteen soon.'

8

When winter approached the preachers did move on to the towns, to Eddie's relief. Everyone could now forget all about that Bible studying and hymn singing. But his brother couldn't seem to get over it. Eddie didn't understand what had got into him; it was as if Jack had contracted a fever. He wasn't pulling his weight around the place. Also, he went over to the Miller farm more often than Eddie liked. He knew Janie remained true to him, she was his girl. It was other fellows he was worried about.

Suspicion kept him on edge. He couldn't decide if Jack went over to the Millers for the Bible study or to make eyes at Janie. It was starting to dawn on him that Janie had been taken in by this God-bothering bunkum like everyone else. He worried that Jack might be gaining an advantage in that department, an advantage he, Eddie, might not be able to make up.

He'd had few opportunities to see Janie, or to be alone with her. There weren't enough places on the farm where a bloke could have a quiet smoke by himself and think. There was the outhouse. Sitting there one morning, Eddie puffed on his pipe and mulled over this problem of Janie and the God-bothering. He wondered whether he should go over to the Millers and be quite open about his courting. He was old enough now, though he wasn't so certain Janie's father would agree. A sudden thump shook the walls of the outhouse, making him jump. It was heavy enough to rattle the whole flimsy structure.

'Hey!' he called angrily. 'What's that?' Couldn't a bloke even have a quiet moment to himself?

Echo's voice carried to him. 'Get out of it, you little blighters!' She was chasing someone, probably one of the small boys. 'Eddie's in there!'

Eddie pulled up his trousers, poked his head out from the sugar bag draping the doorway, and flung a few curses towards the retreating backs of two small brothers. They'd thrown a rock at the outhouse, knowing full well he was sitting in there. He growled at Echo, asking why she couldn't keep the kiddies under control.

She came over and gave him a curious look. 'You were a long time in there, Eddie.'

He hitched his suspenders onto his shoulders. 'I were thinking, weren't I.'

Echo continued studying his face. 'About Janie?'

Eddie didn't answer, just gave her a look that he hoped would shut her up, but didn't.

'If you went to the Bible meetings, you could see her,' Echo suggested.

He didn't like the way she was looking at him; a tremor of irritation surged through his stomach. She should mind her own business. Then it occurred to him that Eck was only trying to help. When he stopped to think about it, her suggestion was sensible enough. But in his gut he knew he could never pretend to be converted for anyone, not even Janie. He wasn't the one in the family who told lies, never had been, and he wasn't about to start. And he couldn't go over there without *really* converting; the new Christians could be mighty standoffish with anyone they suspected was a scoffer. He'd already had a few of them giving him the cold shoulder in town.

'You don't want to be left out of things, Eddie,' Echo went on.

Behind them, the bush rustled in a winter wind coming up from the Dasher. The outhouse was at the far side of the yard, away from the house, downwind most days. It was a spooky place at night and draughty at any time.

'What's Jack doing over at the Miller place so much?' Eddie asked her. Echo had always been nosey; she knew most things. Maybe she could answer the question weighing on him.

'Why, he goes for the Christian meetings,' she replied. 'He's been working on his reading and getting much better at it. You should hear him, Eddie – he seems like a grown man sometimes. I'm that proud of him.'

Though her answer should have reassured him, Eddie still reckoned there was more to it. Jack's slicked-down hair and clean shirt whenever he went over to the Millers' seemed suspicious. Walking back up the yard to the house, with Echo chattering away about reading the Bible and praying together and how they all hoped the preachers would come back, Eddie stopped listening. He had his own particular worries.

That evening, penning up the bullocks with Jack, Eddie decided to test the question. He looked sideways at his brother in the lowering dusk. 'That Janie Miller is a corker,' he suggested, and watched Jack carefully.

Jack didn't answer. Pretending not to hear, Eddie thought. The bullocks shuffled and snorted; the smell of them blanketed the yard.

'Well, if the attraction ain't Janie Miller,' Eddie went on, trying to provoke an answer, 'why d'you keep going round there? Is the entertainment as good as at Duggan's barn? If it's that good, I might come myself.' He gave a bark of laughter and wondered if he'd need to carry through with this threat. The thought brought a flash of irritation with the whole lot of them, all the neighbours who'd fallen under the preachers' spell. But Jack only frowned and said it was a serious business, and the Believers didn't want any scoffers around.

'I better stay home, then,' jeered Eddie but Jack wouldn't be drawn into a fight about it. He just slapped the pen shut, looped the wire over the post to keep it that way, and loped off into the night yard.

Eddie was none the wiser about whether his brother might be trying to court Janie. He remained suspicious. He might have to ask Janie herself about it, next chance he got. It began to occur to him, a dim idea flickering at the edge of his consciousness, that he'd never be really sure until they were married. They were both sixteen, or close enough. Slowly, an amazing idea began to form in Eddie's mind, the shape of a future.

Meanwhile, Jack kept going on and on about believing, and converting, and getting saved, always haranguing the family, never shutting up. It appeared he'd gone converted himself and he kept saying he couldn't wait for the preachers to return in the spring. Eddie wondered if his brother would really get immersed like the rest. At first, Eddie was just bemused, but when Jack went on and on and on about it, he lost his patience.

'Why are you constantly haranguing about the bleedin' Bible?' he asked, but Jack took no notice. 'Jack, you're off your head. We got enough to do right here without worrying about the bleedin' afterlife. We got to get this clearing done, and this rubbish burned, and then if you want to pray, you can bleedin' pray for the frosts to keep off.'

'You should come to a scripture meeting, Eddie,' Jack said. 'When you read the Bible, well, you find out there's better times ahead. You can have forgiveness! There's God's heaven waiting for you. And those already passed over, they're waiting too!'

'Give over, or I'll knock your block off,' Eddie warned.

They ended up in a fist fight that time, though their father busted it up pretty quick. Eddie wouldn't have minded an excuse to give Jack a good thumping.

9

Eddie watched Father leaning on the fence rail of the yard, staring towards the bottom paddock, his shoulders hunched against the rain. This wet weather better ease soon, Eddie thought, or the mould would strike the wheat when it came through. They'd had some severe frosts too, and frosts could kill off the first sprouts. Jack, in his usual froth-headed way, had recommended prayer. He claimed that a prayerful request to the Lord for a turn in the weather would likely be answered. Eddie was openly scornful; Father merely doubtful.

This worry about the weather and the winter food supplies hung in the atmosphere of the farmhouse like a foggy miasma. Eddie made an effort to put aside his exasperation with his brother and they worked together to set rabbit traps. Rabbits were skinny, but better than nothing. Any fresh meat was welcome, to add to the turnips and cabbage, the withered potatoes and the dwindling side of bacon. It took a good few rabbits to make a decent meal, though.

Eddie went over and over that day Amos got himself shot. The trudge through the sticky mud of the bottom paddock, the little fellow hopping along behind, calling out that he could help skin the rabbits. His head of spiky yellow hair cut short by Mother, his bandy little legs, his hand-me-down boots that didn't fit, his hero worship of his two big brothers. Eddie had loved that little blighter.

He tried to recall the moment he pulled the trigger of his shotgun, what he'd seen as he sighted along the barrel. Only a couple of rabbits – that was all. He was certain Amos had followed Jack, that the little fellow had run to the other side of the paddock, that he was nowhere near the warren. How could he have got there so quickly? Why, he could barely pull his boots in and out of the mud. Eddie would never have fired if he'd thought the kid was nearby.

The kid should have been with Jack; Jack was in charge of him, he should've watched out for him. And another thing – didn't Jack raise his gun at the same time? Eddie was sure he did. He could see it in his memory. He thought he'd heard another shot too, almost at the same time he'd fired himself – or even a moment before. And didn't Jack admit to their parents that it might have been either one of them? What had Jack muttered to the others? What lies had he spread?

Over and over, Eddie turned the story. To shoot your own little brother!

When he saw the boy on the bed and Mother's face, he'd known Amos was gone. He'd spent hours in the bush that night, not coming home until morning. It had been cold, he remembered feeling the cold, but the icy feeling came from inside, not outside. It was a long time before he could shake it. He spent more and more time away from the farmhouse, more time fishing. Whatever had happened out there, Amos was dead now, and buried, and Mother in floods again.

Grannie looked unruffled in her corner by the stove. Eddie took a kind of comfort in seeing the old lady there, day in and day out, unchanging. Sometimes he wondered if the death of Amos had touched her at all. It was hard to tell.

Coming back from the creek at daybreak one day, with a decent haul of blackfish, he found her awake and starting a pot of boiling water on the stove. He remembered how she used to hum while she worked, usually one of those old songs about sailing ships or bushrangers. There was one about someone named Kathleen. Who was Kathleen? Her own mother? *I'll take you home again, Kathleen, across the ocean wild and wide.* That morning, bringing in the blackfish, he realised he hadn't heard Grannie singing for quite some time. He gave her a good hard look while her attention was on the pot and decided she'd taken the little boy's death just as hard as the rest of them.

It was a relief when the weather finally began to warm up, but Eddie still couldn't shake his mood. He wondered if it was this constant, lurking confusion in his mind that had put off his aim at the cricket match down at Dawson's paddock. He bowled his first 'overarm' ball that day, but it turned out none too 'friendly' when Jack copped it in the knee.

He hadn't meant to hit his brother. Not consciously, anyway.

10

By the time of the cricket match, the preachers were back. One of them, that Fenny, had even come to Paradise and prayed over the wheat crop. Eddie could hardly believe that Father went along with it. Then the weather improved and it looked like the smut wouldn't take the wheat, and of course that set Mother on to saying how the preacher had saved the wheat. As if the weather would've changed, whatever that bloke did.

The two preachers spent the afternoon nattering in the kitchen. Eddie knew Mother was pleased to have them there, those 'gentlemen' as she kept calling them. He watched as they doffed their hats and acted all high and mighty, treating her like she was a fine lady, just to get the use of her kitchen fire and a pot of tea. She'd made them some of her biscuits too.

Eddie spat in the dust. Ever since Fenny had started in with praying for the wheat crop, he felt that Mother had fallen under the preacher's spell. Soon enough she'd be getting herself doused in the creek, like Jack. He shook his head at the thought; he just couldn't understand it.

He went into the house and found Mother with her ear against the kitchen door, shamelessly eavesdropping. Her round face was flushed. She put a finger to her lips. Since the door to the kitchen was both flimsy and ajar, the voices of the two men could be clearly heard. The younger one was talking about his wife and kiddies back in Melbourne.

Eddie's mind shifted as he tried to imagine what Melbourne was like. You read about it in the paper sometimes. He'd heard they had gas lighting in the streets, theatres, and stone buildings. He supposed there was a proper dock at their port – loads of spuds from the north-west coast were shipped across to Melbourne. Timber too. He'd always thought of the city as a place where a lot of building went on. There was a bloke from Barrington decided to go over there once, looking for work. Eddie tried to remember if he'd ever come back. He didn't reckon he had.

Before the preachers left Paradise for the winter, Mother and Echo did go off to be dunked, just as Eddie had feared. Though he'd enjoyed watching the first baptisms, he surely didn't want to see this one. He was disgusted to think of his mother and sister making such asses of themselves. He stayed at the farm with Grannie.

That Hubbard was a proud one and he'd soon be strutting around boasting about his creek being used by the preachers. A lot of the blokes he met at the inn were like that these days; so pleased with themselves, calling themselves 'saints' as if everyone but them was a wretched sinner.

He lingered beside Grannie as the wagon rolled off, feeling irritable. Grannie yabbered on a bit about the *Anglican church*. She was a rum old stick, but you could laugh at her funny sayings. Then she said something that gave him food for thought. Gave him his idea.

As Eddie approached the inn in Sheffield, he noticed the usual cluster of men standing at the verandah rail, ale pots in hand. Eddie thought about looking around for the Coleman brothers, to see if they had any news of the English cricket team touring on the mainland. Or he might see if he could cadge a copy of *The Examiner*. Eddie could read well enough, though he rarely bothered. At the inn, he could pick up the latest news of prices. Last he'd heard spud prices were still fluctuating wildly. Wheat was a better bet this year, and Father could look forward to a good price now it seemed the crop had come through without the smut.

Eddie also wanted to talk to George Heyward about a matter he'd been turning over in his mind.

A rumble of gruff voices came from the verandah. The men of the district were a mixture, like any place, Eddie supposed, though he'd never been beyond the jetty at Emu Bay. Some of the locals were great talkers, waving their arms as they spoke, holding forth as if they stood on a soapbox. Others were listeners, like Eddie. There were the good-natured ones, such as George Heyward, who kept the peace when the rough-natured ones became too forthright. An image came to Eddie's mind of a row of ravens.

As he walked up to the verandah, eyes turned on him. In town, people looked at you, assessing your business. Grannie said it was always that way in the towns. It wasn't to Eddie's liking. Today the men not only gave him some good long stares, they stopped talking among themselves. With a prickling of his skin, Eddie felt that he'd been judged and found wanting, though where that came from he didn't know. Some of the men turned away. He noticed Arthur Dunstan and his brothers among the crowd, their spiky straw hair unmistakable. They seemed quite at home.

Eddie stopped dead in his tracks. He wondered what they'd all been talking about. Suddenly he wasn't thirsty anymore. He whistled the dogs, Rags and Tippet, to heel, and set off for the sale yards. He'd have a smoke and wait there.

Amid the ruckus of the sale, the auctioneer calling and the farmers doing business, Eddie was able at last to get hold of George Heyward. He told George what he was after – a lease, on terms he could afford. Eddie had no money at all, and no way of making more than a few bob from rabbit skins, but he knew you could get a lease sometimes in the back blocks for no money down, and agreement to give a percentage of your crops. The lessee had to clear rough scrub, that was part of such arrangements, and improve the lot, which went to the good of the landowner. But you could occupy the place, and all you had to do was get the land to produce. Eddie was confident he could coax potatoes to grow. He understood soil and he had faith in the chocolate loam of the district, which was there underneath if you cleared the scrub and ploughed it over, ringbarked the trees and got in the seed potatoes.

George Heyward listened to him carefully. He was a good bloke and one of the smart ones. And he didn't ask Eddie if he'd gone converted yet. George pointed out that Eddie had no bullocks, and no money for seed potatoes, but Eddie said his father would help. If George helped too, Eddie reckoned he could do it.

'A place with a hut,' said Eddie. 'D'you know of somewhere?' George ruminated for a while, then said he did. But it was a long way out.

All the better, thought Eddie, looking around at all the ravens at the inn with their backs turned to him.

11

Eddie was aware that his sister had a beau. He remembered sharing a smoke with the bloke after the first revival. At least the bloke wasn't a God-botherer. Trust young Eck to choose well. But Henry soon left for the highlands for the summer season and, judging by his sister's long face, she wasn't happy about that. Eddie told her he'd be back in the autumn, but it didn't make much of a difference.

The weather grew warm and people started gathering again for picnics down at Dunn's Swamp nearly every Sunday afternoon. Eddie was keen on the picnics – they were a chance to meet Janie, but the neighbours were ruining things this year. Most of them insisted on praying over the food and singing hymns all afternoon. Eddie would just grab a bite to eat then head off into the bush.

He waited for Janie in their special place. With his elbows resting on his knees, he sat on a fallen log under the fern canopy and rehearsed in his mind what he had to tell her. To ask her. Soon her white pinafore flashed through the bracken and he opened his arms as he always did. But today he had serious things to discuss. Perhaps she sensed this, because she was subdued and didn't giggle as much as usual. She'd developed a cough, which interrupted almost everything she said. When he asked about it, she told Eddie it was nothing; Mother had a remedy from Mrs Coleman and reckoned it would clear up soon.

'I'm so glad we're here, where there's no-one else around,' she said.

He sensed that she had news for him too. He pulled her down to sit beside him. 'There's just us, Janie. What is it?'

She hesitated, then lifted her hand and stroked his face. 'It was that bad about Amos,' she said. She looked as if she might cry. 'Thank goodness the winter has lifted.'

A shaft of sunlight filtered through the man-ferns. Eddie's thoughts, so clear a moment ago, became confused. He didn't want to talk about Amos. He hadn't spoken about that to anyone. But the thought that Janie might be able to understand how it had been, the idea of someone to share it with – sharing hadn't occurred to him before. He pulled her closer and kissed her hair.

'Mother's better now,' he said. 'She don't cry so much. A couple of nights a week I get a good haul of blackfish.'

After a few minutes of snuggling in his arms, Janie gave a muffled little sound, almost like a sob.

'What is it, love?' Eddie asked. 'There ain't nothing to be done about Amos, poor little blighter.'

'It ain't only Amos.'

'What then?'

She couldn't seem to go on. He was at a loss, and sat holding her for a while. Then he recalled the serious business he had to discuss with her.

They bent their heads together.

As soon as Eddie turned sixteen, Father gave him the responsibility of driving the bullocks to the jetty. Spuds were Eddie's specialty; he knew soil and had a good sense of when to sow and when to dig. Many of his ideas came from listening to Grannie who knew a good few things about potatoes, or *praties* as she called them. Usually he managed to sell the full load, though you never could tell what you'd get. This last year, some loads had barely brought in what they cost to produce.

Returning with the empty dray one grey afternoon, coming up

from Barrington along the rough track that passed for a road, Eddie mulled on the difficulties of cultivating potatoes and on his own plans. His future was firming up, and he whistled one of Grannie's tunes, one of those Irish ones. Grannie had put the idea into his head and George Heyward had helped him on the right track. That talk he'd had with Janie at the picnic – he could hardly believe she had agreed so readily. When he'd told her he knew of a place he could lease, that it had a hut where they could live and they ought to be married, Janie had flung her arms around him and cried her eyes out. At first her tears had worried him, but she said they were happy tears. She said he'd made all her dreams come true, and she seemed to forget whatever had been worrying her. It was a miracle. Now he just had to talk to Father – the final step – and their plans could be put into action.

Ahead, ambling down the West Kentish road, he saw a black-coated walker carrying a big canvas Bible bag. Feeling generous with the world, Eddie pulled up his bullocks. 'Whoa, Snowy,' he called to the leader, adding the odd clicking signal that instructed the animals to halt. 'Offer you a ride into Sheffield?' he called to the walker.

The man stiffened and turned. He eyed Eddie up and down. 'Ain't you the Hatton boy?'

'One of 'em,' said Eddie.

The man raised his chin, the better to examine Eddie. 'The one that ain't baptised?'

Eddie paused and spat. 'You want a ride or not?'

'Our Lord never rode in a wagon, and I am no better than our Lord.'

Eddie could feel warmth creeping into his face. 'And neither did He wear great black boots like yours, friend,' he said, and whipped up Snowy and Tiger and rolled off down the road.

Eddie had become used to incidents like this but that didn't mean he liked them. It was his view that the Lord would not approve of such rudeness. In all of Mother's Bible stories when he was a kiddie, he'd never heard the Lord was in favour of one man thinking he was any better than another. That wasn't the Lord Eddie had always been told of. And neither did he believe in this new God, the one who wanted a bloke to be always praying about every blessed thing, and get himself dunked in the creek besides.

Eddie was fed up with his family's God-bothering, their remarks about his unsaved state, and Jack's constant praying. It made Eddie angry. Jack was so sure of being right and so quick to tell a bloke he was wrong. It was high time to move out.

As the wagon rolled down the road, Eddie rubbed a hand over the stubble on his chin and pulled his hat lower over his eyes. His Adam's apple worked up and down and it took him a few minutes to get over the insult of the black-coated Christian. Eddie had never liked those types. From the day those two preachers rode up, his instinct had told him to be cautious. He knew you always welcomed travellers out in the bush – how else would they all get on? He'd received such hospitality himself, a bit of food and a bed, if he had to stop somewhere on his journey back from the jetty. But something about those two strangers got Eddie's goat right from the start. He wasn't sure why, even now, when all the rest of his family had succumbed to their preaching.

He hoped Janie would settle down when they had their own place.

12

When Eddie told his parents he'd found a place with a cottage out at Staverton, where he could lease enough space for two paddocks of potatoes on good terms, they said nothing. They both appeared dumbstruck.

'Well, it's more like a hut, only one room, but I can put a verandah along it and it'll be good,' he added. 'And I can get some fences up, if you'll lend me Lark and Linnet for a while. And the second wagon.'

'Oh, Eddie!' Mother eventually said.

Father grunted, tugged at his beard, and said he reckoned that would be all right, lending the two bullocks. For a while. Until Eddie got his first spuds in. He also agreed to donate seed potatoes, though reluctantly. There wasn't a big supply.

Over the next few days the farmhouse at Paradise was filled with low-voiced conversations and rustling air currents as the family began to splinter. Eddie had the sensation that he'd caused something momentous. It filled him with a kind of pride to know he could direct his own fortunes, that he was an independent man. He could see that Jack, when he heard about it, was envious. Eddie couldn't help feeling a little thrill, knowing he'd secured Janie and been first over the line into manhood. But these things soon began to seem childish; he had bigger matters to attend to. A stack of items – an axe and a hoe, timber and nails, rolls of canvas and bags of seed potatoes, hessian and rope – piled up beside the bullock stall, things he'd cadged from his parents.

EDDIE

He visited Janie's place often, helping her to get her things together. They'd be gone soon. She seemed as excited as he – more, even. Her father hadn't looked too thrilled when he'd first been told about it, but Janie pleaded with him, and he'd come around. Her mother's reaction was harder for Eddie to read. Eddie reckoned she wished Janie had chosen Jack, if she had to have one of the Hatton boys. But he had no real basis for that, just a hunch. Mrs Miller seemed willing enough to help Janie get ready for her new home, and said she'd come over to visit as soon as they were settled. Eddie hoped they wouldn't have too many visitors. Their own cottage should be theirs to do as they wanted. And that meant no praying and Bible reading.

Echo watched him make his preparations. Eddie would miss Eck the most of anyone, after Mother.

'Can I come and see you?' she asked. 'If Father will bring me over? How far is it to Staverton?'

He rubbed mutton fat into his boots, wondering how long the pair would last – he'd have to be careful – and looked up at his sister. For Echo, he'd make an exception. 'Janie and me would be right pleased to see you, Eck. It's a long way out, but Father might bring you sometime.'

'How will Janie get in to Assembly on Sundays?'

Eddie's mouth twisted. Janie's mother had asked him the same question, and he'd dodged it, mumbling something about getting his own wagon soon. Though he hadn't said so to Janie, in his heart he was glad to be getting her away from all that humbug.

'I reckon she'll have to give that a miss for a while,' he said.

'When will you and Janie be married?' asked Echo. 'Will we all come to the wedding?' She kept her head lowered over the britches she was mending, but the stiffness in her shoulders showed she was alert for his reply.

'We can't get hitched until we can get over to the Wesleyan chapel at Latrobe,' he said, 'or until some preacher comes through again.'

Echo looked up at him then, a quick glance. 'What does Janie think about that?'

Eddie decided that young Eck asked a lot of questions. 'Janie and me reckon we're married already. Good as.'

When they reached the hut in Staverton in the borrowed wagon, unloaded their supplies, staked Lark and Linnet for the night, and lit the first fire in their hearth, Eddie wondered why he hadn't made this move earlier. His spirits hadn't felt this fine in his whole life. Night was approaching and the mountain stood indigo-blue in the twilight. While Janie fixed up a temporary bed for them he wandered outside into what was now his own yard and enjoyed a thoughtful smoke. The mountain stood close here, much closer than he remembered from the only other time he'd seen the place, when he came out to inspect the lease. In the dusk, the purple rock seemed like a fine backdrop to the life rolling out ahead of him.

It took Eddie a few weeks to fell the saplings invading his rough paddocks and drag them into temporary fence lines. He tried to get started on the ploughing too, while he still had the use of the bullocks. Often he found himself working the slopes of his two paddocks well into the dusk, until Janie would call to him.

They'd been out on their own for several weeks when it became clear to him what Janie hadn't been able to confess earlier: a baby was on the way.

The idea of this came as a shock at first but soon Eddie found himself looking forward to it. He'd be a man with a son, on his own farm. If he could just get the hillside ploughed before he had to return the bullocks, if he could get the spuds in, if the weather held, if the baby arrived strong and healthy – that was a future any man could be pleased with.

Out at Staverton, Janie's cough got worse.

'I can't seem to shake it,' she said one night as they sat beside the fire. Far gone with the child, the cough shook her thin shoulders and made her belly tremble. Eddie wondered if his son could hear it, inside. He placed his open palm on Janie's stomach and rubbed gently.

'When I take the bullocks back to Paradise, I'll ask Grannie for a remedy,' he said.

The animals and the borrowed wagon were due to be returned soon. He'd have to walk back to Staverton. Another grating cough shook Janie's body and she agreed it'd be good to have a remedy from Grannie Eliza. Her complexion glimmered pale in the firelight.

'And Eddie, love, could you ask about the preachers? Ask if they're back yet?'

'What d'you want to know about those shysters for?'

'Why, they bring all the news. And they have the latest remedies.'

Eddie relaxed, mollified. Remedies were fine. For a moment he'd thought she wanted prayers. He got enough of those when her mother and sisters came out to see her. It was clear to him now that the women had known about Janie's condition for some time, for longer than him. The secretiveness irritated him. But he could also see that Janie took comfort from her mother, from her advice, and she liked showing off her little home. Mrs Miller didn't come often; it was a two-hour journey each way.

He supposed that if those preachers did return, he and Janie could get married, officially. He didn't mention this to her in case it raised hopes for something that couldn't be delivered; she seemed happy enough with things as they were. He rubbed her belly again affectionately.

The day he returned the bullocks to Paradise, he met Echo standing in the yard, watching the wagon roll in. She walked over to greet him and ask about Janie. This was the first time Eddie had seen Echo since he'd left. He narrowed his eyes. Her gait seemed careful, not the skittering run of the young girl he remembered, always chasing the kiddies around the yard. Familiar now with the signs, he thought he knew what was up, but he didn't ask. Indeed he hadn't yet told anyone about Janie's baby, his son on the way.

Mother gave him a prodigal's welcome – he hadn't had such a good feed in ages. She'd got some mutton from somewhere and the stew steamed rich and aromatic, with potatoes, turnips, green peas and bacon. She knew how to use pepper berries to give it some kick too. But Jack started the meal off with a sour turn when he insisted on his Bible talk.

'*Now he that ministereth seed to the sower both minister bread for your food, and multiply your seed sown, and increase the fruits of your righteousness.*'

Eddie found himself surprised at how deep Jack's voice had grown. He didn't remember it that way. He tucked into the mutton stew and the damper and the apple pud that followed, and let out a contented sigh when he'd finished.

'I thought you'd have brought Janie with you,' said Mother.

Eddie knew the moment had come. He had to tell them.

'Well, that'd be no good, because I got to be walking back. And Janie ain't in no state to walk that far.'

He paused to let the news sink in, and it only took Mother seconds. She leaped up and grabbed him around the shoulders, exclaiming and chattering.

'That were quick,' remarked Father from behind his beard.

They piled him up with damper and apples and turnips to take back, but he couldn't carry too much in his swag. Grannie gave him a bottle of new remedy, a blend made up of native hops and tea-tree bark, watercress and white poplar. She had the recipe from the preachers, who'd said it had done well in other districts. 'Tell her to take it with molasses if it be too sour tasting,' she advised. Echo hugged Eddie fiercely and asked him to tell Janie she missed her awful much. 'I hope she'll be all right when the baby comes,' she whispered, sounding frightened. He raised his eyebrows.

'Why wouldn't she be? Women pop out babies all the time. Look at Mother!'

'But will there be someone to help her?' Echo asked.

Eddie thought for a moment. He hadn't got that far with his planning. 'I suppose there's old Ma Parker at the next farm. And Janie's sisters come sometimes. Staverton ain't the end of the world, you know.'

'Seems like it is, sometimes,' Echo replied.

Eddie set off for his tramp home. He had twenty miles to walk.

13

Janie's coughing started to plague his dreams. It even plagued him when he couldn't hear it, when he was down in the paddock trying to get the spuds sown. The ground was poorly ploughed; it had more rocks in it than anywhere he'd ever seen.

One Sunday, Janie asked if she could go to Assembly. She thought her father might come and fetch her, she said, if she sent a message. Eddie fired up, and Janie cowered a little at his shouting. He told her they had no need of them Gospel 'howlers', then stomped off to his work.

Summer was ending when the baby was born. The birth was mercifully quick, and Eddie spent the whole episode down in his paddocks, grubbing fiercely at a stubborn stump, until Janie's sister called him back to tell him it was all over. She showed him the wizened features of his son, the small body wrapped tight in a swaddle. Janie's sister had stayed for a couple of weeks, but she couldn't stay forever. There was little room, for one thing, and she had complained the whole time about how cut off it was. The Miller women had been to visit once or twice in the first days, but it was a long way for them to come. Sometimes Janie spoke wistfully of her mother and her sisters, and said she wished they could see how the baby was growing. To Eddie's eyes the child hadn't grown much at all.

On Sunday mornings Janie would pull out the Bible her mother had given her and sit running her finger along the lines of some passage or other, though she didn't keep it up for long. Always tired these days, always coughing, she abandoned her reading soon enough. Eddie supposed it was having the baby to look after; she seemed always to be feeding him.

Eddie hadn't yet managed to build a verandah, though he still intended to. His plans were feverish and detailed and unattainable until a crop came in. He had to spend long hours out rabbiting, rabbits being their only source of fresh meat. The few shillings he might get for the skins were welcome too. Rabbits were keeping them going.

Janie didn't ask again about going to Assembly. Eddie had no cart or animals to take her there, even if he thought it was a good idea, which he didn't. He had no trust of the Gospel Hall crowd, thinking themselves better than anyone else. If Janie sent a message to her father, if old Miller came out here and took her and the baby away, Eddie feared she might never come back. Her mother might say that Janie needed looking after; that haunting cough was not improving, even with Grannie's remedy. Eddie felt sure that once Janie sent a message to her family to take her away from Staverton, he would never see her back, nor his son neither.

He watched anxiously for the child to grow, to show some signs of changing from a helpless infant into a sturdy boy. As Eddie dragged through the rough warrens in the foothills, going round his traps, looping rabbits onto his stick, he thought of his son somehow replacing Amos in the world. In producing this new boy, he had made right the loss of the other.

When he had walked off a bout of bad temper and came home to her they would lie in the cold hut under the only two blankets they had, often with the baby between them. Eddie repeated again and again they had to keep a fire going *day and night*, but she couldn't seem to manage it. He often arrived home to cooling embers in the hearth and had to go out again to find some kindling to restart it.

As the coals glowed in the rough hearth, and their baby slept, Eddie held his wife close and buried his face in her hair.

Echo

1

A straggly group of seven or eight children wandered along the track from Paradise into the hamlet of Sheffield. Echo Hatton, tall and thin and wearing a once-white pinafore over a greyish linen house dress, was the oldest and in charge. Her little brothers and sisters ran on ahead, jumping on the frosty puddles they found here and there, laughing as the glassy ice splintered. Every now and again she yelled to the smaller children to stay on the track.

'Little pests,' she muttered under her breath.

Her sister Charlotte, younger than Echo and small for her age, walked beside her swinging a stick through the ferns at the edge of the path. Both girls had long hair tied back with string and carried their tucker, a bit of cold mutton bird and a knob of bread, in bags made from flour sacks slung across their chests.

'Give over with that stick, will you?' Echo said to her sister.

Charlotte tossed the stick aside. 'What d'you reckon about Mother the other night? I thought she'd never stop crying. Are we all going to starve?'

'We got the mutton birds now.'

'If we starve, Eck, we'll have to leave the farm and go into town, into Latrobe or even Launceston, that's what Eddie says.'

Echo had heard their big brother say this too, probably to scare the little ones. 'Town' – a frightening place, where town kids would call them names, or even fight them, and they'd have to miss school and work all day long. That's what Eddie reckoned.

'We got the mutton birds now,' she said again.

Before walking into the schoolroom Echo stomped her muddy boots on the grass verge. Her bottom lip curled in disgust when she saw the other children rushing in without this precaution, scattering chocolate soil clods across the floorboards. As she turned, scowling, ready to yell at them, the schoolmaster appeared. He bent his head to his desk, fished for his stick, then thundered down among the rabble of children in a good-natured way, herding them onto the benches behind the wooden desks. Echo waited beside her friend Janie Miller until the teacher got everyone under control. It took a couple of slashes with his stick.

Mr Pullen smiled at Echo and Janie from among the foliage of his great white beard. 'Good girls!' he trumpeted.

Thomas Pullen's voice was famous in the district, and Echo imagined it carrying out of the open door and across the street to the Sheffield Inn opposite. It must be like a stage actor's voice, so Echo thought, though she had never heard a stage actor.

Three charts decorated the schoolroom walls: a map of the island, a drawing of an Aboriginal man with stiff red hair, and a portrait of the Queen in England. Mr Pullen handed out the readers. He had a tattered supply of these dusty, green-covered books, shipped out from Home to educate the children.

'Geography, boys and girls!' cried the schoolmaster, pointing to the map of their island hanging on the wall. With his stick he indicated the direction of New South Wales – 'North!' He had the children sing out the compass directions as he pointed – 'East!

South! West!' Nothing showed on the map in these other directions.

'Now open your readers, children, to page twenty.'

The children complied, some with more difficulty than others. Echo, a good student who had been coming to school for years now and at fourteen was, strictly speaking, too old to be there, found the page and began to read to herself. '*Van Diemen's Land*,' she read, '*is neither a pleasant nor a safe country to live in, for the greatest part of the settlers are men who were wicked in their own country, and become still more so here.*'

The teacher directed the children's attention to a diagram reproduced in the reader that showed the mountainous regions of the island. He started on a story of bushranger days, a tale of desperate criminals hiding in the bush and attacking farmers' homesteads. Echo only half-listened. She read on. '*The children of such parents are not likely to be brought up to any good. It is better to live amongst the fierce wild beasts than amongst depraved and hard-hearted men.*'

Echo considered asking Mr Pullen about these *hard-hearted men*. Were there any in their district? Her father was a settler. True, he could be strict and didn't stand any nonsense, but he surely wasn't wicked? She began to raise her hand, but the teacher had moved on. He was talking now of the round river stones the Aboriginal people carried from the Mersey all the way up the Gog mountain to grind their ochre. The Gog range, a line of low hills, lay grey and sketchy to the east of the Hatton farm at Paradise. According to Mr Pullen, the Aborigines had a special ochre mine up there. Echo knew of this mine, in fact she had been there, and she had a question about it. She pushed her finger into the air until the teacher noticed her.

'What'd they do with this ochre?' she asked.

Mr Pullen pointed to the picture on the wall of the Aboriginal fellow with red ochre gummed all through his hair, covering his head like a knitted red cap. 'They mix it up with seal grease, to make it stick. This fella was a big chief,' said Mr Pullen in his booming voice. The face of the big chief stared down.

The children eyed the picture on the wall with looks of disbelief. Echo thought of her oldest brother Jack, who had shown her the path up the Gog mountain to the mine. Once he took her and Eddie up there, following a faint trail through the foothills until they came to a place scattered with stones. He'd learned the way from one of the Coleman boys, that's what he had said. Jack only took them up there the once, and insisted on keeping the way to the mine secret. When Echo asked him why it had to be secret, he said it was so those Dunstans didn't learn of it and take all the river stones. The stones made good ammunition and those Dunstan boys were trouble. At a place where the track to the Hatton farm ran between thick scrub and a high rock that no farmer had been able to move, they hid a stash of stones. The Dunstans had several times ambushed the Hattons at that spot. Jack worked out a whole battle strategy and muttered about 'surprise tactics'.

When he spoke of battles, it reminded Echo of Mr Pullen's lesson on Napoleon, the King of France. Napoleon sent explorers to Tasmania, the teacher said, and they made maps and drew pictures for their king. He said a Frenchman had drawn the picture of the chief with the red ochre in his hair. Mr Pullen told the children they might all have been born French, and he laughed from deep inside his big belly. The British Queen frowned down from the schoolroom wall.

Echo flipped through her reader, trying to ignore the girls sitting on the bench behind her. They were giggling and snickering and, as

Echo well knew, laughing at her old pinafore and her hair tied back with string. Daughters of the storekeeper at Barrington, the girls had new dresses of white cotton and their mother had curled their hair in rags. No farm work for them.

Janie, the same age as Echo and her best friend, pressed against her shoulder and said, 'Don't worry, Eck, we'll get them later.'

Echo turned to pretty Janie, whose bright blue eyes were full with tears that hadn't yet dropped, and said, fiercely, 'I don't care about them girls *at all*.'

When Lottie's ankle was broken and Eddie fought Arthur Dunstan and they all arrived home with Eddie bleeding everywhere and Lottie out in a dead faint, Echo ran straightaway to fetch their mother. In her experience, Mother always knew what to do with blood. Echo knew enough to fetch a rag and soak it in the bucket of creek water so Eddie could staunch his nose. She decided it was only a nosebleed; Eddie's nose didn't look crooked or anything. He didn't complain of pain, though Eddie never complained about anything hurting. What a good fighter Eddie was! He'd shown that Arthur Dunstan.

Inside the house, lying on the mattress, Lottie didn't look too good at all. Echo hovered near her mother's elbow, ready to boil some water or bring a rag or a remedy, or heat some broth, or whatever Mother needed. In the end, it was Grannie who got up from her chair and made the compress, and then the lanolin smoke. Echo darted between Mother and Grannie, intent on what had to be done, what could be done.

Lottie recovered eventually. She had a busted foot forever though, and needed a brace. Echo, rarely sorry for anyone, felt sorry for Charlotte.

2

Out in the yard, digging for worms between the bean plants, Echo found something small and white. She examined it, wondering who had left it there, certain someone had. She slipped it into her pinafore pocket to add to her collection. The yard was busy that morning. Jack's axe rang and the wood splintered, the bullocks snuffled, Father called '*Haw! Haw!*' as he wheeled his team to the left, and Mother called out again about collecting the eggs. Echo stood, shook out her skirt, and stomped over to the chicken coop where her little brother Amos, his braces undone, was amusing himself chasing the chooks.

'You don't find eggs like that,' Echo growled, and hitched his braces roughly onto his shoulders.

Emerging from the coop, Echo noticed Jack was finished with the kindling. He had to get over to the Vineys' place, he told her – old man Viney had a few extra rabbit snares he could borrow, but Jack didn't fancy the two-hour round trip. 'Show us the shortcut, Eck,' he asked, wheedling.

'What'll you give me?'

'Why, I got a terrific rock here, a bit of the mountain.' He reached into his britches pocket. 'I found it when Eddie and I went up there that time. Picked it up at a place where the Minnow comes down and makes a waterfall. You can have it for your collection.'

Echo examined the treasure. Dark grey-blue, a dull shine, shaped like an arrow, with hard pointed edges. 'Is it from the Aborigines?'

Jack had told her about Percy's ancestors and the things they left behind, and how Percy could find treasures like this if he listened hard enough. Echo would like to hear such stories herself, but Jack said she couldn't, her ancestors were from the Old Country.

'Nah, I don't reckon it's from them,' he said now. 'I expect it's a bit chipped off the old mountain. Maybe the leprechauns did it!'

Echo frowned. Was he pulling her leg? He often laughed at Grannie's stories, but she didn't think he should laugh at leprechauns. According to Grannie, they could be naughty. She turned the rock over again and decided it was worth her while. She would show Jack the shortcut. They set along a track heading north-west from their yard.

'I know this way already, Eck,' Jack protested.

'Shut up and follow me.'

Within minutes, she stopped near a fern-choked dip beside the track, a small gully that looked steep and impassable. With her arms outstretched, she parted the foliage and led Jack under a big old man-fern and into a magical glade beyond. Her brother followed; she liked the way he trusted her. She led the way downwards, along a faint trail beside a trickling creek. The water had made the ferns lush here and their greenery filtered the autumn sunlight into sprinkled shards of emerald.

'You sure about this?' Jack asked in a low voice. 'Is it really quicker?'

Echo looked at him, surprised at his doubt. 'Ain't I always right?' She turned and walked on through the light-dappled bush and within minutes they emerged on the fence line of Vineys' property.

'You're a ripper, Eck!' Jack said as he climbed the wooden rails. 'Wait for me though, or I won't know the way back.'

'Oh, I got to go,' Echo said, turning back to the bush. 'You come home the long way.' She ducked into the greenery before Jack could protest, then watched him shrug his shoulders and go off to fulfil his errand.

Wandering homewards, Echo sat to rest under the high canopy of a spreading man-fern. The forest pulsed with a sense of autumn fruitfulness. The furry fiddleheads on the ferns had spread wide and the birds seemed quieter. She lay down, looking up through the fronds and the sassafras branches, listening to the faint singing. Then among the leaves, under the myrtle bushes and the bracken, she noticed some shiny purple mushroom caps pushing through the sour-smelling humus. Reaching forwards, she plucked a few and scooped them into her pinafore. She noticed others, less gaudy, walnut-coloured with spindly brown stems, and she gathered these too. Brushing the earth from their caps, she nibbled a little, then a little more. Lying beneath the fronds, she watched the green world spin above her. She was late home, and Mother made a fuss.

That evening, after she'd eaten her small share of the pottage of root vegetables and boiled mutton, Echo went out to pen up the chooks. It was dark and still in the yard, the chickens roosting. She paused at the fence line, peering into the bush with night eyes. The undergrowth rustled with snorts and grunts, whistles and growls, as if the animals were holding a carnival.

Disobeying Mother's rule, she ducked under the fence and walked a little way into the bush, following an old trail. Though the big eucalypts near the house were all dead, long-since ringbarked, the undergrowth was dense. Deeper in the bush, where the ground sloped up towards the foothills of the mountain, the gums were still living – except for one or two of the old ones, ancient trunks long died off from age, damp shelters like caves formed in their hollow trunks. Echo knew the best one and she kept some of her treasures in there. She thought of it as her hideout. Following the trail, she startled a devil gnawing at a possum carcass in the underbrush. It dropped its meal and opened its slathering jaws wide, hissing, showing a cavernous red throat. Echo jumped back, but after the first surprise she wasn't afraid. Devils didn't like interruptions when they were eating, that was all.

Wandering through the bush, she became unsure of the way back. On an old tree long fallen – maybe a hundred years ago – she stopped to think. Fronds of feathery white fungus sprouted along the log like the frills on a petticoat. From between the layers of damp, rotting timber she saw the blue glow of the night mushrooms, unremarkable in the daytime but luminescent in the dark. With her night eyes, she looked for pricks of light in the undergrowth, listened for songs, watched for trembling through the ferns. The night cooled, silky air turning chill. For ages she didn't hear the calls from the direction of the house.

Mother cried wildly when Echo finally emerged. 'Echo Hatton! What are you doing, frightening me like that? Don't you know little children get lost in the bush and never come home to their families?'

Mother covered her tears with blustering anger. Echo smiled to reassure her, brushing twigs from the front of her pinafore. 'Don't be bothered, Mother. The bush ain't that scary.'

When Father came back from the jetty and Mother told him about her escapade, he spoke sternly, with barely controlled temper. 'Eck, don't you go out in the bush at night *no more*.'

She considered his fierce expression, his beard twitching with emotion, and she remembered the story of her sister Caroline, the little child drowned in the Mersey.

'All right, Father,' she said, deciding to be docile. She hung her head a little, to show it.

Mother told that story of Caroline so often, repeated like a lesson. The celery-top pine near the farmhouse, with the crude wooden cross, had always been a kind of shrine. Echo and the others knew why Mother lingered there. They knew the story of drowned Caroline, but it was hard to believe she'd been a real girl. Caroline had somehow changed from a two-year-old child into a cautionary tale.

As for the dangers of the forest, Echo believed in those stories even less. On the contrary, she loved the bush: the ferneries and secret burrows, the wallabies and badgers and spotted quolls who made tracks through the bracken, the treasures she sometimes found, the curiously-shaped rocks. And the sounds – there was much to hear in the bush if you lay still under the fern canopy. She wasn't sure if the rustling and singing she sometimes heard came from Percy Coleman's ancestors, or from the Irish fairies. Maybe both.

3

Sitting at the table in the smoky kitchen, Echo opened her journal. She'd reached the part in her story where her mother stood in the yard thinking about planting flowers by the door of her house. Roses, she'd told Echo, though Grannie said waratah might be just as good. Echo thought this idea of the flowers could be the end of her mother's story, but then she remembered she hadn't written about how the mutton birds had saved them. Her pen scratched along the lines ruled in her book. The air in the room was fuggy with the odour of cabbage and a whiff of Grannie. Eddie began talking about some strangers who'd come up the bridle track and arrived unannounced at the Clarke place. Preachers, Eddie said they were.

Echo put down her pen to listen. She'd never seen a preacher, not even a Wesleyan.

After this news, and everything that happened afterwards, a long while passed before she went back to her journal. For a time, the goings-on in the district were so fascinating that she couldn't be bothered wondering about the past.

The day the preachers visited the Hatton farm, Echo almost missed them. She was down among the ferns with Amos. 'No noise now,' she said to him, holding her hand over his mouth. 'I'm going to take my hand away, but you're not to make a sound.' Amos struggled a little, but nodded as best he could. Echo slid her palm from his lips, watching him, her face only inches from his. 'No noise, or the fairies won't come out. You want to see them, don't you?'

Amos nodded again. 'But Eck,' he whispered, 'Mother will be calling for you soon. It's almost time to be making tea.'

'I'll go. But first we have to finish what we're doing.'

She grabbed him by the wrist and led him farther down into a gully until they reached a place where the man-ferns grew as high as verandah posts, the fronds forming a canopy that arched over their heads like a green roof filtering the sunlight.

'In here, Amos, and keep quiet.'

They stepped into the shadowy interior of the sacred refuge and crouched on the crackling brown fronds. Echo flapped her palm to show Amos he should be silent, and they listened. Soon the murmuring and rustling came; she'd heard it plenty of times before and knew it to be always there, you just had to pay attention. Watching Amos, his absorbed face scrunched up with the effort of listening, Echo tried to judge if he could hear it too. At least he tried, not like her older brothers who just laughed when she spoke of it.

Echo had known about the secret sounds since she'd been old enough to crawl. As a little girl, she'd thought the sounds were baby animals, hidden. Then Grannie came to live with them and told her stories, and Echo understood that the sounds were fairies, or sprites, or one of those magical creatures Grannie talked about, one of those Irish goblins. Now she was older, Echo was convinced the rustlings and singings were made by something Grannie didn't know about. After all, they were in Tasmania, not Ireland. The Tasmanian bush had its own kind of fairies, and Echo reckoned probably only children born here could hear them. She was trying out her theory to Amos and watched as his little eyes screwed up.

'D'you hear anything?' she hissed.

His eyes popped open. 'Yes I do!' he whispered back. 'I reckon I hear . . . a snake!'

Echo let out a little puff of annoyance. She wanted the boy to hear the magical sounds, the Tasmanian fairies. But as she turned away from him she did see the tip of a whip snake slithering into the bracken. 'You were right!' she whispered.

Amos had been right about Mother too – soon they heard her calling from the house and both scurried back to the yard. Echo was surprised to see two horses tethered, and even more astonished to see the two strangers sitting at their old kitchen table. At least the table was scrubbed clean; Mother had been anticipating this visit. Grannie sat in her usual place by the stove, grinning at the newcomers, beaming with delight. The scent of apple cake, fresh-baked that morning, disguised the usual boiled-cabbage odour of the kitchen. Mother was rattling the tea things and she waved at Echo to take over as soon as she appeared in the doorway. The two visitors were getting a fine old welcome.

As she set the kettle on to boil and took down the tea caddy, Echo examined the visitors with sideways eyes. They looked to be quite old blokes, one especially. The younger one had a Scottish voice, same as Janie's father. He wore his curious red whiskers in fluffy sideburns, and a wide handle-bar moustache split his face in two. It was a marvel to see these gentlemen in their own kitchen in Paradise, but Echo felt she should be cautious. What did they want?

When Baby coughed, one of the gentlemen pulled out a paper and began to write down the ingredients for a remedy. He had the paper, and a pencil too, right there in his pocket. He wasn't to know that Mother couldn't read, but Echo would read it for her later. Then the red-whiskered gentleman noticed Echo beside the teapot, and he asked if she could say the Lord's Prayer. Of course she could! That one was easy enough.

In the end, she recited the whole of Psalm 121 with no mistakes. The red-bearded Scotsman smiled so kindly when she finished, Echo's insides swirled with pleasure. The whole incident left her quite well-disposed towards the visitors – though it was still unclear what they wanted.

On the bush telegraph, the Hattons heard of the preachers calling all over the district. Echo hoped they'd come back to Paradise. She would be pleased to recite for them again. In preparation, she tried memorising Psalm 23, another good one: *The Lord is my shepherd; I shall not want. He maketh me to lie down in green pastures; he leadeth me beside the still waters.*

Then came the night of the revival in Duggan's barn. She'd never heard of a *revival* before, in fact she'd never heard anyone preaching before, unless the schoolmaster counted. Grannie talked of *Anglicans*: so often they had heard her stories about getting married in a church. In Echo's mind, 'Anglicans' conjured a picture of tall, imposing people with loud voices, dressed in white.

Up at Duggan's, squashed between Mother and Grannie, she craned her neck and watched. Even though the preachers weren't tall men, and wore ordinary black coats, there was something entrancing about the way they stood and raised their arms, and the way the whole barn fell quiet before them, listening to the lift of their voices – not loud at first, but growing and growing like the sun rising behind the mountain range.

Echo sat with her mouth open and her eyes wide; later she could not recall the passing of time. She did join in the singing, that she remembered. Mr Pullen had taught the children some of those hymns. The rumble of the barn full of people growling the melodies, sometimes women's high voices soaring above the rumble, sometimes women shrieking and then one or two fainting right away and the crowd appearing to sway and tremble – these were Echo's memories later, but in fact she could never quite recall what had actually happened in Duggan's barn. Only that it was terrible and exciting and everyone talked about nothing else for ages afterwards.

4

The path between the Hatton farm and the Miller farm was beaten hard and flat and made for easy walking. No-one knew who'd first made the path, but Jack said it was the Aborigines. Echo thought it could be so; it seemed an old path to her. On a late autumn day, in blustery weather, the winds blowing down from the slopes of the blue mountain, Echo and Janie walked together. Janie's family had been at the big revival in Duggan's barn, and, like most people, the events of that night had left her excited and unsettled.

'Did you see Arthur Dunstan there, Eck? He was there. His whole family were.'

'What about it? Everyone was there.'

Janie kicked at a stone. Her boots were holding up pretty well, unlike Echo's second-hand pair. The stone skittered off into the ferns. 'D'you like him, Eck?'

Echo flushed. 'D'you mean like him enough to kiss him or something? I surely do not. That Arthur Dunstan is a bully.'

'I seen him looking at you a few times, that's all. Don't get mad at me.'

Echo picked up a stick and took a few swipes at the bracken. The girls walked on in silence. Janie pulled her shawl around her shoulders against the wind.

'Father says I won't be going to school no more after the wheat's planted,' Echo said. 'Not in the winter, and not after that neither. He says I'm too grown for school now and I should be helping Mother more.' This development had been preying on her mind ever since Father had given her the news.

'Oh, I ain't going back to school neither. Mother says I'll be marrying soon enough.'

Janie was a few months older than Echo. From the way she spoke, anyone would think she was looking forward to getting married.

'Is that so?' Echo said.

'Yes,' Janie replied happily.

There was more silence, as Echo digested this news. 'Who, then?' she asked, after a minute or two.

'What?'

'Who do you like enough to marry? One of my brothers?'

Janie giggled and grabbed Echo's arm. 'We'd be sisters then, wouldn't we, Eck?'

They were within a mile of the Hatton farm, and Rags came racing up the track to meet Echo. As the dog approached, he gave a short bark of recognition and ran a few rings around the girls.

'What are you doing, Rags, old boy?' Echo said. 'Father will be that mad if he finds you away from the farm. You should be working.' She bent down to rub the dog's ears, and forgot for a moment about which of her brothers might marry her best friend.

Janie moved onto another topic of interest. 'Them preachers came to our place, Eck. Did you know? That Mr Fenny the other night got Mother and Father kneeling down and praying, right in our kitchen! Mother and Father are both going converted!'

She was almost breathless with the excitement. Echo walked on silently for a while, considering, Rags trotting alongside. Ever since the revival meeting, her brother Jack had done nothing but talk about the preachers. He kept hoping there'd be another revival. But Eddie only snorted whenever anyone mentioned it. Echo reached into her bag slung across her chest and pulled out a couple of knobs of hard bread, handing one to Janie.

'I reckon I might go converted too,' Janie said, 'like everyone else.' She took a bite of bread.

'Why?'

''Cause then I can go to heaven after I die.' Janie paused for a moment. 'That's the main reason.'

'My brother Jack is mighty interested in the preachers.'

Echo watched Janie to see how this went over. From the way she'd seen Jack looking at her friend, she thought he certainly liked Janie enough to marry her. Lately, however, it was dawning on her that she might not have the full story. She'd noticed that sometimes Eddie had eyes for Janie too. It was confusing – life these days seemed to be moving quickly. Even Janie, her best friend, appeared to be somehow different. Echo wondered if she kept secret plans, plans Echo couldn't imagine.

'Yes, I reckon Jack will go converted,' Echo said, fishing for a response.

'Will he, Eck?' said Janie, chewing. 'What about Eddie?'

'Eddie don't think much of the preachers. He only thinks about growing spuds, and getting them sold, and he says them preachers can't help him do that. He says only plain hard work can help him.'

'Oh,' Janie said, and fell quiet. 'Don't Eddie want to go to heaven?'

'I don't know, Janie. I ain't asked him about that. But he reckons the preachers are full of hot air.'

The girls came to a fork in the track where they needed to part, Janie to the left, Echo to the right. With Rags at her heels, Echo said goodbye to her friend and went off down her fork in the road, still wondering which of her brothers Janie liked enough to marry.

No-one had heard the Dunstans' taunts for a while but Echo still proceeded cautiously. She wanted to avoid them, to avoid the trouble they brought. She was glad to have Rags with her on this late afternoon, with dusk advancing. But the dog ran on ahead – sniffing the home yard, she supposed – and then she heard the shuffle of boots. Echo paused. Arthur Dunstan appeared from around the bend. She stepped back into the ferns, but not quickly enough – he'd seen her. Arthur stopped too. They eyed each other.

'Get on past then,' Echo said after a minute, her face flushed.

Arthur took a few steps towards her and stood in the middle of the track. He stared right at her, grinning, his fists propped on his hips. The wattlebirds in the myrtle trees shrieked, as if chuckling. Something skittered away under the ferns, avoiding the scene. Arthur took a few steps towards Echo, then stopped again. He was a full head taller than her.

'Hey Eck,' he said, winking. His mouth twisted in an expression that might have been a grin, but had a queer lopsidedness to it.

'Go on past then,' commanded Echo. She tried to sound bossy, as she did when she ordered her little brothers and sisters around, but this seemed to make no impression on Arthur. He reached out one large hand and took her arm above the elbow.

'Get off!' she cried.

'Come on, Eck, I seen you looking at me.'

Echo stared into his face for a shocked minute. Then wresting her arm from his grip, she dashed away down the track, never stopping until she reached her own yard, the bush flashing past her, full of laughing bird calls.

5

The mountain was always there, every frosty morning and every cool afternoon, and Echo often spoke to it as if it listened. Sometimes it answered back. Though she didn't always catch the reply, she liked to know it was listening, part of the living world that surrounded the farm.

Glowing violet in the dawn light, the rocky dolomite face looked down at her once again as she collected the milking pails. She had a few questions today – for a start, she'd like to know exactly what was going on down at the creek. Clanking the pails against her thighs, she walked over to the cow shed. Chilly air snuck down her dress collar, misty-white breath puffing in a cloud in front of her nose. Early milking wasn't the worst job; splitting kindling was harder, especially with a frost on the woodpile. Echo liked milking; the flow of milk felt generous, a blessed certainty of farm life. She leaned against the warm flank of the cow and tugged on the udder. White goodness splattered into the metal bucket.

'You are a good one, Bess,' she whispered. 'You are a good one.'

Mornings at Paradise often broke like this, sweet and fine. When the sun climbed and light began to wash the mountain face, the mist would lift from the Dasher River flats and the whole world woke clean. Peace reigned in the cow shed, though the yard was noisy enough. The chooks made a real racket, and the dogs, Rags and Tippet, were already whining for a scrap to eat. They'd wait a while yet. Mother had Baby to feed before the dogs.

Echo carried the pails of frothy milk back to the house. When she reached the kitchen, Mother was standing in front of the wood burner with Baby grizzling on her hip. Echo put down the milk and brought out tin cups for the kiddies. The smallest boys were in a lather this morning; they couldn't shut up about the baptisms in the creek.

'We're going! We're going!' they yelled, racing around the kitchen.

'Give over,' their father growled.

'Have your milk, boys,' Mother said, standing at a great black cast-iron pot of stirabout on the stove.

'Get out of me way, you little menaces,' said Echo, swatting at her brothers. On her second swipe, the flat of her hand connected with the ear of one little brother and he howled. 'And stop that yelling!' she added.

It didn't make any difference; the boys took no notice of her. Hauling a two-day-old loaf and a bread board from the dresser, she thumped them onto the table and began to hack off chunks, first handing one to Father. He sat waiting for porridge, his thin haunches bent onto a chair. A lot of work fell to her, the oldest girl. Lottie tried to help, but she couldn't do so much with her lame foot. The other little sisters were too young yet; they were only good for feeding scraps to the chooks and collecting eggs. Even then, they broke some.

Eddie came in, letting cold air through the kitchen door. He and Jack sat at the table with their father. All three already had their boots on.

'You coming to the creek, Father?' asked Jack.

Father finished his slow chewing. His beard moved up and down rhythmically. Eventually he said, 'Reckon I will.'

Echo lifted her eyes from the bread board. She so wanted to see these immersions. 'Ain't it too cold for swimming?' she asked.

He bit off another mouthful of bread and looked vacantly across the kitchen. Echo had the impression he felt as puzzled as she.

Jack snorted. 'They ain't going *swimming*, you chump. They're going to be *immersed*. That's different.'

Eddie laughed. 'Not so different, I reckon. It'll be a good show if those preachers do it.'

When they'd visited the Hattons, the preachers hadn't seemed like crazy men who would go swimming on a frosty morning. They'd seemed like sensible gentlemen. Echo wondered if she'd missed something.

'We're going! We're going!' yelled the little boys again, still dashing about.

'Can I go too, Father?' Echo asked.

'Ask your Mother.'

She went to the stove and took Baby from Mother. The little ones clustered around with their tin bowls, and Mother began ladling porridge.

'Can I go, Mother?'

'If you've done your work, 'course you can. We're all going, if these boys calm down and get theirselves ready.'

Echo turned to Jack and Eddie. 'I'm going too!'

'Help me with this first, Eck,' Mother said, scraping out the last of the porridge, then opening the door to heave the cast-iron pot into the yard.

Setting down the baby, Echo dragged the pot to the water bucket and began washing out the sludgy remains of oats, scouring the pot clean for the next batch. The sun had risen and the mountain looked different already, benign and sleepy, unimpressed by the excitement building down at the creek. Echo scrubbed at the stubborn clumps, attached like glue to the black iron. Right now, when she wanted to be done with her chores, the lumps seemed to stick harder than ever. She finally finished, stood, and stretched her back. Before she went to the creek she should change her pinafore, though she didn't have a clean one; she only owned two and washday was four days off. The racket from the kitchen suggested that the family had got itself ready. Echo hurried to join them.

'You coming, Grannie?' she asked the old lady, who was licking the last scraps of porridge from her bowl.

'Yes! Eddie says he'll take me.' Grannie was bright-eyed this morning, as excited as the rest of them.

A crowd had gathered on both banks. The creek, the Dasher River, meandered through the farms in Paradise. At the place chosen for the baptisms, men had been working for days digging out a waterhole deep enough for the dunking. Echo and several of her little brothers lay on their stomachs on a small rise, their grubby pale faces lined up in a row, mouths hanging open, eyes widening at the sight of so many people all in one place.

'Must be thousands of them!' she whispered.

'Don't be an ass,' Eddie said, standing behind her. 'There's not a thousand people in the district.' He squinted at the crowd. 'Couple of hundred maybe.' He stood with one hand on his hip pretending he saw sights like this every day. Then he said, 'I'm off' and headed away to climb into the low branches of a gum tree.

As he was easily tall enough to see over the heads around him, Echo didn't know why Eddie wanted to climb a tree, but plenty of other boys were doing the same thing. She shivered; a chill hung in the air and she recalled the frost this morning when she went out to do the milking. Would anyone wade into the creek on such a cold day? It was hard to believe. In Paradise the farms were long and narrow, each claiming its own bit of creek or river frontage. Today everyone had gathered in a field that belonged to the Mason farm. And *lo-and-behold!* here came Mrs Mason, walking down to the creek, with her grown boys helping her. A fellow in a black suit and hat followed them.

'Who's that fella?' asked Echo.

'Why, you chump,' said Jack, sitting beside her. 'That's Preacher Fenny. He's going to do the dunking.'

'No! He might drown her!'

Jack laughed. 'Just watch, Eck,' he said, but he sounded uneasy himself.

The children gawped at the proceedings down at the water's edge, the handshaking, the greetings they couldn't quite hear. Mrs Mason wore her best house dress. She hesitated at the riverbank – then in she waded right up to her armpits. The preacher held onto her elbow and waded in beside her, still in his suit, his hat pulled down on his head as if he was going visiting. The crowd murmured and shifted like a herd of sheep, shuffling and alert, not knowing what to make of this. Then a collective gasp rose as Mrs Mason went under, tipped backwards by the preacher. He seemed to be talking all the while; Echo could see his lips moving but could only hear a vague murmur. Then Mrs Mason rose up, spluttering and flapping her arms and wiping water from her eyes. The preacher waved his arms too and cried out things Echo couldn't hear. She pressed her fist against her lips.

Mrs Mason sure did look half-drowned. Then *lo-and-behold!* if she didn't let out a glad shout that floated up the riverbank, like the sound of a currawong calling in the forest. 'Hallelujah!' She climbed from the creek with a grin all over her face. Hands reached down to help her; they hauled her up and someone wrapped her in a blanket. None too soon, either. Whistling started from the trees as she stood in her dripping wet dress, the fabric clinging to her body. Mrs Mason must have been freezing cold.

Eddie, up in the fork of the gum tree, gave a loud snort when he saw this. Echo heard and glanced up at him. She shivered in the damp grass. A skinny boy with high cheekbones had climbed up near Eddie, a bloke she'd noticed sometimes hanging around in town. His face seemed angular and soft at the same time. Echo had found it hard to forget. Once, she'd passed him on the track, near the junction that leads down to Beulah, but they hadn't spoken. Now, on the hillside, she reached behind to pull her dress down; she didn't want any boys looking at the backs of her knees, not even that good-looking one.

Though Mrs Mason had climbed from the water, the preacher still stood there waist deep in the creek. Even from the hillside Echo could see him shivering.

'Praise the Lord!' came his faint cry. Then he called something about 'received in Heaven' and 'rejoicing'. A small cheer went up. Echo looked up to the sky, half expecting some sign, some inkling of all that rejoicing going on up there. Certainly some rejoicing erupted down by the creek. People began singing. Quavery women's voices floated up to the children, '*Shall we gather at the river, Where bright angel feet have trod, With its crystal tide forever, Flowing by the throne of God?*'

'Are they singing about *our* river, Jack?' Echo asked.

Her brother had been quiet during the immersion, not whistling and calling like the boys in the tree. 'No, you chump,' he said. 'It's the river in heaven. The one you cross over when you die.'

Echo wondered if this meant Mrs Mason would die, but decided she seemed too happy for that. After Mrs Mason, a whole line of people waited to wade into the creek and have the preacher dunk them. He continued to cry out things that Echo could barely hear but she couldn't drag her eyes away. This had turned out an even better show than the revival in the barn. The quavery singing went on, winding up to Echo on the hillside: '*Yes, we'll gather at the river, The beautiful, the beautiful river, Gather with the saints at the river, That flows by the throne of God.*'

'What's them "saints by the river", Jack?'

'Them's the ones who've died.'

'You mean like Caroline, who drowned at the ford when Father drove the cart to Paradise?'

'Yes, she'll be there.' There was a thrill in Jack's voice when he said this; it seemed he really believed it to be so.

The idea entranced Echo. Mother would be glad of that news, she thought – if you get yourself dunked, you can go to heaven and meet up with the ones who've died. She looked around for Mother and Father. They were standing near the boundary fence farther down the hillside, with the Clarkes and some of the Clarke children.

'We should tell Mother about that, Jack,' she suggested.

But Jack was gazing down the hillside as people lined up to be immersed in the Dasher, wading in, then going under, then emerging with joyous shouts. Echo stared too, hardly breathing at each moment of immersion. Wet grass brushed her cheeks and her pinafore was becoming damp. When the baptisms were finally over, she stood, cold from lying in the grass, and headed home with her family. As they wandered back across the paddocks, Jack said he'd counted fourteen people going into the creek that day.

'In our own creek, Noah!' Mother said in wonder.

Father grunted. It did seem a marvel.

Eddie said it'd been a good show, but he would never let a black-coated preacher in a hat dunk him in the river.

6

The hours of daylight grew shorter. Snow fell on the mountain, as if to remind everyone in the district how close they were to the highlands. The snow would be deep on Middlesex Plains and out towards Cradle Mountain, where stockholders ran their herds on land not yet fenced off. Jack's mate Percy Coleman had brought his sheep down from there; he said it looked like a freezing winter ahead. Jack always listened to Percy, and Father often went along with whatever the Colemans reckoned, so long as it wasn't to do with prospecting. Father had no faith in prospecting. Echo rested her cheek against the flank of the cow, the one reliably warm place on the farm.

Down in the bottom paddock where her brothers were burning off, Echo could hear the noise of an argument as she approached. The sound of voices raised in anger mingled with the barking of the dog, running ahead of her. Plodding through the mud, she was bringing tea in a stone bottle wrapped in flannel to keep it warm; the boys had left without it and Mother had sent her. Echo's feet were cold; she had holes in her boots again. The cold infected her all over. She didn't like the way her brothers fought these days; they never used to be so angry with each other. She didn't like the way Eddie had taken up cursing.

As she crossed the paddock, the raised voices became more distinct.

'Why d'you go on and on at me about the bleedin' Bible?' she heard Eddie say.

She couldn't hear Jack, who stood beyond the pile of tree trunks and branches.

'Jack, you're off your head. We got enough to do right here without worrying about the bleedin' afterlife. We got to get this clearing done, and this rubbish burned, and then if you want to pray, you can bleedin' pray for the frosts to keep off.'

With her boots sticking in the mud, Echo approached, her feet making a sucking noise with each step. The flask of tea, hugged against her chest, felt warm and comforting. When she reached the pile of fallen timber she could hear them more clearly.

The whole family knew by now that Jack was convinced by the preachers. He was always haranguing them to read the Bible; he even wanted Mother and Father to go converted. Echo could understand Eddie's irritation.

'When you read the Bible, you find out there's better times ahead. There's God's heaven awaiting for you. And those that already passed over, they're waiting too!' said Jack.

'Give over, or I'll knock your block off,' said Eddie.

Jack didn't give over, and Eddie eventually lost his temper, took a swing, and Jack took a swing back. When Echo heard the sickly thump of fists connecting with jaws, she let out a shriek. Their father, across the paddock with the bullocks, rushed over and busted up the fight quick smart, pulling the boys apart and demanding they give over or he'd show them why. Father had never liked brawling in the family.

Then Amos was shot, and though Mother and Grannie worked hard they couldn't save him.

Echo was left numb, hardly able to grasp that he was gone. This wasn't like Caroline's death, a story from the past. It was Amos, her own little brother, whom she'd belted around the ears often enough when he wasn't careful with the eggs, whom she'd taken to visit the fairies under the ferns. She'd mended his britches and fed him pea soup. He'd sat agog when she read *Robinson Crusoe*, and yakked all the time about becoming a terrific rabbitoh who could skin them as fast as Eddie. He had been an annoying little brat. Oh, she had loved him. Mother went back to crying her floods, and Echo didn't know how to help. She shed plenty of tears herself, though Grannie said it did no good.

Still, when Echo read the Bible words at the burial, Mother seemed to take heart. It seemed she really believed she'd meet Amos again in heaven. Was it true? Grannie said it had been a good service, as good as Anglican. Echo worried they'd not done well enough for her little brother. They'd buried Amos without a preacher. Mother said they never had one for Caroline, and Father said they had to look out for themselves. Jack said Mr Fenny reckoned they could be Christians on their own. Still, it didn't seem enough. For a while, when the frosts had melted in the afternoons, Echo went back to her old habit of creeping under the ferns in the bush to watch the green light splinter above her.

Winter seemed to last forever at the Hatton farm, with Mother always wringing out her apron. Baby wasn't thriving as she should. The dogs whined whenever Echo went out to the yard to see if the hens had laid even one egg – sometimes, feeling lucky, she found one, precious and warm. The bullocks shuffled, unexercised. Echo pressed her cheek against the flank of the cow as she milked her, morning and evening.

The excitement that had taken over the district when the preachers arrived faded, almost forgotten on the cold farms. No school for Echo now, just mending and scrubbing, milking and stirring, carrying the baby on her hip and mopping up her mother's tears.

Closing her book and cleaning the nib of her pen, Echo wondered if she'd keep going with her story. It was all very well to write down the words of her mother's songs, or describe the first hut, or record the stories of Caroline or her own birth or the time her parents met in the hayfield. She even got up the courage to write of losing Amos, and now she felt she'd written everything. When it came to her convict grandfather, she had no intention of writing about him. Grannie told plenty of stories, but the thought of an old convict who used his fists on Mother made Echo's stomach churn. Neither did she like the tales of *collisions* with the Aborigines, because she knew what had happened to them.

Uncomfortable feelings began to assail her. Walking in the forest, lying under the spreading man-ferns, sinking into the strange vibrations she sensed in her thickening body, Echo sometimes felt new mysterious pangs of longing. She wondered if it was the bush speaking to her, or growing into her somehow. With her eyes closed, she ran her hands up and down her thighs, onto her emerging breasts. Did the Bible have anything to say about these new sensations that both thrilled and worried her? She supposed it did – there seemed to be a Bible reading for everything. Turning onto her back, she nibbled at a mushroom cap and watched the green world spin above.

The girls who were Echo's age, her friends from school, had left and were at home helping their mothers – they were growing into women. Mary Viney had recently passed her sixteenth birthday and had married already. Janie too had turned sixteen and wore her hair differently. Echo thought of her mother chuckling and winking when she spoke of courting at the picnics. What lay ahead? Her thoughts turned to Arthur Dunstan and that time he'd grabbed her on the track and she'd run away like a scared pademelon. The Dunstans never came to the picnics. Probably a good thing.

Then she had Jack and his conversion to wonder about. These days he seemed full of hope and happiness, sparked by his strange encounter with the Lord while he was out chopping firewood. Echo wondered if she might one day experience an explosion like that herself. It seemed unlikely, but then sudden conversion hadn't been on anyone's mind before the preachers arrived.

7

Down at Dunn's on an afternoon in early spring, Father pulled the dray up alongside several others. Jack took the leading reins and tethered the bullocks to stakes. Jumping down, Echo helped her mother unload the small children and the picnic provisions – cold meat and knobs of bread and a few wrinkled apples saved since the autumn. Father submerged some bottles of home brew in the creek to chill and the family spread out on the grass beside the Clarkes and the Millers and the Vineys, the whiskers and the aprons, the milky babies. Echo looked about and saw some of her friends, those she knew from school, wandering away together, in twos and threes and larger groups. She found Janie, and they sat together on a fallen log at the edge of the clearing, munching an apple each.

Echo considered the best way to ask Janie the question that was bothering her.

'Does Jack still come over to your place for them Bible meetings?' she asked, coming at it from an angle.

Janie laughed. 'Yes, he does, though he ain't getting any better at reading.'

This irritated Echo. 'You didn't ought to laugh at him. He was never too good at schoolwork.' She paused, considered her apple core. 'He's a terrific bullocky, though.' Across the clearing they could see Jack checking on Lion and Blue Boy.

'Oh, yes,' Janie said happily. 'He showed me his whip cracking once. It was marvellous.'

'Did he?' Echo puzzled over Janie's smiling face, and watched her watch Jack with his bullocks. 'What about Eddie?'

'What about him? He don't come to Bible meetings, you know that, Eck.'

Echo sighed. 'I know he don't.'

She glanced around the picnic ground but couldn't see Eddie anywhere. Nibbling one last bit of sweet white flesh from her apple, she concluded that her mother must have been mistaken when she'd said that about Janie and Eddie, about them courting. *Could Janie be courting?* Wouldn't that mean babies and your own house? An unaccustomed shyness made her unsure how to ask about these things. She tried to imagine Janie in charge of a kitchen like Mother's, with a baby on her hip. Mother was fourteen when she married, so she said, but she might have that wrong.

'Want to come down to the creek? I know a good blackberry place,' suggested Echo.

But Janie had to go and help her mother. Echo wandered off on her own, her brow furrowed.

The three girls from Barrington, who used to tease Echo at school, were at the picnic and sat on a patch of grass at the edge of the clearing. Echo did not care for those girls one bit; she did not want to encounter their taunts today. When they saw Echo, they called to her to come over, laughing behind their hands when she turned away. They wore white dresses and wide sun hats. Echo shook out her pinafore and raised one hand to smooth her hair. Her mother had twisted it into a soft braid for her this morning. The girls continued to call and laugh. Echo tossed her braid over her shoulder and headed in the other direction.

'Echo! Echo dear, come over here!'

Echo quickened her steps. The girls got up and followed her, as if they would not let her get away. 'Echo! Echo! Come and talk to us!' They laughed, like little witches.

Increasing her pace, trying to look as if she had something urgent to do, Echo hurried into the bush. Her legs felt oddly rigid, and she stumbled a little. The girls followed, laughing slyly, creeping up behind her, moving from tree to tree. She couldn't get rid of them. They stuck like a cow pat on boots. She pushed deeper into the forest and the girls in their white dresses fluttered after her.

Trying to shake them off, she dived up a side track. It was barely there, just a faint path where someone might have pushed through before. Soon the bush enclosed her and she couldn't see the girls any longer, but their shrill calls still sounded faintly behind her. Panting a little, she crouched behind a fallen log and ducked her head into her arms, curling up as small as she could, like a possum in a tree trunk. She stayed that way for a long time, until the shrieks died away. Then she uncurled her body and sat in the quiet forest, her refuge.

A boronia bush grew beside the fallen log. Idly, Echo broke a twig from it and sat stripping off its tiny leaflets and miniature pink flowers one by one, letting her heart settle. She felt angry, yes she did. Mainly at those girls, chasing her like that. Why did they think they could chase her, Echo Hatton, if she didn't want to talk to them? On the farm, she could make the little kids do what she wanted. At home, she ran things her way. But those girls took no notice.

Echo knew whatever they said would be stupid. It would be about clothes and hair. She didn't care about clothes and hair. As long as her boots lasted, that's all she minded. She picked off more leaflets, staring hard at each of them between her grubby fingertips. When she had nothing but a stripped twig left, she sighed and leaned back against the mossy log.

A young bloke stood a few yards distant, looking straight at her. It was Henry, though she didn't know his name just then. 'I was that startled,' she would say to him afterwards, 'it was a wonder my heart didn't stop.'

Henry lived at Beulah, he told her. His clothes were poor; worn and almost ragged. When he took off his hat, his thick brown hair stood up in roughly cut tufts. The planes of his face angled like the facets of a rock, punctuated with a long straight nose – he was a fine-looking boy, if you got past the grime.

When she asked him, Henry said he was about twenty years old, though he could not be sure. His people moved around a lot, he said; his father went prospecting. They'd lived at Lorinna for a while, and once they'd been down at Waratah. Henry had taken to the prospecting too. Tin, they looked for. But the rabbiting kept him going. He got a bit for the skins, and the meat.

He told Echo all this, that first day in the bush, after he sat down next to her beneath the ferns. She told him about the screeching girls in their sun hats, and he said he'd heard them.

'Bloody stupid sheilas,' he said.

Echo smiled at him gratefully. He was awfully good-looking.

8

Henry took to visiting the Hatton house, walking over from Beulah, about five miles along the bush tracks. When he reached the farm, he would approach the yard and stand shuffling by the fence post. After a while he'd lean on the post with his hat tipped over his eyes, looking up now and then at the house, almost furtive. He would wait until Echo spotted him.

'Eck, what are you doing at the window?' Mother called.

Echo pretended to be polishing the window glass. The front windows had proper glass and were Mother's pride and joy and she never minded having them polished; Echo could waste plenty of time doing the polishing. She would lean her forehead against the windowpane, watching Henry beside the fence post, tall and skinny and diffident. She looked out; from beyond the Hatton fence, he looked in. She wondered if he'd ever move, if he'd ever make it to the door. It seemed as if he'd planted himself outside forever. Growing impatient, worried he'd leave if she didn't fetch him, Echo would go out and bring him into the yard. In the kitchen, the first time Henry came, she waited until Mother turned from the stove.

'Here is Henry,' she said, 'from Beulah.' As if that explained him. 'Cup of tea?' Mother offered.

Echo felt nervous about having this visitor in the kitchen with Mother and Grannie. Probably they would be looking him over. 'Sit down, won't you?' Echo said, waving him towards the chairs at the table. She was holding her breath, looking from Mother to Henry, from her past to her future, though she didn't think of it like that at the time. She had no way to imagine ever leaving her mother.

When Henry had gone and Father came in from his day's work, Mother was real quick to tell him all about the visitor. She described him as 'Eck's suitor'. Echo wasn't sure how she felt about that. Henry was described and dissected, discussed and pondered. On his next visit, he shook hands with Father, but neither man said much.

Later, as the discussions of Henry continued, Father seemed doubtful. He was even poorer than the Hattons, that was obvious to everyone.

'He's only a rabbitoh,' Father said.

Echo found this unfair, and she explained to Father about prospecting, and the tin diggings, and how Henry could strike it rich one day.

'I don't want you marrying a rabbitoh. Nor a prospector.'

'I got to marry sometime,' Echo said, though it sounded strange in her own ears, to say that.

'Is he converted?' Mother asked. 'Is he baptised?'

'I ain't asked,' said Echo, 'and I've got to finish this mending, those girls are so careless with their things.'

She bent her head over her sewing, but she noticed her parents look at each other, raising their eyebrows.

Henry came to see her most Saturdays, sometimes during the week too. He turned up at any odd time; he wasn't constrained by farm work like the Hatton boys. When Jack met him they shook hands, but he didn't seem to take to Henry.

'I have to say, Eck, I reckon he's bone idle,' Jack said. 'He don't seem to do much work.'

Echo punched his arm. 'Don't you say that, Jack Hatton. Henry works real hard, just not at farming like us.'

'Give over, Eck. I'm only saying – what's the bloke doing wandering about all day?'

When Henry visited Echo, and Mother agreed she could leave off her jobs, the two of them went for walks in the gully below the farm, sometimes as far as the forest in the foothills of the mountain. Henry turned out to be a good bushman – he knew some tracks even Echo hadn't found, and she thought she'd been everywhere in that forest. He told her stories about sleeping out in the highlands, and he knew how to make a fine bush mattress out of saplings and man-fern fronds. He showed her, and they lay together and watched the first stars appear in the dusk. He pointed out some of them that he said had names, a thing Echo had not known.

'Those ones are the Tasmanian Tiger,' said Henry pointing to a cluster of stars that did seem to outline an animal. 'The natives call him wurrawana corinna. That's their name for the tiger.'

Echo was impressed. Even Percy Coleman had never spoken about that. 'I do love to hear you talk of the stars, Henry.'

'You can see even more, if you go up high.'

'Up the mountain, you mean?'

'Sometimes I been up there,' he said, 'but I'm talking about up the highlands beyond Cradle. Up there, you can see every bloomin' star like it were close enough to touch. Sometimes I reach out my hand to see if I can gather some.'

She gave a little chuckle at that.

'Don't laugh at me, Eck.'

She put her hands on his cheeks as they lay on the ferny bed. 'I'm not laughing at you, love. I'm laughing at the lovely thought of the stars. Like jewels in our hands.'

'I'll take you up there, Eck. Up to the highlands.'

'When?'

'Any time you like. How about on our honeymoon?'

'Oh, Henry! I don't reckon Father and Mother will allow it. Getting married, I mean.' The idea made her feel shy.

'They'll come round,' he said, as if it would be no problem at all.

But Echo thought there'd be trouble.

They talked this over for a while, their faces close in the ferns. Henry's arms were around her, the forest dusky. Echo hadn't noticed the day fading away so fast, pressed warm against Henry.

'Look, Eck,' he said, rolling onto his back. 'See how many stars have come out.'

When she tipped her head back, she could see the sparkles of light pricking the sky. The dark, protective bulk of the mountain loomed over them.

'Dear old mountain,' she said, 'always there.'

They laughed and stretched their arms up high and pretended they could scoop up the stars.

'Them stars is yours, Eck, any time you look up.'

'If it don't rain,' she said, and started giggling.

They laughed again and embraced and Henry kissed her, and before she knew what was happening he began pulling off her blouse and taking down his trousers, and she said, 'Oh, Henry, we ain't married!' and he said, 'I'm marrying you right now, Eck', and she felt warm and content and never so happy in her whole life as in that moment under the stars.

Afterwards, Henry said he would tell her father right away they were going to get married with a preacher, as soon as one turned up.

Echo pulled her clothes back on and snuggled up beside her husband. 'What if we made a baby?' she said. 'You better tell Father real soon.'

9

Mr Fenny and Mr Braithwaite returned to the district in the spring, and it seemed like the old exciting times were back. Another revival was announced, this time out at Wilmot. Mother pestered until Father agreed to take her. Of course Jack was keen too. They went over in the wagon and managed to snag a seat on a form made of planks set up outside the door. There were too many people to fit inside the Wilmot Union chapel – more than a hundred tried, though the chapel had been built to hold only thirty. Men had taken out the chapel windows, so everyone could hear. From her seat, Echo had a good view inside. Preacher Fenny sang with his palms outstretched as if in invitation, '*Come home! Come home! Ye who are weary, come home!*' Something about the singing made her feel as if the whole crowd, everyone there, the preacher and the neighbours and Jack and her parents, were embracing her all at once. '*Earnestly, tenderly, Jesus is calling, Calling, "Oh sinner, Come home!"*' Beside her, Mother heaved a sigh. Preacher Fenny started on his sermon. He spoke on a text in Matthew, the one where Jesus walked upon the sea, '*But straightway Jesus spake unto them, saying, "Be of good cheer; it is I; be not afraid."*'

'Oh my word, ain't he an eloquent one!' Mother whispered.

The Celtic burr in his voice was a pleasure to hear. Something about it reminded Echo of the singing she used to hear under the ferns, when she'd been younger. Mr Fenny spoke of a 'constant question' arising in the hearts of the Lord's people: how were they to get 'power over the sins and temptations' that beset them? 'Brothers and Sisters,' he cried in his powerful voice, 'the word of God is full of the answers!' He waved his Bible aloft. 'Every page gleams with light! Light to help the weary, troubled, failing Saint to find the rest and the strength that God desires His children ever to enjoy!'

All the congregation fell quiet as they waited for the answer to these mysteries. The preacher let a pause sit silent for a moment. Then he took a pace forward. 'In one word,' he said, 'the remedy for all our failure is: Jesus!'

Everyone seemed affected. Echo didn't hear any scoffers at all and supposed they must have stayed away. Or maybe everyone in the district was convinced by now. She'd heard it said that Mr Fenny's preaching had converted many a scoffer, turning them into Believers. Except Eddie, of course.

That night in Wilmot Mr Fenny preached for more than an hour. The night air chilled, but Echo hardly noticed. The singing went on and on, hymns following one after another. Pretty soon everyone was humming along or singing out loud. A few just sat still, stunned-looking, listening to the words, '*"Almost persuaded" now to believe; "Almost persuaded" Christ to receive; Seems now some* soul to say, "Go, Spirit, go thy way, Some more convenient day, On thee I'll call."

Jack nudged Echo when this hymn began and she looked up but couldn't read his expression in the half-light. There were so many hymns that night. 'Almost Persuaded' had some people weeping. Echo assumed they were the *anxious* ones. '*"Almost" is but to fail! Sad, sad that bitter wail – "Almost – but lost!"*'

The preachers gave their benediction at about eleven o'clock but the people wouldn't let them go. The crowd pressed to the front of the little chapel, jostling each other, pleading for one more prayer.

'Could we go up?' Mother asked. 'I would surely like to speak to Mr Fenny, personal.'

'What for?' Father said. 'Ain't you heard enough of him for one night?'

Jack looked like he wanted to stay too, but Echo had to get up early for the milking. She peered into the interior of the Wilmot chapel, thronged with women and men pushing to the front, murmuring and exclaiming. The preachers couldn't persuade the people to go home. Some ran after them in the dark when they tried to leave. Mr Fenny's voice was cracked and hoarse from speaking and singing. It seemed like the whole crowd had a fever. The preachers had spoken of the Lord like He was a nourishing food – what had they all eaten that night?

Eventually Echo and Father convinced Mother and Jack to climb into the wagon. Father turned the bullocks and the wagon creaked off down the dark track. Jack said he'd counted fifteen hymns sung. Echo sat swaying beside him in the back. She mused on all the ideas that had filled the chapel that night: ideas of believing and praying every day for preservation from a life of sin.

'D'you reckon I live a life of sin?' she asked Jack.

He thought over her question. 'Well, Eck, I think we all do, seeing as we haven't gone converted to believers and got immersed. That's my understanding.'

'Even Mother?'

Jack considered this point. He never rushed into things. 'I reckon. Even Mother.'

Echo was quiet. The preachers often said how hell awaited non-believers. She didn't like the sound of that.

'Probably we should all believe,' she said after a while.

Jack bent his head towards her. 'It ain't so simple as that, Eck. Ain't you seen how the preachers cross-examine them who says they believe? They make sure you understand what you're about before they do an immersion. That's why they harangue people for so long. To make sure they know what the Bible says.'

'D'you think I should read our Bible at home, like you do?'

Their parents sat hunched on the front bench of the wagon, dark silhouettes against the grey, moonlit bush.

'Maybe you should give it a go,' Jack said. 'I reckon you could be saved if you wanted, Eck.' He leaned closer to her in the dark, his shoulder pressing against hers, and whispered, 'I seen the light, like I told you. I heard the Lord down in the paddock and the words were like a burst of light for me. I reckon I'll get immersed soon.' He spoke eagerly, keeping his voice down. Echo stared into his face, inches from hers. 'Only hear His Word and believe!' he said. 'That's the whole truth, Eck. Hear and believe.'

In the dark, sparks of light flickered, the eyes of animals flashing in the lantern glow, pinpoints that lasted only a second or two as the wagon passed. Echo turned away from her brother and sat quietly, wondering if Henry would come to one of the revival meetings. When she'd asked him, he'd said he never wanted anything to do with the God-botherers. They were not for him, he'd said. Echo wondered if they were for her.

She felt the attraction of the preachers' performances, the sense of riding a rising tide with her neighbours, a curiosity about what it might feel like to see things as Jack saw them, to experience that same flood of confident happiness that seemed to have enveloped him. She thought about the moment Jack had described to her, many times now: the moment when he was out chopping wood, when he had his vision of the Lord, when the voice of the Lord spoke to him and the sky filled with glorious light.

Staring into the dark bush, Echo wondered what it would be like to see the forest bathed in heavenly light and to hear the angels, and the word of the Lord, like Jack and Janie and Mrs Mason and all the others.

Her stomach clenched with a kind of thrill, and she hummed the last hymn under her breath, 'Almost Persuaded'. That might describe her. Was this what being *anxious* felt like? Butterflies in your stomach and a swimmy sensation inside your head, almost like a headache? Would Henry come to watch, if she got immersed?

10

When Mr Fenny came to the farm, Echo remembered the excitement of the revival last autumn, and of the singing out at Wilmot, of Jack's enthusiasm for the Bible, the neighbours wading into the creeks, the promises of heaven and Mother reunited with Amos.

Still, when Mother and Father were finally convinced to go down on their knees in their own kitchen, she did feel taken aback. It seemed unlikely that praying could stop the mould infecting the wheat. And yet she felt that something momentous had come into their kitchen, and she grabbed Mother's hand and knelt beside them.

They closed their eyes and listened to the preacher exhorting the Lord to save the wheat crop. Echo squeezed her eyelids tight and tried hard to believe, but she found it was not a thing you could just summon. She wasn't sure she *truly believed* the Lord could save the crop, could change the weather specially for them. She worried that if her believing turned out to be merely hoping, it might not be enough; she might be the one that allowed the crop to fail. A tremor shook her at this disturbing thought.

When the prayer was over, Father sat on a kitchen chair but didn't say anything. Echo saw Mr Fenny watching her father's face. He must have seen doubts there, in the twitching beard or the furrowed brow, because he took a deep breath and began an exhortation. He became eloquent.

'Can you trust in Him?' asked Mr Fenny in his musical voice. 'Oh, cast out this terrible sin of doubt and unbelief, this sin that robs you and robs God!'

Father glanced at Mother, who dabbed her eyes with the corner of her apron. Echo thought Mother seemed a little desperate, as if she *wanted* this to be true – that you could pray for a good wheat crop, and the Lord would answer, and that was all it took. It sounded too easy, and things were not generally easy.

'Unbelief robs you of the peace and joy that ought to be your portion!' Mr Fenny went on. 'Let us hearken to the words of Jesus: "only believe".'

Her mouth open, Echo sat listening to the melodious voice. The old kitchen disappeared in the swirl of the words, as if it were not good enough for these grand ideas of God and peace and joy. The preacher spoke with the voice of an angel, calling heavenly music down for the family. Mother started to weep, her shoulders trembling and Mr Fenny took her hand and told her to leave all her worries with the Lord. He and Father shook hands and they walked out to the visitor's horse, hitched in the yard, and stood talking together for some time. Mother sat, dazed, still sniffling into her apron.

Echo gave herself a shake – she felt woken from a kind of dream – and went to fill the kettle. Jack, who had listened to it all with his elbows on his knees, stared into the fire.

Not long after, Mother declared she would ask to be immersed. This didn't come as a surprise to Echo. In fact, she'd been thinking the same thing herself ever since the revival at Wilmot and the amazing prayer for the wheat. Not wishing to be left behind, Echo announced she would be immersed too. They would be baptised together. It gave her an unaccustomed feeling, to think of this – a swirling combination of excitement and happiness and fearfulness. It would be all right to do it with Mother, she thought.

When Henry next came and took her for a walk, Echo told him about her conversion, the thrill she felt with the decision made, the way the world looked different to her now. She found it difficult to say exactly what she meant. Her tongue kept stumbling, and she looked up at Henry – so much taller than her – wondering if she'd explained herself. 'I feel like I really belong now,' she said, 'with everyone, and the Lord watching over us all. And when I pass over the river—'

'What river?' Henry asked.

'I mean, when I die – then I'll see Amos again, and the others who've died . . .'

'Who else has died?'

Echo sighed and broke a switch off a young tea tree. She used it to swipe at the bushes along the trail as she tried to explain these Biblical ideas to Henry, ideas that had seemed so clear out at Wilmot when the preacher spoke. Henry just grunted. She invited him to come to Hubbard's place for the baptisms and he said he might. Later, Echo thought maybe he only said that to please her.

When the day came, Jack drove them over in the wagon.

'We're lucky with the weather, Eck,' Mother said. 'Thank goodness it's warm.'

When they got to Hubbard's farm, there were dozens of people gathered on the banks of the creek. Echo scanned the throng and looked up into the trees where boys had climbed, searching for Henry. But she couldn't see him anywhere. This was disappointing, but at least Janie was there.

Echo watched as her mother was dunked, before rising up spluttering and grinning. It didn't look too bad, but even so, Echo hung back as she waited for her turn. She was wearing her chemise and house dress – she refused to take off the house dress. When Mr Fenny, standing in the creek with his hat and coat on, called out 'who is next for the Lord?' Echo scuttled down to the creek, conscious of all the eyes watching her. She rushed into the water as quickly as possible so she didn't have to think about it. The water struck colder than she expected and she gave out a squeak as she went in. Jack was there on the bank. 'Eck! Stop that squealing!'

The next thing she knew, Mr Fenny had her by one arm and put his hand on the back of her neck, and said kindly, 'I baptise you in the name of God the Father, and of the Son, and of the Holy Ghost,' and he dunked her backwards. She came up gasping for air.

Mr Fenny cried out, 'Hallelujah! Another saved for the Lord!'

Echo didn't stop to think about being saved. She leaped out of the creek and Jack hauled her onto the bank. Janie stood ready with a blanket. With one eye on the boys in the trees, Echo pulled the blanket around herself.

'Look after her, Janie!' Jack yelled, grinning.

Janie smiled at him.

Peeking out from the tent, Echo searched the nearest branches, and the crowd on the riverbank, but Henry wasn't there. She'd tell him all about it later. He would surely be pleased.

Sometimes Echo daydreamed about where she and Henry would live when Father finally agreed they could marry. Perhaps they could find a hut in the highlands – it was lovely country up there, so Henry said, even though it was two days' walk from town. She'd make a home the same way Mother had when the Hattons first came to Paradise – plastering newspapers on split-timber walls, and shoving slices of man-fern trunk into the gaps; a wooden chimney and an open fire, a sugar bag hung over the doorway in place of a door, rabbits for meat. Echo felt excited by this vision of home building; she couldn't wait to get started. But she'd have to leave Mother behind, and Lottie and Grannie and Father and her brothers, and Janie and all the new Christians too. Rubbing her palm over her belly, she conjured Henry's face, and felt better.

Janie had turned sixteen and had also been baptised, and sometimes the girls discussed the lessons they heard their parents talking over, the ideas the preachers had brought into the district. Once Janie asked a question – what to do if a husband believed, but his wife did not? Sure enough, the answer was in the Bible. They found a verse in Corinthians: *For the unbelieving husband is sanctified by the wife, and the unbelieving wife is sanctified by the husband.*

Echo wondered why Janie wanted to know about that, seeing as Jack certainly believed. She looked across at her friend, at her intent expression as she considered the meaning of 'sanctified'. With her Bible open to the passage, Echo read on to herself, seeing the command: *to avoid fornication, let every man have his own wife, and let every woman have her own husband.* As a farm girl, she knew what 'fornication' meant. She wondered about the strange thrum in her own body and thought of Henry.

Summer came and Henry went away to the highlands for the season, promising Echo he'd be back by the autumn when the weather began to cool. He'd be trapping up there – possums and wallabies – and could make good money from the skins. It was a worry that he had to go, but surely Father would relent when Henry came back with some money in his pocket.

11

Staverton was a long way out, more than twenty miles from Paradise. Eddie had moved out there with Janie and Echo hadn't seen either of them for months. She wasn't sure if he ever married Janie – there were gossips in the district who called their new baby boy 'illegitimate'. Eddie, for his part, had said he and Janie would marry as soon as they could get over to the Wesleyan Chapel at Latrobe, or when he could lay his hands on a preacher. But the preachers had gone from the district again, and the gossip went on.

The fact that Janie had chosen Eddie had surprised Echo at first. She'd been sure it was Jack who was courting her. When Eddie was preparing to move out, Jack had thumped him, which confirmed that she'd been at least half-right about that.

Since the wheat crop had come in and made a good harvest, Father had been able to buy a new horse and cart. This made for easier going than the bullocks and was quicker than walking too, depending on the state of the track. Father said he'd drive them over to Staverton in the new cart.

'I'm that keen to see the baby, Eck,' Mother said.

'And Eddie too,' said Echo. 'He is my brother, even if he ain't a Christian. We ain't seen him in ever so long.'

Jack refused to go.

'Why are you so set against Eddie? Can't you forgive him?' she asked.

Jack, chopping kindling, slammed his axe into the wood. A wattlebird chattered nearby. 'Eddie can do what he wants, but us Christians has made a commitment to the Lord to eat and drink only with those who would share the Lord's supper with us. It's the difference between right and wrong.' On the last word, he thumped his axe into the wood again and splinters flew. The wattle birds chuckled.

'Ain't that a bit harsh, Jack? He *is* our brother.'

Jack stood and rested his axe on the ground. He raised his forefinger at his sister. 'The Lord says we have to refuse the evil and choose the good, and that's what I'm doing. If you can talk Eddie into coming into the fold, good-oh. But I've given that a try, and it didn't work.'

'I want him in the fold too, Jack,' Echo said, 'otherwise he won't be in paradise – I mean heaven – when we all get there.'

'And he won't be among the ones who are raised when the Lord comes again! I don't know why the silly bugger won't listen.' He raised his axe and went back to chopping.

Echo supposed Jack hadn't got over losing Janie. As to the rest of his talk, in her opinion Jack was being a bit exclusive, with this business of not speaking to any unbelievers. She didn't reckon anyone should shun the new baby, even if Eddie remained a scoffer. Jack went on and on about how Eddie wouldn't believe in the Lord, but Echo suspected his antagonism had more to do with Janie than anything else.

Steep hills rose between the Hatton place and the Staverton farm where Eddie was trying to grow potatoes on the edge of real mountain country. The blue dolomite ridge loomed over the paddocks and the land dropped away into deep gullies. The road took a roundabout route. When Father saw how steep the paddocks were, he gave a whistle.

Eventually the cart reached the yard behind Eddie's house, which wasn't much more than a hut. Echo wondered how Janie had got on with having the baby way out here. Mother said her older sister had come to help, though she'd gone home now.

Janie cried out happily to see them, and went to call Eddie from the bottom paddock. In the distance, they saw him look up and lean on his pitchfork. He shaded his eyes against the sunlight but he didn't climb up the hill. Father started on down to speak to him. The paddock was that steep; it must have been a horror to plough.

Janie brought out her baby boy from inside the hut. She looked too young to have a baby. Though much thinner than in their schooldays, she was still pretty – even beautiful – but she seemed worn out and had a loose cough that racked her every few minutes. Lines ran from her nose to her chin. Maybe she hadn't yet recovered from the birth. The baby boy was only a few weeks old.

'Why's Eddie not coming up?' Mother asked, the baby crooked in her arm.

'Is he angry about us visiting?' asked Echo. 'I thought it was only Jack and him at odds.'

Janie sighed. The baby began whimpering and Mother rocked him. 'I don't know, Eck. He seems mad about everything these days.'

Tired eyes, milky with fatigue, gazed at Echo. Janie's house dress was grubby and the baby didn't look well. The new mother showed them into her home, and Mother walked up and down the one room of the hut, rocking the baby and cooing; he seemed calmed by her touch.

Janie lifted her hands to her face; for a moment Echo thought she would cry. 'Oh, Eck! Eddie's that upset all the time. The paddocks are mighty hard to plough, and he says it'll be a season or two before we're producing. He spends a lot of time out rabbiting, that's what's keeping us going. But when he comes back, he's always in a mood.'

A narrow shelf was nailed to one wall and on it sat a few enamel utensils, a candlestick, and an earthenware jar in which Janie kept a little salt. Beside these necessaries sat a small useless item, a china figurine in the shape of a clown, no bigger than a teacup. Its glazed colours flashed tiny notes of red, yellow and blue. Echo knew this clown – it had always been Janie's treasure, she'd had it for years, a gift bought from a show in Launceston, given to her by a visiting relative. Echo clicked a soothing noise, put her arm around her friend's shoulders, and promised to talk to Eddie.

But outside, she couldn't get Eddie to come up from the bottom of the hill no matter how she called. When she walked down the slope to search for him she couldn't see him anywhere, nor her father. She didn't know the tracks around Staverton like the ones around Paradise. She climbed back up the roughly ploughed hillside to the little hut. Mother had set Janie to feeding the baby, and put the kettle on to boil.

After some time, Father returned – but without Eddie. When Echo asked about her brother, Father said they should let him be, he was not in the mood for visiting. Eddie had asked to borrow the bullocks again, he said.

'That'll set Jack off,' Echo remarked.

As the Hattons climbed into their cart, Echo told Janie to send word if she needed any help. A boy at the next farm down the road, Parkers, would surely take a message for her.

On the journey home, Mother spoke of the baby.

'So they named him Max,' she said. 'There ain't no Max on our side of the family, but perhaps it's from the Miller side.'

'It's a good name,' Echo said. 'A good strong boy's name.'

'Pity he's not as strong as his name, though,' said the new

grandmother. 'Looks to me like that little mite ain't getting the nourishment he needs.'

'Janie's doing the best she can,' Echo said. 'It is her first baby.'

Echo didn't spend as much time out in the bush now she was older, but occasionally she'd still wander down into the ferny gully below the farm to collect blackberries or mushrooms. She often daydreamed about lying with Henry under the stars. She hadn't seen him for weeks.

'He'll be back soon,' she said into the soft green fronds. 'Oh, he better be back soon.'

Dry ferns crinkled under her like a welcome. She remembered when she would visit the fairies here, when she brought Amos to see if he could hear them, the time when she believed in fairies, when she talked with the mountain and heard some answers too. There were still occasions when she looked up to the mountain and wondered if God lived up there. It would be a good location for Him – he'd be able to see the whole district. Even Staverton.

12

Since that visit to see the baby Echo had been keeping her ears open for news of Eddie and Janie, stuck as they were way out there on the boundary of the district.

'There is a reason that lease is so cheap,' Mrs Clarke said one Sunday at Assembly in the new Gospel Hall. 'You can't farm on the side of a bloomin' mountain.' Echo also heard that Mrs Miller was worried about her daughter. Janie couldn't get in from that Godforsaken spot to attend Assembly, not with a small baby. Someone whispered it was not only the distance keeping Janie away, and heads nodded knowingly. Echo wondered what they meant, these gossips. Their remarks made her uneasy.

When Echo asked, Mrs Miller said Janie's sisters had been out to Staverton just last week. The baby was growing slowly, though Janie's cough remained a worry. Mrs Miller sounded fussed and said Staverton was too far away. Eddie should give up and move back closer to town, but Echo couldn't see how that would work. Eddie couldn't afford a lease closer in, and she couldn't see him living at the Millers, nor at their place, with Jack as he was.

She decided she must visit Staverton again, no matter how far it was, and pestered Father until he agreed she could take the horse and cart. As he helped her hitch the horse to the shafts, Mother bustled out of the kitchen with her arms around a bulging basket covered with muslin.

'Here's some things for them, Eck. Some bread I made, and a bit of last year's blackberry jam.'

'Oh, Mother, that will be good! And Father gave me a half-bag of turnips.'

Echo wedged the basket into the tray of the cart, along with the turnips and two blankets that she hadn't told her mother she was planning to give away. The journey would take a couple of hours, so she set out early. Frost still lingered under the bracken and the cartwheels crunched along the track from the house.

'Be careful, Eck!' Mother called.

Echo had been as far as Sheffield alone before, but this would be a longer journey, out to the edge. The horse, named Creamy, trotted out fresh and eager to get along; they made good time.

Drawing up at the hut at Staverton, Echo called hello. No-one answered. A stony silence sat about the place. Climbing down from the cart, she went to the rough door, made of split palings like the rest of the hut. It stood ajar. Pulling it open, she stepped inside.

'Eddie? Janie?'

She didn't see her brother at first. He sat, still and silent, on a tree-stump stool. He was leaning forwards, elbows on his knees, his head hanging down. After a moment, he seemed to notice her and jerked back his shoulders. The movement made Echo jump.

'Eddie! It's me! Whatever has happened?'

She couldn't get him to speak. He seemed stunned and the look in his eyes frightened her. In the gloom, for there was no lamp lit and the windows were small, Echo then noticed Janie lying on a sugar-bag mattress. She couldn't see the baby.

'Where is the baby, Eddie? Is Janie sleeping?'

A faint whimper came from the mattress. Echo went over and found the tiny boy tucked in beside his mother.

'Janie!' Echo said urgently. 'Is the baby all right?' She brushed Janie's cheek, icy cold. Echo rocked back on her heels with a cry, then grabbed the baby up in her arms. She stood shaking in the middle of the hut, staring first at Janie, then at Eddie. When her wits returned, she pulled a rough blanket over the mother's pale face.

Echo sat holding her brother tightly. At first she couldn't stop weeping for Janie, but she had to think of the baby so she controlled her grief. She tried to think what Mother would do, what Grannie would advise. The little one was tucked between them, barely whimpering. She didn't know how to feed him, but she knew bread and turnips weren't food for a baby, nor even blackberry jam.

Eventually Eddie, clinging to her, told her in broken, disordered sentences how Janie had been sick for weeks, coughing and growing thin, and this morning she didn't wake up. The Adam's apple in his throat rose and fell in jerks.

'It's my fault, Eck,' he said. 'Bringing her out here, where she don't have her mother or nothing. And that bloody land—'

'Are you hungry, Eddie? Mother sent some bread.'

He had no stomach to eat, he said, but she fetched the bread from the cart. The baby's head lolled as she held him.

'What about Baby Max? We have to get him some milk. We have to take him to Mother right away.' The baby's eyes were clouded, his small limbs limp. 'Eddie, I'm that afraid. What if Baby dies too?' She tried to rouse him with her urgency.

Eddie bent his forehead to his knees and began to sob. Echo was trembling – from fear, from anxiety, from a searing wish for the world to make sense. But she had no time to name these things. Practical matters needed her attention.

She got Eddie to stand and insisted he wrap Janie's body in the blanket and carry her out to the cart. He sobbed all the while. Echo tipped her mother's provisions from the basket and swaddled the baby with the muslin. She covered the bundle with a blanket. Fetching Eddie's hat and gun from the hut – they seemed the only possessions of his worth worrying about – she yelled at her brother to climb onto the seat beside her. Then, remembering, she ran back and took Janie's small china clown from the shelf.

'Giddy up, Creamy!' she cried, and the cart set off.

They were not long out of the yard when Eddie stirred and spoke the first clear thing he had said. 'Mother Parker, at the next farm – she has a baby.'

Echo looked at him, hope rising. She drove Creamy at a rollicking pace along the rough track and soon swerved into the next farm. Mrs Parker hurried out to see what the commotion was. When Echo told her, breathless, that Janie had gone, and lifted the baby from the basket, the woman understood immediately. She gathered up the little one and took him into her kitchen.

'He'll be all right now, Eddie,' Echo said to her brother. 'Come on down while Mrs P. feeds him. Have some of Mother's bread.'

Eddie accepted the bread but refused to go into the neighbour's kitchen. He leaned against the cart, chewing slowly, swallowing as if the bread were a lump of coal. Echo stayed beside him.

'She'll be in heaven now, Eddie,' she began hesitantly. 'Janie, I mean.'

He turned blank eyes to her. 'I'll never see her again. I won't never be able to tell her I'm sorry.'

'Go on, Eddie. It ain't your fault she had the consumption. You ain't to be blamed for it.'

'I shouldn't have brought her to live out here.'

'Well,' suggested Echo, thinking about the Bible lessons. 'You can ask forgiveness if you want. The Lord forgives those who are truly remorseful.'

Eddie straightened and rubbed his eyes. 'Oh, Eck, I surely am remorseful. About a lot of things. But why should the Lord, or Janie, or Mother and Father, or anyone, forgive me?'

'Mother and Father don't blame you for nothing, Eddie.'

'What about Amos?' he shouted, and dashed his palms on his thighs.

Echo's thoughts clouded for a moment. Many months had passed since Amos had been shot out rabbiting. Had Eddie been carrying around guilt about that accident for all that time?

'Eddie, that was an accident,' she said slowly. 'Father knows that. Like the accident he had when he lost Caroline in the Mersey.'

Eddie's head came up at that. He looked as if he hadn't thought about things in that way, until now.

'Tell you what,' suggested Echo, 'I can say a prayer for you. They call it – *intercession*. Then the Lord will know you're sorry, and He'll forgive you. Perhaps you can find peace that way. And you can see Janie again in heaven.'

She took hold of his arm and stepped close to him. His head dropped, like a defeated fighter. He didn't reply, nor object, so Echo closed her eyes and began her prayer of intercession, as she'd heard the men pray in Assembly. She didn't know if the Lord would forgive Eddie, she didn't know if he needed forgiving, but she reckoned it might be his best bet.

Her prayer finished, dwindled to its benediction, its Amen. She dropped Eddie's arm, left him leaning on the cart beside Janie's body, and walked over to the fence line of the Parkers' yard. Gazing towards the mountain, she wondered why Janie had to die, if the mountain could offer any explanation for such a tragedy, whether the Lord could do anything to restore Eddie's heart, grant him some peace, some redemption. Looking back at him over her shoulder, at his slumped form, remembering her proud brother and his wish to build his own farm, she wondered what the Lord's plan could be. She wondered if people should try to struggle against Him and go their own way – Eddie had surely failed.

'What d'you reckon, old mountain?' she whispered. 'You used to have the answers.'

Mrs Parker, the neighbour woman, came out of her kitchen with the baby wrapped in a shawl. When Echo peeked at him, his breathing seemed stronger.

'He's well fed now, dear. I suppose you're taking him to your mother?'

'Yes. She'll know what to do.'

Mrs Parker sighed. 'It's terrible sad.'

With the well-fed baby tucked back into Mother's basket and with Eddie beside her, saying nothing, Echo headed the horse and cart home to Paradise.

About halfway there, with the noon sun riding high in the sky, Eddie stirred and asked if she'd like him to drive the horse for a while. This seemed encouraging and Echo handed over the reins. Mercifully, the baby continued to sleep.

'What'll you do now, Eddie?' Echo asked after a while. 'Will you go back to Staverton when we've buried Janie?'

He sighed. 'No point in that, Eck. That place will never pay. And how could I live out there without Janie? It was supposed to be our home.'

'Mother once warned me it wasn't so easy to build a home.'

Eddie stared ahead, watching the track between the horse's ears. 'D'you reckon Mother will take in the baby?'

''Course she will, Eddie. Why ever wouldn't she?'

'Well, she's got quite a few to look after already.'

Echo snorted. 'One more won't make no difference. You know how Mother is.'

Eddie drove on, deep in his thoughts. Echo sat beside him for a few miles, saying nothing. As they neared the hills of Paradise, she made a suggestion. 'You might think of going out to the tin diggings at Waratah, Eddie. I've heard from . . . someone I know, that tin prospectors can make a bit of money out there.'

He turned and looked at her, his lips twisting in a half-smile.

'You don't reckon Jack will want me around the place, ay?'

Eddie had always been a sharp one. 'What about the prospecting? It'd do for a time.'

Eddie said nothing for a while, then he sighed. 'You're right, Eck. I might try it.'

The cart entered a stretch of ringbarked forest and they arrived home in Paradise.

13

The new arrival didn't much change the routines at the Hatton farm. Baby Max was soon absorbed into the family, taking the place of Alice, now a toddler, at Mother's breast. No wonder Mother lost count of the kiddies sometimes, Echo thought. Grannie seemed confused about the new arrival, asking where it came from. She had trouble keeping all her grandchildren straight in her old mind.

With summer drawing to a close, Henry returned from the highlands. The day Echo saw him walking up the track and into the yard, she hurried out to meet him, flooded with pleasure and relief – then stopped, feeling suddenly shy, unsure.

'Eck!' he exclaimed. She saw complete surprise on his face. But he recovered himself in a moment, stepped forwards, and threw his arms around her.

Jack made a fuss about getting hold of a preacher real quick, although Echo didn't care. They finally found a Wesleyan over at Latrobe who travelled to the farm and married them. Grannie told

Echo her new husband was handsome and she was lucky to find one that wasn't a convict.

Henry said he knew a farmer out at Lorinna who would give him a job, and a hut to live in too, and they would go there after the baby came. Echo asked him about his family, his own father and mother, but he said they were away, prospecting or trapping, he reckoned. She would meet them someday. No use in thinking about that. Better to plan their own future.

The idea of her own home out at Lorinna was a joyful thought and a frightening one at the same time. It hadn't gone so well for poor Janie. But Echo didn't have the consumption, so she supposed she'd get on all right. She delighted in imagining: tucking her baby into a wooden cradle lined with a sugar bag and the blanket her mother had knitted. Keeping the fire going *day and night*. Carving slices from a side of bacon – Father said he'd give them one to start them off. She'd find the tracks through the bush out at Lorinna, and listen to what the mountain had to say, and lie with Henry again under the stars. Sometimes she wondered if Janie had dreamed of such things.

Baby Max squalled from the corner by the stove and Echo heaved herself up to attend to him.

'He's hungry again,' observed Grannie. 'Better take him to your mother.'

Echo cradled Janie's baby close to her breast and imagined feeding her own soon.

Burying Janie had nearly undone them all, it was that sad. The Millers, Janie's father and mother, wanted a burial place in the new Sheffield burying ground. Eddie insisted on being the one to dig the pit. Jack said he'd help. Echo marvelled at the reconciliation between her brothers. That day when she and Eddie arrived home with the baby and Janie's cold body in the cart, Jack had let out a low whistle, as if he knew bad news had arrived.

'What is it?' he'd called.

Echo had shouted, almost hysterical, the exhaustion of it all finally overtaking her. 'Get Mother!' she'd shouted to Jack. 'Janie's gone!'

'Janie?' Jack rushed to the cart and stared up at his brother. Eddie climbed down from the bench and turned to the bundle wrapped in the back of the cart. Wordlessly, he began to lift Janie, but the strength in his arms failed him and his sobs welled up again. Understanding seemed to spread through Jack like blood soaking into a rag. Echo had Baby Max to concern her, but she did wonder if her brothers would choose this moment of all moments to start another argument. She remembered that Jack had loved Janie too. But instead of yelling at his brother, as Echo feared he might, Jack grabbed Eddie around the shoulders and hung onto him as if rescuing him from drowning. He didn't say anything about prayer nor forgiveness nor anything that sounded like a sermon. Between the two of them, they carried Janie's body into the house and laid her carefully on one of the beds.

'Who is that?' Grannie asked in a wobbly voice.

Clutching the baby, Echo glanced across at the old lady and thought that Grannie would soon be shrouded herself. 'It's Janie, Grannie. Died of the consumption. And here I have her baby boy.' Pulling back the baby's wrappings, she showed his face to Grannie, who peered at the puckered little mouth and soft baby brow.

'Ay, Susannah will be in floods again,' the old woman remarked.

As it turned out, with so much needing her attention – Janie to be laid out, the baby to be fed, the prodigal son to be welcomed home, to say nothing of Echo's own condition – Mother did not indulge in her usual floods, not much anyway. Echo watched her getting on with things, keeping the home together, sitting in the evening light to nurse the baby, talking quietly with Eddie. Jack did end up saying quite a few prayers, but he confined them to the usual prayer time after tea, and he made no remark if Eddie decided to go outside for a smoke for the duration.

When it came to digging Janie's pit, the two brothers worked side by side. The soft chocolate earth gave way easily. There was singing when she went in. *When all my labours and trials are o'er* – 'The Glory Song'. Janie's father did the reading. Jack had been asked, but he said he couldn't do it.

When the birth pains started, Echo had her mother and her grandmother beside her, and her sister Rosetta too, carrying basins and bringing her water from the bucket. At her own birth, her mother had lain on a sugar-bag mattress on the floor, and she insisted Echo should lie on the floor too, even though they had proper beds now.

'There's a lot of cleaning up after a birth,' Mother said, 'and anyway, you'll find it easier to push.'

As it turned out the birth came easily for Echo, though it began much earlier than Mother had calculated. A tiny slippery girl slid out into the world on the floor of the kitchen in Paradise to be cradled by her family. Echo peered into the squashed little face and waited to hear her baby's first breaths.

14

Eddie and Henry had a devil of a time reopening the pit at the Sheffield burial ground. It should have been a quick job, since it wasn't that long since they'd buried Janie in the same grave. But the soil seemed sticky this time as if it didn't want to give.

Jack read from Psalm 121, Echo's favourite: '*I will lift up mine eyes unto the hills, from whence cometh my help.*' It was a cold day, and Susannah crossed her arms over her chest, hugging herself and sniffing as Jack read: '*My help cometh from the Lord, which made heaven and earth.*'

After it was done, Eddie announced he'd be leaving. He was going tin prospecting with Percy Coleman and his brother. That mine lease they'd got at Mount Claude was looking good, and they had another in the offing, and Perce said he'd cut Eddie in cheap. Eddie could get enough money from the rabbit skins and a bit of borrowing to get started. He said he wouldn't mind travelling farther out for the Coleman boys – down the west coast even, the farther away the better, Eddie reckoned. He said those Colemans were real optimists. He liked that about them.

No-one in the house could stop weeping that first week. Henry said he would go away up country as soon as they'd buried her, and he would be taking his wife with him. Echo, dry-eyed at last, held Max wrapped tightly under her old brown coat. She'd carried him everywhere, against her breast, ever since the day her own baby girl was born dead.

Mother said she'd miss Baby Max, and Eddie too, but most of

all she'd miss Echo, her oldest girl and her favourite. They held each other close, and Mother cried fit to burst when the day of departure came. Echo cried too, but she wasn't given to tears at every turn. The baby under her coat, the hut at Lorinna, Henry, a home in the back country – she focused on these things. The sad graves had to be left behind. But she would miss Mother, no doubt of that.

She'd written new names in the family Bible when Mother had asked: two births, two deaths, one marriage. Mother said Echo should take the Bible with her, since she was the one who could read best, so she did. But she didn't bother taking her journal. At the last minute, she remembered Janie's little china clown, and she took that too. For years afterwards people would ask where it came from.

Henry borrowed a wagon and Father helped him load it with whatever tools and provisions could be spared: the side of bacon, a bag of spuds and one of turnips, several blankets and Mother's second-best cooking pot. They also took a small wooden cradle that had been intended for the baby granddaughter.

Eddie helped Grannie out into the yard to see them off. Two borrowed bullocks were harnessed to the yoke; they'd have to go back to the farmer at Lorinna once Henry had transported his family to their new home. Out at Lorinna, they'd be isolated, but that didn't bother Henry. It'll be best, he said. It'll be grand, in fact. They'd be able to get on with their own business, with no-one watching. It was the one thing that gave Echo comfort, the thought of her own home with Henry and the baby, snug against the world.

The borrowed wagon creaked into motion and rolled out along the track lined with the white skeletons of dead trees, into the back country beyond the mountain.

Author's Note

The story of the Hatton family is loosely based on my own family. Eliza Wise was a real person, as was her convict husband Benjamin Walters. One of their daughters married a farmer and settled under the aura of Mount Roland in the Kentish district and raised a large family. They were living there when Christian Brethren evangelists arrived in 1874 and swept the people up in enthusiasm for revivals and creek baptisms. The family became strong 'Gospel Hall' adherents – except one son.

Acknowledgements

This novel was written in the nurturing environment of the Creative Writing Department of the English Faculty at the University of Sydney, guided by amazing teachers and benefitting from a stimulating atmosphere of inquiry and debate. My thanks, firstly, go to all those I encountered there – the scholars, the teachers and my fellow students.

Hugely grateful thanks to Belinda Castles. I doubt this novel would exist without her guiding hand, her faith in the project, and her nurturing support of a sometimes floundering would-be author. I was so lucky to have had such a teacher, supporter, mentor and guide as my first reader.

Particular thanks to Brigid Rooney, who was the first to show faith in my project about the Christian Brethren in the backblocks of Tasmania. Brigid guided me rigorously through the early research process, keeping my ideas focused and my feet to the fire.

I also owe so much to my creative writing teachers Fiona McFarlane, Beth Yahp, Vanessa Berry, Kate Lilley and Anwen Crawford. Thank you.

Thanks also to Peter Minter for his careful advice, and to Meg Brayshaw for sparking important ideas on writing Australian literature about the past.

A special shout-out to the members of my hugely supportive

writing group who have read their way through many iterations of 1870s Tasmania, and in particular to the beta readers of the manuscript, Dennan Chew, Amina Jansz and Lucy Mushita. The critique and support of this tight-knit group were invaluable in equal measure. Also Julie McElhone, constant comrade through it all; Sandy Bullon, who supplied several bright ideas; and Kyle Davis, who always reads everything I ask him to.

Special thanks are also due to Kentish local historian Alan Dyer, who granted me a long and thought-provoking interview in April 2019. Many of the incidents, names and details of the times are gleaned from Alan's *God Was Their Rock*, a history of the arrival of the Christian Brethren in the Kentish district. I also owe my title to him.

I am also hugely grateful to Penguin Random House and the judges of the Penguin Literary Prize 2022 who showed such faith in my novel, and for everyone at PRH who has shepherded the book out into the world. Without you, my characters may never have emerged from the past to remind us of who they were. Forever grateful.

And to Jess, Sophie and Evan, always there for me.